SKIES OF FIRE

A NORA ABBOTT MYSTERY

SHANNON BAKER

SEVERN RIVER
PUBLISHING

Severn River Publishing
www.SevernRiverBooks.com

ISBN: 978-1-64875-503-3 (Paperback)

ALSO BY SHANNON BAKER

The Nora Abbott Mystery Series

Height of Deception

Skies of Fire

Canyon of Lies

The Kate Fox Mysteries

Stripped Bare

Dark Signal

Bitter Rain

Easy Mark

Broken Ties

Exit Wounds

Double Back

Michaela Sanchez Southwest Crime Thrillers

Echoes in the Sand

The Desert's Share

Standalone Thrillers

The Desert Behind Me

To find out more about Shannon Baker and her books, visit

severnriverbooks.com/authors/shannon-baker

To Dave: Home is wherever I'm with you.

1

Sylvia LaFever simply had to have it. *If the Trust won't give me an advance, I'll force Eduardo to pay for it. I'm going to make him the wealthiest man on the planet.*

But of course, he wouldn't want anyone to know that.

Sylvia stared at the photo of the Chihuly chandelier on her laptop. She'd never have another chance at something so perfect for her dining room. At $90,000 it was a steal. The Trust could cough up the money. *They owed it to me.*

A squeaky voice broke into Sylvia's thoughts. "I've finished the initial calculations on the refractory angle but it seems like we're way off."

Sylvia slammed the top of her computer closed. "Nice work, Petal."

Petal stood in front of Sylvia, a mass of dreadlocks on a too-skinny body. As usual, layers of gauze and hand-knitted rags swathed Petal. She mumbled, "When the plume excites the ionosphere, are we monitoring the disturbances in the 100 km range to see if this leads to short term climatic alterations?"

Questions, chatter, like a million needles into her brain. Sylvia bestowed a patient smile on Petal. "It's complicated and I don't have time to explain it to you. If you earn your PhD we can have a more meaningful conversation about the principles behind ELF and short term climate fluctuations."

For god's sake, Petal's eyes teared up. She swallowed. "I just wondered because the coordinates bounce the beam to South America."

Sylvia rolled her chair away from her desk, the wheels rickety on the plastic carpet guard. *I deserve better than this drafty space tacked on to the aging farmhouse that Loving Earth Trust is so proud to call headquarters.* The slapped-up dry wall and builder-grade windows are bad enough but they'd simply laid industrial carpet atop a concrete floor with minimal padding.

Rust-colored carpet. *Disgusting.*

Maybe the sparse computer equipment covered the Trust's simplistic climate change modeling project, but for the magic Eduardo demanded, she needed more sophisticated hardware.

Sylvia stopped short of patting Petal on the arm, never sure when Petal showered last. "If you do as I tell you and watch and learn, you'll gain more knowledge than asking me questions all the time."

Petal nodded and wiped her nose with her sleeve. "Will we need to change the angle of the tower?"

Sylvia pressed a finger up to her mouth to silence Petal.

Petal retreated to her particle-board desk shoved into the corner of the room amid the used file cabinets the Trust provided for Sylvia. Dented metal with chipped beige paint, they maintained the same thrift store style of the rest of this dump.

I should still be in Alaska running the HAARP facility. I wish I could see their faces when they understand their mistake in firing me. Thank god Eduardo understands my genius.

The October chill filtered into the office but Sylvia forgot the temperature while she opened her laptop and emailed the art broker to secure the Chihuly. A knock on the thin door of her office disturbed the glow of acquisition. Sylvia glanced at the time on her computer. Ten-thirty.

The door opened without an invitation and a frowsy woman poked her head inside.

Sylvia sounded more welcoming than she felt. "Darla. What are you doing working so late?" The Financial Director of Loving Earth Trust didn't often stick around after four o'clock. No one at the Trust did. Sylvia, on the other hand, worked long hours. As expected of a creative genius.

Darla stepped further into the suite, as Sylvia called the 30 square foot addition to give it more class than it deserved.

Darla stood just inside the door and gawked at the maps tacked to the walls. Sylvia changed them periodically so the office appeared dynamic. Darla's dumpy jeans and scuffed clogs fit right in with her hair—the color of spoiled hamburger, hanging in shapeless strands to her shoulders. The woman had no style. But then, those environmental types seldom worried about fashion.

Darla twisted her hands over her heavy, udder-like breasts. "We need to talk about your project."

Actually, Darla coming here saved Sylvia the trouble of going to her. "Absolutely. I've made some necessary equipment upgrades. I'll turn in an expense report tomorrow and expect reimbursement right away." How much could she get the Trust to pay her?

Darla cocked her head as if she hadn't understood.

A rustle of clothes reminded Sylvia that Petal sat at her desk. Sylvia brushed her hand through the air. "You can go now, Petal."

Petal slipped almost silently toward the door. Darla and Petal exchanged looks as if Sylvia couldn't see them. Underlings always hung together, driving home the truth: It's lonely at the top.

As soon as the door closed behind Petal, Sylvia addressed Darla. "I can give you a trend analysis of the climate change with respect to beetle kill so you can answer questions at the board meeting."

Darla smelled ripe, like a true naturalist. *God, why couldn't these people shower regularly?*

Darla's bushy eyebrows drew down in a frown.

"I found the missing money."

Sylvia didn't care about Darla's petty bookkeeping problems. "That's nice."

Color rose in the accountant's face. "I don't know how you got the money out of your restricted funds without the passwords but you need to return it."

Minions. Always bothering her with their problems. Sylvia wouldn't let

Darla weasel out of paying her. "If Mark approves the funds for equipment, which I assure you, he will, you need to cut me a check."

Darla shifted from foot to foot. She peered at the ceiling and the floor. "I don't know what's going on, but money is missing. Big amounts."

Was she suggesting Sylvia somehow caused *her* bookkeeping errors? Sylvia strove to sound maternal. "I'm not the accountant but I know you're good at what you do. You'll just have to find it."

"The auditors will see it right away even if the board doesn't discover it." Darla's voice broke.

Just because Darla was a terrible accountant didn't make it Sylvia's problem. "Sometimes when I have a particularly vexing problem, I sleep on it and things are better in the morning."

Darla's porcine eyes sparked with fear. "You stole $400,000." She trembled.

Sylvia stood. "You're crazy."

"You're not doing any work on climate change here. Everyone knows it. But you're doing something. I'm going to the board and tell them."

Pathetic Darla, so jealous. She needed to learn her place.

Sylvia slid her desk drawer out. With a voice like cotton candy, Sylvia said, "Go home. Sleep on it. I'm sure you'll feel differently in the morning." Sylvia straightened and pulled her arm up.

Darla gasped.

Sylvia loved the feel of the Smith and Wesson 638 Airweight revolver. The grip caressed her palm and at slightly less than a pound, even her delicate wrists could hold it steady. The gold plating on the barrel coordinated pleasingly with the pearl grip.

When she'd bought it, she thought it might be an extravagance. So elegant and deadly—just like Sylvia—and she'd had to have it. Now it proved an expedient tool for chasing off fools.

Darla backed into a file cabinet and inched toward the door. "You wouldn't shoot me."

Sylvia raised her eyebrows and smirked, holding the gun steady on Darla, loving her feeling of command. Only a few people had Sylvia's audacity. She was truly extraordinary.

Like a quail in the brush, Darla panicked, turned tail and raced toward the office door.

Sylvia couldn't resist and followed her down the short hallway to the kitchen. She laughed to watch Darla tugging on the kitchen door and stumbling down the steps to the dark backyard.

Still laughing, Sylvia pointed the gun into the night and fired. How could she not? It would be like holding potato chips in your hand and not eating them. Besides, frightening Darla provided extra insurance that the nitwit would write that big check tomorrow.

In Sylvia's life, insurance was a good thing.

Chuckling, she locked the kitchen door.

2

A cyclone roared in Nora Abbott's ears. Her gloved fingers clung to the cold stone and she fought rising nausea. She forced herself to scan the horizon, to broaden her view and take in the vast expanse opening below her.

The sharp rocks at the mountain's summit seemed like teeth about to shred Nora. The thin, cold wind tugged strands of hair from her ponytail as Nora concentrated on the big picture. Maybe gravity anchored her to the rock, but she felt as if she'd fly off any moment and kite into the impossible openness of sky. Then she'd fall. Down the expansive sweep of the cliff face, through the struggling brush at the tree line so far below her. She'd crash into the pines and rocks as the air grew thicker. Finally, she'd lie in a heap of bones and torn flesh.

Like Scott. Her husband. Forever gone.

No.

Far away, across the vast sky, peaks met her gaze, smattered with snow left from last winter. As far as she could see there was nothing but the Rockies, strong, solid, never-changing. No houses, office buildings, cars or people. The early morning clouds hung low and Nora wished for the bright Colorado sunshine to burn away her fear.

Okay, enough of the dramatics.

Today. Now. This is the day she'd overcome her dread.

No more of this craziness. She'd reclaim her lost love of the mountains and the sky.

Nora made herself come up here today after hearing a prediction of the first snow of the season for next week. After that, they'd close the road and she'd spend another winter cowering in town.

Up here on Mount Evans, the most accessible of Colorado's fourteen-thousand-foot-high peaks, the world opened before her. It was as if she balanced on a pinnacle between space and earth, held by only a brush with the stone.

Normally the summit would be packed with tourists, since they could drive to a parking lot a quarter mile down and take the narrow, rock-strewn, switchbacks to the summit. But this early, only a dozen people in twos and threes scrambled over the boulders, inching toward the edges to admire the colossal views. Nora occupied a perch alone, tucked as close to the mountain as possible, afraid to slide her foot an inch toward the edge.

Even if you didn't have to strap on a pack and climb for days to enjoy the grandeur of the view, the short hike and the precarious footing at the summit required some level of fitness. Not one square yard of the top area lay level. Boulders and rocks perched at odd angles that necessitated scrambling just to get from one dangerous visage to another.

She inhaled.

So far, so good.

Maybe she wasn't the Fear-Conquering Goddess, but she was working it.

Despite the jagged rocks and uneven footing she *would* overcome her fear. At thirty-two, her health good, her balance as steady as ever, she wasn't likely to sail off the side.

Except.

Scott had been in awesome shape. And yet he'd gone over the side on the mountain in Flagstaff. But he hadn't fallen. He'd been pushed.

Her breath caught in her throat.

Don't think about that.

And Heather. She couldn't save Heather, either.

Apparently, her flight from Arizona to Colorado hadn't been far enough to shield her from the memories of their deaths.

Nora started to tremble. A fissure opened somewhere inside her right temple. It spread downward and branched off, racing across her skin, splintering her control.

Stop it!

Falling apart would not bring back the people she loved.

Nora clenched her fists and imagined her insides of jelly hardening into steel. Her heart slowed slightly. The crashing hurricane of blood eased enough she heard the screech of a hawk. The world stretched below her— endless mountains, their tips white against an impossibly blue sky. The crisp air brushed against her cheeks.

Feeling more stable, Nora eased forward, leaning away from the mountain and toward the future. Any day, any moment, her life could change. She might soar, like that hawk. Any moment.

With one more gaze across the limitless mountain range, Nora shuffled across the boulders and scree, making her way to the trailhead down to the parking lot.

That's when she saw it.

At first, it was a flash of blue against the rocks. This far above tree line, she didn't expect much color aside from the tiny flowers hiding in cracks.

She gritted her teeth. Probably a bandana or cap left by a tourist.

But it got worse.

He stood in front of her. Hatchet in one hand, feathers in another. His fierce mask with its plug mouth faced her.

"No. Oh no. Go away."

Nora slid to her knees.

A figment of her imagination. Of course the kachina in front of her wasn't real. Kachinas were Hopi. They belonged in Northern Arizona, not the heart of the Rocky Mountains in Colorado.

That is, if kachinas really existed. Which they didn't.

She squeezed her eyes shut. *You don't exist. You're not real.*

The black blanket appeared at the edge of her inner vision, creeping toward her brain. She couldn't breathe, could only feel the wild thump of her heart trying to burst from her rib cage. She refused to open her eyes and let them lie to her again.

Paralyzed by panic, Nora curled into herself.

"Are you okay?" A little girl's voice cut through the thunder of fear.

Nora fought back from the blackness. With Olympic force of will, she opened her eyes.

Of course the kachina had disappeared. Nora sucked in the cold, thin air in relief. He never stuck around for any other witnesses. It made no sense that he chose to show himself to Nora, a white girl with red hair. As if it made sense for anyone to see the phantom kachina at all.

A cartoon of gauze and yarn swirling in color stood before Nora. The girl— or woman— Nora couldn't tell, hovered in layers of skirts, sweaters, leggings and scarves, topped with a wild growth of dreadlocks bunched on top of her head and twining around her face like Medusa's snakes.

Her appearance seemed as bizarre as the kachina, but her slight build with her small face and tiny hands didn't harbor much threat. More than that, she her timid gaze behind a pair of John Lennon—pink sunglasses, disarmed Nora.

"Are you okay?" she asked again.

Nora inhaled good air. Like a child in the throes of a nightmare, she felt relief in the presence of another person. "Yes. I'm fine."

The girl eyed her skeptically. "Having trouble with the altitude? If you aren't acclimated, you can get disoriented this high."

Of course. That explained it all. Nora could have kissed this strange mountain imp for giving her an excuse. Nora considered the parking lot several switchbacks below them. Just a small journey to safety.

The girl helped Nora stand. "I'll walk you to the parking lot. You'll feel better as soon as you get lower."

I'll feel better as soon as Hopi spirits quit popping out at me. But Nora smiled as best she could, for now satisfied the kachina had retreated to the depths of her very sick mind.

"I'm Petal," the girl said.

The name fit. "I'm Nora."

Nora ought to be embarrassed but she welcomed the steady hand on her arm. Far from an easy stroll, the trail was nothing but a pile of rocks that required concentration to navigate. Though traveled by countless tourists every summer, the trail could be easily lost. The switchbacks angled back on themselves in unexpected places and it was easy to find yourself off-trail, going around the side of the mountain with nothing below to stop a fall.

Someday Nora would be agile and fearless again. She had climbed the backside of Mount Evans in high school; today she'd driven. Driving to the top of a fourteener was nothing short of cheating. You should have to work to be rewarded with the view from the top of the world. But today was her test. If the kachina hadn't swept in, she would have passed.

Petal walked Nora to her Jeep. She waited while Nora dug into her jeans pocket for a key. "Your first fourteener?"

Nora unlocked the door and Abbey, her aging golden retriever opened his eyes. He sat up from napping on the driver's seat. "No. I've lived in Boulder most of my life. But I haven't been climbing recently. What about you? Did you hike the whole mountain?"

Petal shook her head. Her voice sounded frail, as if she'd rather not speak at all. "No. I caught a ride up."

Abbey eased from the Jeep and nosed the tire. He lifted his leg. Abbey finished and walked back to sit by Nora. "Thanks again for helping me down."

Petal nodded and stood still.

"Where is your ride?" Nora asked, mainly because Petal seemed to expect the conversation to continue. Nora motioned for Abbey to get in the Jeep.

Petal shrugged.

That's what Nora suspected. "You hitched?"

Petal nodded again, solemn.

Nora leaned into the Jeep. She pulled a backpack and a couple of paperback books from the bench seat in back to the floor. She picked up an extra ski cap and gloves from the passenger side floor and tossed them on top of the books and waved Abbey into the back seat. "If you don't mind riding in a muddy old Jeep, climb in."

Petal shook her head, her dreads bouncing. "Oh no. You don't have to do that. I'll get a ride."

"I know I don't have to. Where are you going?"

Petal studied her Chacos sandals and thick wool socks. "Boulder."

"Me, too. Let's go." Nora felt almost cheerful at being able to help someone.

Petal seemed to argue with herself for a moment then her thin lips turned up in a tiny smile. "Okay. Thanks."

She clambered into the Jeep and Nora backed out, already feeling better. Nora cranked on the heater in the rumbling Jeep, the smell of dog hair mingling with Petal's organic odor.

Petal turned in the seat and scratched Abbey's ears. "Your dog is nice. Her name is Abbey?"

"His. Named after Edward Abbey. One of the earliest conservationists." Nora braked and eased to the inside of the narrow road as they met an SUV. She'd rather hike than drive this strip of pavement carved along the mountainside.

Petal nodded. "I know."

That surprised Nora. So many people had no idea about Edward Abbey. "What do you do for a living?" Oops. From Petal's appearance, she might not be making a living. Nora cursed her rusty social skills.

Petal didn't seem offended. "I work at Loving Earth Trust."

Nora knew the name. "That's great. They, you, have done some good work, especially with open space in Boulder."

Petal turned from Abbey and pulled her feet under her. "What do you do?"

Nora maneuvered the Jeep around a tight corner, holding her breath and avoiding glancing at the edge of the road that slid into oblivion. "I'd love to work for an environmental group."

"Really? Why?"

Why. The answer involved so much history, so many regrets. "Redemption."

Petal's soft voice sounded shocked. "You're such a nice person, I can't believe you've done something you need to atone for."

"I'm not that nice, believe me."

Petal shook her head, sending the dreads waving again. "I can read auras. They don't lie, and yours tells me how good you are."

Nora smiled at her. Clouds scuttled across the sun and the Jeep felt chilly even with the heater blasting.

"No. I mean it," Petal said. "Yours is deep red. That means you're grounded and realistic and a survivor."

Not too long ago Petal's words would have made Nora scoff, not in someone's face, but inside, at least. Now dead Hopi leaders visited her on mountain tops and spoke to her in dreams. Who was she to judge?

Petal regarded her. "What is a kachina?"

Nora's hands tightened on the wheel. "Why do you ask?"

Petal cast her eyes down at the floor. "You said something about a kachina when you were on the mountain."

Raving. Super. They ought to lock me up.

"A kachina is a Hopi spiritual being of sorts. Hopi are a tribe in Northern Arizona. The kachinas are not really gods, but they're not human, either. There's about three-hundred of them and they can represent things in nature or—" she forced her voice to remain neutral—"they can be spirits of ancestors."

Petal accepted the explanation as if Nora had described an interesting recipe. "Oh."

They rode in silence for a while, Nora holding her breath at every tight switchback. It seemed like walking down would not only be safer, it would be quicker. Finally, Petal asked. "What do you think you should do for your redemption?"

Nora shrugged. "I'm not sure. I'm an accountant and I've been applying at environmental places all over town with no luck. I hate to give up and go corporate. But I need a job."

Petal's face lit up. At least, it seemed to from what Nora could tell behind the rose glasses and that bird's nest of hair. "Accountant?"

"Business manager, MBA, accountant—all that left brain stuff."

Petal squirmed like an excited child. "I knew there was a reason I met you up there. The universe introduced us to each other."

Nora raised her eyebrows at Petal.

Petal clapped her hands. "I think we have an opening for a financial director."

Nora wanted to feel optimism and excitement at an opportunity but she held back. "I already applied to them a month ago."

"It's a new opening," Petal said but the delight evaporated from her face.

"Our Financial Director disappeared a few days ago and no one knows where she went."

"She just disappeared?" Like the kachina on the trail?

Petal hung her head. "I think it might have been my fault."

"I'm sorry," Nora said and meant it.

Petal sat upright. "But this is like *my* redemption. Darla left, but you're here and I found you."

Nora tried not to get her hopes up. "That's nice of you to say, but the Trust wouldn't be hiring already, with your director only being gone for a couple of days, would they?"

Petal's mouth turned down. "They were getting ready to fire her. Maybe that's why she left. Anyway, her taking off without a word to anyone was the last straw. They already have an ad set to run in this week's paper."

Nora didn't wish the old director ill, but this opportunity gave new meaning to *serendipity*. "Thank you for the head's up. Will you do the hiring?"

Petal's eyes sparkled. "Not really. But sometimes, I can suggest things."

The girl's excitement penetrated Nora. Maybe fate had jumped in and rescued her. "I'd love if you could get me an interview."

Petal smiled. She resembled a playful elf. "Done."

3

For the first time in too long, Nora joined the morning masses on their way to jobs the following Monday. Constructive, worthwhile, paycheck-producing jobs. Nora needed to work, had worked since she was sixteen, even while earning top grades in college and grad school. The last year of unemployment had depleted more than her cash reserves.

But no more. Look at her: A job! Loving Earth Trust wasn't just a job, either. It was a dream position. She'd called the Executive Director as soon as she'd returned from Mount Evans. He remembered her resume, called her in for an interview the next morning and hired her that afternoon. Two days after her failure on the mountaintop, her wheels gained traction.

Sunshine blazed from the east, sparkling on the morning. Nora turned from her apartment parking lot onto Arapahoe Street, happy to see the students with book bags strapped to their backs making their way toward campus for their first classes. There was something about people heading out for productive days, fresh from the shower, hair and clothes spiffed. Ready, expectant.

Finance Director with Loving Earth Trust. Score!

While not as well-known as The Sierra Club or The Nature Conservancy, Loving Earth Trust had earned a reputation in Colorado for getting results. Founded in the early seventies to spearhead open space in Boulder, they'd done good environmental and restoration work through the years. More than raising money and wringing hands, the Trust produced science to influence lawmakers to protect wild places. They sent volunteers out in the field for trail maintenance and landscape restoration. Now she was their financial director.

"And you get to come with me," she said to Abbey, stroking his silky head as he sat in the passenger seat keeping a keen eye on traffic.

Boulder's Flatirons rose to the west and Nora felt like saluting them. Flaming maples shouted good morning with their deep scarlet leaves contrasting to the golds and oranges of the less showy trees. She loved her town in all its outdoorsy quirkiness. The People's Republic of Boulder. The land of bicycle commuters, hippies, audacious entrepreneurs. Liberal, green, often down-right weird. Right where she belonged.

Nora's phone vibrated and she flipped it open.

"How are you?" Abigail. Again. Loving or smothering were the same in Abigail's world. It didn't help that Nora and Abigail were as alike as a Birkin Bag and a North Face backpack. In Nora's case, the backpack tended to be smattered with mud and repaired with duct tape.

"I'm the same as I was fifteen minutes ago, just a little closer to work." Nora waited at a stop light on Broadway in downtown Boulder and watched a young woman and man in business suits in earnest conversation. They cross the street in front of her, followed by a scuzzy gray-haired guy whose canvas pants barely stayed on his skinny hips. Behind them, two young women pedaled across in spandex biking shorts, colorful jackets and helmets.

"What did you decide to wear? Did you pack a lunch? You're wearing make-up, right?" Despite living in the woods in Flagstaff, Arizona for the last year, Abigail hadn't lost her high esteem for appearance. A magician, Abigail managed to look nearly perfect at all times.

Nora waited at the light. "Turquoise velour sweat suit. Sauerkraut and sausage. The darkest, skankiest Goth I could shovel on." Although Nora wore her copper-colored hair straight around her shoulders, she'd earlier told Abigail she wore a ponytail just to irritate her.

Abigail exhaled. "No need to get snippy. I'm only concerned."

Nora rolled her window down a few inches to smell the fresh morning.

"Sorry. I'm nervous. I'm wearing jeans and, sorry to say, not much in the make-up department. As for lunch, Abbey and I will probably take a walk." Although Nora admired Edward Abbey, he also served as a good excuse to use a name that would forever irritate Abigail Podanski. Her mother would prefer she call her dog Fido.

"Jeans! You brought your dog to work? Oh, Nora." Abigail couldn't sound any more disappointed if Nora wore a bathing suit to a cocktail party.

"It's an environmental trust. I'll be hanging at the office with enviros, not power-lunching with the rich and famous." She rubbed a pinch of Abbey's soft hair between her fingers before pulling her hand away to shift gears. "And Abbey will probably sleep all day on my office floor."

Abigail's voice sounded distracted. "I know you were desperate for a job but that place is not up to your standards."

Nora pulled the hatched closed on her emotional cellar. She refused to let Abigail irritate her. "I wasn't desperate."

"If you say so. I've told you a hundred times you should have kept more of that money from the Kachina Ski sale instead of setting up that trust for me. In fact, you shouldn't have set up that trust at all."

The money Nora received when she sold the ski resort should be enough to keep Abigail in a decent living standard for the rest of her life. The problem was that Abigail enjoyed a higher-than-decent standard and if Nora hadn't locked it down and kept herself as executer, Abigail might run through it too fast. It had happened before.

For her part, Nora didn't keep much of what felt to her like blood money. She'd figured with her resume and business skills, even if she insisted on working in the environmental sector, she'd land a good job in no time. She hadn't planned on a wrecked economy.

"This job is perfect for me, Mother."

"But the salary is so low."

"Sadly, I'll have to forego the spa weekends and month-long cruises with you."

The sun dazzled the flower beds and brick pavers of downtown. Nora drove past the offices and shops, beyond the county buildings and library and out of town on Canyon Boulevard, along Boulder Creek

Abigail probably thought Nora was serious. "If you'd get a real job you wouldn't have to make those sacrifices."

The paved bike trail along the creek gave way to a gravel path as the highway narrowed in the canyon. The creek rushed along, as happy as Nora to be going someplace.

"I'm almost there. Let me talk to Charlie." At least he was proud of Nora working for the Trust. Charlie had been Nora's buddy long before he ended up as Abigail's fourth husband. A situation more bizarre than anything Nora had experienced—and she'd been in a vortex of bizarre.

"Charlie's not..." Abigail trailed off. "Charlie's not here."

Nora nodded. He probably headed out early for his day of relatively harmless eco-terrorism. After his stint in Vietnam, Charlie had returned to his cabin outside of Flagstaff and did his bit for the environment by blocking forest trails with logs and rocks to keep dirt bikes and quads from shredding the forest.

"Tell him hi for me." Nora's stomach churned, like a kid on the first day of school. Where would this new adventure take her?

"Okay." Abigail sounded unsure. "Nora, I probably should tell you..."

A voice interrupted Abigail. It sounded like, "Can I take your order?" Since Abigail usually didn't venture from the cabin before her lengthy morning beauty regimen, it must be the television.

Just outside of the bustle of town heading into the canyon, a graveled clearing off to the side of the road supplied parking next to a bus stop. One person stood under the bus stop sign. Nora considered him. A shrunken old man, swallowed by a canvas work coat, he stared down the road as if watching for the bus...

The canyon walls disappeared and ice raced through her.

"I have a kachina for you." She stood in a crowd in the Flagstaff courthouse lobby.

He touched her arm. A withered slip of a Native American, he wore a long, threadbare tunic, leggings and moccasins that reached to his knees. Deep wrinkles lined his face like wadded parchment and skin sagged around his eyes.

"I have a kachina," he repeated in that soft voice cracked with age.

"I don't want to buy a kachina," she said.

"Not to buy." He reached into a canvas bag and pulled out a doll carved from cottonwood root. "For you." The doll had a scary mask with slit eyes and a plug mouth. A bright blue sash fastened across his shoulder...

Her two right wheels dropped off the pavement and Nora jerked the steering wheel to pull the Jeep back on the road. It fishtailed but righted itself.

"Nora?" Abigail's voice squawked from the phone in Nora's lap.

Nora grabbed the dropped phone. "Had some traffic."

"Where are you now?"

Nora spotted a road side. "A couple miles past Settler's Park. About to the Trust."

Nora braked and turned left. She rumbled across a wood-planked bridge over the creek. Loving Earth Trust occupied a rambling old house in Boulder Canyon, butted up to the mountain side. Gables and windows, extensions and extra rooms jutted out at weird angles giving the place a disjointed feel. The picturesque front porch descended to a sparsely grassed front yard with a rail fence separating it from the packed dirt parking area. Only three other vehicles sat there. Beyond the lot, a one-lane road ran along the creek bank, but it petered out after a couple hundred yards. A large wood barn stood behind the house. Towering mountains and pines assured that the house stayed in shadow most of the time. It was beautiful, of course, but a chill goosed Nora's flesh.

"Here we are," Nora said. "Gotta go."

"Have a good day, dear. We'll talk soon."

Too soon, no doubt. That wasn't fair. Abigail had been supportive and encouraging since Nora had moved from Flagstaff a year ago. At times, Abigail had been Nora's only human contact.

Now it was time to start over. Be normal. Have a job. Friends. Maybe a social life. "Hold on, Cowgirl. Just start with a job, okay?"

If that went well, maybe she'd stop talking to herself.

She ran her fingers through Abbey's fur. Good thing first days of work didn't last forever. Too bad second days and then the first week, and month, full of anxiety and nerves followed. In no time, say a millennium or two, Nora would feel right at home.

She filled her lungs, imagining the air had magical powers to make her appear confident and smart. "Let's go," she said, pretending she talked to Abbey.

Abbey jumped out as if he'd been coming to work here every day for years. Nora leaned into the back of the Jeep and hefted out a bushy potted plant. She rested the terra cotta pot on her hip and steadied it with her arm. She had larger and heavier pots at home but thought this would work in an office. The long, wide, deeply green leaves rose from the pot and cascaded, leaving her room enough to peek over the top. She slammed the Jeep door shut.

4

Nora and Abbey crunched along the frost-skimmed dirt of the parking lot and up the old wooden stairs. The wide porch creaked as they crossed. Nora balanced the plant on her hip and opened the door, letting Abbey take the first step into their new digs.

Although Nora had bosses and structure in jobs before, this was her first Real Job. She'd gone from her undergrad to business school and right into running the ski resort in Arizona without the entry-level introduction to her career. Now she held a management position and answered to the Executive Director and the board. Gulp. But she needed to act like that was no big deal to her.

They stood in what appeared to be a large living room, complete with a stone fireplace on one end, window seats on the front porch side, a flight of stairs off the other, and some Mission style padded chairs scattered about. Whoever built this around the turn of the century must have had means to make it so spacious. As it was, the cost of this sucker, with the size and location along the creek outside of Boulder, could probably save the earth and a few other planets.

Mark Monstain, Executive Director, walked into the room carrying a take-out cup with a Mr. Green Beans logo. Nora gave him the benefit of the doubt and assumed the green in Green Beans meant the cup was recyclable. He stood about five eight, all rounded edges, with a belly in the early stage of drooping over his belt. He wore the same ensemble as he had at her interview, a white, short-sleeved shirt, tucked sloppily into black dress pants. Despite thinning hair at the crown of his head, he had to be about Nora's age. Not the typical build and dress of an outdoorsman and rugged environmentalist. More like a grocery store clerk without the apron.

"Good. Right on time." He punctuated the unfunny remark with a giggle. Nora noticed in the interview he tended to insert an annoying high-pitched giggle into nearly every sentence. She'd teach herself to ignore it. For this job, she'd ignore a roaring grizzly bear.

"I see you've brought a plant to liven up your office."

Thank you, Mr. Obvious.

"And your dog."

He'd told her bringing Abbey would be fine. "Did you say my office was upstairs?" The plant bit into her hip and she felt awkward standing in the lobby/living room with both hands full.

He didn't move. "You don't remember me after all, do you?"

Uh-oh. Awkward Alert. She hugged the plant. "I'm sorry."

"From Earth Club at Boulder High?"

"Oh, of course." *Mark Monstain?* She had no clue.

She wracked her brain to recall the flabby lips and chubby cheeks. Earth Club was little more than a group of idealists handing out flyers on weekends and railing against what they thought of as humankind's war on the environment.

"I'm not surprised you don't remember me. You were a senior when I was a freshman." He giggled.

At the interview she'd felt a vague sense of familiarity, similar to the way she felt about anchovies. She'd tasted them once as a child, had a lingering memory of nausea and never wanted to try them again.

The pocket of Nora's jacket vibrated. It had to be Abigail calling back. Even if her hands weren't wrapped around her plant, she wouldn't answer.

He sipped his coffee and began as if she'd asked. "I went to CU after Boulder High and graduated in environmental engineering. I started here as head volunteer coordinator and worked my way up. I've been here longer than anyone else."

"You're doing a great job." What else could she say?

He nodded. "Well, let me show you your office, then." He led the way up the stairs.

A sunny mezzanine opened on her right with a shared area and several offices lining it.

"This is where the volunteer program lives." Giggle, snort. "They log about four thousand man hours a year on our various projects from trail maintenance and open space restoration to range research and of course, the beetle kill problem. They're all out in the field this week taking advantage of the weather before the snow flies."

The plant tugged at Nora's arms, a heavy accessory to drag around on a house tour. Abbey followed, not acting impressed.

They wound around a hallway that opened into an office area with a large desk. A copier and other office machines sat on a counter. "This is the copy room. This computer has a graphics and design program to make fliers and whatnot."

If this tour lasted much longer Nora's arms would give out and the plant would crash in a heap of terra cotta and roots.

A narrow servant's stairway opened to her left. "The kitchen is down there. Three years ago we added a sweet addition for Sylvia LaFever. You've heard of her, I'm sure."

Nora hadn't. A faint odor of burnt toast wafted from the stairwell.

"She used to work for the government at the HAARP facility in Alaska. You know, doing all sorts of research on the ionosphere and weather and things." He rushed along as if Nora understood what he talked about. She had heard of HAARP, of course. But didn't know much about it.

Mark rubbed his hands together. "We're lucky to have her. She's doing landscape modeling in regard to beetle kill and climate change. Real cutting-edge research."

Nora didn't know how cutting edge since she'd read studies showing the slight increase in temperatures facilitated an extra breeding cycle each year for the deadly beetles. If Nora knew about it, it couldn't be all that new. Maybe Sylvia LaFever's research dug deeper.

Mark pointed but kept them on the winding maze of odd-shaped offices. The old floor groaned as they wandered down the hall. The rooms probably served as bedrooms once but now walls cut them into tiny offices. "This place is enormous."

"But you can't beat the location." Snort. "Sometimes when things get hectic I go out on the front porch and watch the creek. We've had this building about five years now. A donor left it to us in her will."

Mark stopped at an open door. Finally, she'd be able to set the plant down and see her office.

"This is Thomas. He works on air quality." Mark lifted his arm to indicate a tall man with bushy dark curls and hairy legs leaning back in his chair reading. A bike propped on the wall in the corner. His orange Life Is Good t-shirt, cargo shorts and stocking feet indicted a casual dress code. His office smelled of the oatmeal he scraped from the bowl resting on his chest. "Thomas, this is Nora, our new director of finance."

Thomas peered at them over his reading glasses. "Welcome."

Mark pointed across the hall. "This is Bill's office, but he's at meetings today. He's our litigator." More offices opened up along the foyer creating a labyrinth. "Fay, She's in charge of Open Space." Another thirty-something with blonde hair smashed into a nest at the back of her head and wisps spilling down her back. Braless in an olive green t-shirt and hiking pants, her firm muscles showed regular physical activity.

Fay turned from her computer and spoke in a creaky voice. "Nice dog!" Abbey responded by trotting in and allowing Fay to pet him.

Panic swelled in Nora. She'd never remember the names and faces and jobs. She swallowed and forced calm.

First day. Don't be overwhelmed.

Eventually she'd figure this out and make friends. It wasn't life or death in one day.

Despite the at least four people and a dog, the house felt empty. Maybe it was too early in the day for environmentalists. They wouldn't necessarily keep the same hours as corporate drones. "Seems like lots of space."

Mark giggled. "Most of the staff comes and goes a lot. Our work takes us to the field and meetings. It's not unusual for the admin staff to be here alone."

More pocket vibrations. Tenacity, thy name is Abigail.

"Just a minute." Mark poked his head in Thomas's office and spoke about meetings and legislation.

The plant dragged on Nora's arms. A window offered a narrow ledge and she stepped to it and rested the pot. Below, a jumble of flowing fabric bounced into the parking lot on a rusted bike. If the window was open, no doubt she'd have heard the clank and rattle of a chain needing oil. The mass of dreadlocks hid Petal's face. Plastic flowers wove through the old bike's front basket and streamers hung from the handlebars. The whole affair resembled more of a circus act than another day at the office.

Petal jumped off the bike, her flowered skirt fluttering around her ankles. She grabbed a satchel from the basket, flung the strap over her shoulder, and sprinted to the front porch.

"That's our Petal," Mark said from behind her. He scowled and checked his watch. "She works for Sylvia."

"Seems like there are a lot of different activities going on here."

He grinned and motioned for her to continue down the hall. "We're proud we're involved in all kinds of matters affecting the environment. We've got a great board and lots of funding."

Nora heaved the plant back up to her hip, switching sides. "Must be complicated accounting to keep so many programs and funds straight."

A shadow darkened Mark's face. "Darla wasn't up to the job. You'll get it in top shape in no time. From what I remember, you're super-smart and a great organizer."

That's a lot of confidence based on her presidency in a high school club. But Nora knew numbers. She understood accounting and could retreat into the safety of spreadsheets, where mistakes could be corrected and everything made sense.

"Do you mind me asking why the last Finance Director left so abruptly?"

They approached the end of the hall. Her office had to be close. Mark reached into his pocket and brought out a jangling set of keys. "Frankly, Darla was a flake. I'm not surprised she bugged out."

No one checked up to see why? That seemed strange.

Mark inserted a key into a heavy wood door that was probably original with the house. He giggled as he pushed the door open and stood back for her to enter. He opened his arm with a flourish. "Ta da."

Nora inhaled and stepped into the office. The long walk, talk of a disappearing Financial Director and locked doors had her expecting some kind of *Exorcist* moment with papers swirling through the air, maniacal laughter, darkness and debris filling a sulfuric atmosphere.

No overactive imagination there.

Windows lined this large corner office. Lavender paint with mint green trim brightened the walls. Plants sat on the window sills that accented a view down Boulder Canyon. A wicker chair with a chintz seat pad was tucked into a corner next to a cute patio table with a reading lamp. A large cabinet sat in the corner with the doors open. One side held shelves full of office supplies, and the other side was a coat closet. The desk and work space filled up one wall. File folders, papers, notebooks, and documents jumbled across the sizable countertop workspace. After Nora straightened and filed and got the rhythm, the office would be comfortable and pleasant.

Her pocket vibrated again. Never say die. Abigail.

Mark worked her office key off his ring and handed it to her. He pulled a crumpled notebook page from the pocket of his white shirt. "Here are the system passwords. If you change them, let me know. Make yourself at home. I've got to run." He sped away.

"Well, what do you think?" she asked Abbey.

He responded by plopping down next to a filing cabinet and watching her.

"Go ahead and act exhausted, I'm the one lugging this plant around." She eased the plant onto the corner of the counter, shoving papers aside.

"So you're going to replace Darla? Didn't take Mark long to write her off."

Nora whirled around to see Fay leaning against the door jamb. See? Normal colleague chatter. Not a threat. Remember casual conversation? "How long has she been gone?"

Fay shrugged. "Less than a week. Maybe Mark knows something we don't."

Nora surveyed the room. Two painted white wooden shelves above the work surface held porcelain figurines of bunnies and kittens painted in pastels. A snapshot showed a grinning woman, presumably Darla, shrouded in winter gear next to a Pawnee Pass sign on the Continental Divide. Several framed posters with inspirational sayings and landscapes peppered the walls. "Looks like she planned on coming back," Nora said. "She left a lot of personal things."

Fay walked into the office and peeked into the coat closet. She picked up a book from a shelf above the rod. Her voice had a cracked quality, as if she'd been yelling at a soccer match for two hours. "I don't know Darla very well. She kept to herself." She returned the book and picked up another. "Really, I thought she was weird."

Nora shrugged out of her coat. She didn't want to gossip. "How long have you been at the Trust?"

Fay wandered over to the decorative shelf and plucked Darla's picture off the shelf. "I didn't know she was a hiker." She set it back down. "I've been here about five years. I'm wondering how long I'll last."

Nora studied a bulletin board mounted behind the computer. It was strewn with multicolored sticky notes. "Why is that?"

Fay retreated to the door jamb and leaned against it, crossing her arms. Her voice croaked. "You'll see. Used to be all the projects were important. But now days, we've got one star and that's all Mark can see."

Nora leaned her backside on the work counter. She wanted to dive into the mounds of paper. "If the board doesn't like the job Mark's doing as executive director, they can replace him."

Fay's laugh sounded like a rusty door hinge. "Right. Mark isn't ED because he's so brilliant. His daddy is on the board. Mark's not going anywhere."

That answered the question of why someone so...icky... could have such an impressive job.

"So if any of us want to actually do any good, we're gonna have to make an exit."

An uncomfortable silence dropped into the office.

Fay gave that creaky laugh again. "Sorry. I've never learned the art of subtlety. I'll let you settle in. Maybe we can do a hike next week or something." She walked away with a groan of the floor.

A hike sounded way better than dipping down in the dregs of bad attitude. A hike sounded pretty good, actually.

Her phone jumped again. Might as well answer it, Abigail wouldn't stop until she did. "Mother."

"So how's it going? Did they seem to mind you wearing jeans? What about this Mark Monstain?"

Nora kept her voice down. "I'll call this evening and tell you all the details."

"Well, that's what I wanted to talk to you about."

Oh no. That tone. It meant trouble for Nora. "Not now, Mother."

"Nora." Mark appeared as if from magic. "I'd like you to meet our star here at the Trust."

Busted talking to her mother on the first day. "I have to go," she said into the phone.

"What I was saying is that you don't need to call me later."

Nora smiled at Mark and the attractive, petite woman standing next to him. An expensive black business suit draped perfectly over her compact frame, complete with four-inch pumps. Her dark hair curled around an ageless face. She looked like money all dressed up.

"Good bye." Nora tried to balance the pleasant face for her new boss and the firm voice for Abigail.

"Okay. But I wanted to tell you I'm on my way to Boulder. I should be there soon. Surprise!"

An anvil dropped, squishing Nora like Wile E. Coyote in a desert canyon.

5

Nora set the phone on her desk, resisting the urge to stuff it in the soil of her potted plant.

Mark's wet lips turned down in a frowned at Nora, then he gave the same arm flourish he'd used to present her office. He was either profoundly proud of everything at the Trust or liked the gesture. "This is Sylvia LaFever. She's working on the landscape modeling project I told you about."

Nora shook Sylvia's hand. "Mark mentioned climate change and beetle kill?"

While not exactly beautiful, Sylvia's magnetism pulled energy toward her. Dark eyes snapped and her smile commanded attention. "Don't worry about understanding my program yet. It's your first day. How unfortunate to be thrust into a financial maelstrom on the eve of the board meeting."

Board meeting! Mark hadn't mentioned an impending trial by fire. He squirmed and snorted.

A cloud of subtle scent wafted around Sylvia like million dollar molecules of heaven. Abigail would appreciate that. Sylvia clasped Nora's hand. "Was that your mother on the phone?"

If Nora could get through this day without throwing up, she'd be happy. "She's excited about my position here and wants all the details."

Sylvia gave a sympathetic nod of her head, her black curls bouncing just enough to seem alive but not so much as to muss her do. "Family is important but, as I know, they can be trying."

"Tell me about the beetle kill work," Nora said. Maybe she should offer them a chair instead of having them stand in the middle of her office.

Mark inserted himself into the conversation. "Sylvia's work is groundbreaking. She's using some of the science she developed—" his flabby lips formed these words with care to emphasize their import—"at the HAARP facility in Alaska."

Nora raised her eyebrows hoping she appeared impressed.

Mark seemed satisfied with her reaction. "Sylvia was a Senior Project Manager. The modeling she's doing for the Trust uses ionosphere measurements to gauge UA and UV waves and their correlation to the temperatures. She takes all this and overlays it with models of beetle kill. We have our field techs out gathering data on that." As usual, he followed up with a snicker. "When this is published, people will be begging to donate to us."

Optimistic, considering about ten people read scientific papers. "Sounds interesting," Nora said.

"Interesting? Sylvia is a scientific rock star and we've got her here." Although he wasn't actually slobbering he teetered on the verge. "And she's got a killer sense of style." His obvious hero-worship felt creepy.

"Now, Mark." Sylvia bowed her head graciously. "It's all due to Daniel Cubrero's fund raising. His family foundation donates generously."

The name didn't sound familiar to Nora but she didn't hobnob with the super-wealthy types that tended to sit on non-profit boards of directors.

Sylvia's dark eyes rested on Mark with indulgence before she addressed Nora. "It's exciting research. HARRP started as a government program. High Frequency Active Aurora Iononspheric Research Program."

Nora spied a stack of file folders under the desk. She'd love to dig into the work. "I don't know much about it."

No one seemed inclined to sit or at the least, leave her office.

Again, Sylvia showed a patient smile. "The technology is just as complicated as it sounds. Not many people can grasp the concept. Much of it is based on the early discoveries of Nikola Tesla and unfortunately, the bulk of his research was lost when he died in the forties. The program began as a study of the ionosphere to enhance surveillance and communication, mostly for military use. But where it interests the Trust and others concerned about our planet, is how the technology might be used to study the effects of climate change. The Colorado mountain pine beetle kill is one dramatic area to gather research."

"Fascinating," Nora's mind raced beyond Sylvia's words to the haystack of papers on the work surface. The documents and files seemed to split like protozoa, creating new stacks for sorting, identifying and filing.

"That's an interesting plant." Sylvia stepped around Mark to the pot. She ran a red fingernail along one wide leaf. "What is it?"

Nora had a sudden urge to slap Sylvia's hand away. "It's corn."

Sylvia eyed her with skepticism.

"Hopi corn," Nora said. "It's different than what we're used to." *And that's all I'm going to say about that.*

"And the pot designs? Are those Hopi, too?"

Nora had etched the designs into the clay. "Oh, they're just designs. Not significant."

"I don't know anything about the Hopi tribe." Boredom tinged Sylvia's words.

Such an ancient culture, so rich and intricate. And for some reason, Nora didn't want to share it with Sylvia. "They're a tiny tribe in northern Arizona in the middle of the Navajo reservation. They revere peace and natural harmony."

Sylvia stared at the corn for a moment then focused on Nora. "I know you're busy on your first day and I won't take up any more of your time. Why don't we have lunch next week?"

"That would be great."

"If you'll cut my check, I'll be on my way."

Wait. Check?

Nora didn't know what financial software Loving Earth Trust used. Where did they keep the checks? Did they have one general bank account or did each program have its own restricted account? What bank or banks? So much she didn't know, check writing was a definite no-go. "Um." She turned a desperate face to Mark, hoping he'd explain.

He met her with an expectant uplift of eyebrows.

This didn't bode well for a great working relationship. Nora braced herself. "I'm sorry, Sylvia. I need to get acquainted with several things before I spend any money. I'm not even a signatory yet."

Sylvia's full lips turned down in a slight frown. "I understand, of course. But the funding is there. I wrote a sizable check from my personal funds and Darla was supposed to have paid me last week. I hate to disparage her, especially since she's gone, but she was really falling apart lately."

Nora retreated behind professional formality. "As fiscal agent of the Trust, I'm responsible for the finances. I don't feel comfortable writing checks until I have a chance to see what's going on."

Mark frowned. "I can sign the check. Our dysfunction shouldn't be Sylvia's problem."

Flames engulfed Nora as she debated what to do. Her face burned. Should she play nice and make friends or be responsible, buck her boss and probably lose her job on the first day?

Sylvia never lost her expression of expectation. This was a woman used to getting her way.

Tick, tick, tick.

In the kitchen, which sat at the bottom of the servant's stairs at the end of the maze from Nora's office, someone's cell phone jingled, followed by the murmur of a woman's voice.

Did a new stack of papers materialize on the desk?

She shouldn't write a check. She really shouldn't.

Sweat slimed her underarms.

Tick, tick, tick.

Sylvia's foot started to tap. Those had to be incredibly expensive shoes.

Something crashed in the kitchen. A howl like the death throes of a rabbit rent the air, soaring from the kitchen, down the hall, into Nora's office, strangling her.

The sound of death.

6

Sylvia froze. Her mind vibrated with suppressed panic. The scream snaked up the stairs into the base of Sylvia's spine, slithering through her heart. Survival instincts honed in her dangerous childhood told her to run.

Nora leapt past Sylvia and Mark, sprinting through the hall and flying down the narrow servants' stairs. Was she an athlete? She acted like some kind of super hero out to save the day.

Sylvia knew better than to involve herself with others' crisis. She spent three seconds regaining her control.

Mark gave her an exasperated expression. "It's Petal. I suppose we should go see what it is this time."

Sylvia brushed past him. "I'm very busy, Mark. You can handle this."

He whined. "She works for you. I think it's best if you help her."

She instantly calculated her best options. Cooperation. "Of course."

Her beatific smile would do Mother Teresa proud. Great power and gifts had the annoying flipside of great responsibility. Someone always needed her wise counsel or her attention in some way.

Honestly, Sylvia's time would be better spent using her formidable mind solving the problem at which she alone could succeed. But a leader needed to help the little people from time to time. It kept Sylvia humble and human.

When they reached the kitchen, Nora knelt on the floor next to a puddle of gauze and bird's nest of hair. Nora patted Petal's back and cooed soothing words.

As if this nothing of an accountant could possibly give comfort.

Mark crossed his arms and sounded annoyed. "Petal, please try to pull yourself together. We can't help if you don't tell us what's wrong."

Sylvia stepped up. Coddling Petal would only encourage her drama. "Enough of this, Petal. Either tell us what upset you or stop the histrionics and let's see if we can get some work done today."

Nora appeared shocked. She probably thought they should perform a group hug and talk about their feelings. This bleeding-heart attitude, so common among the non-profit do-gooders, demonstrated why Nora slaved as a simple accountant and why Sylvia rubbed elbows with the world's elite.

Sylvia placed her hands on her hips and distanced herself from Petal's current meltdown. She hated this kitchen. It stretched twenty feet end to end and was little more than an extra-wide hallway. The sink and old-time cupboards of thick, white-painted wood ran the length of one wall. A window with a cheap aluminum frame opened above the sink. The counter top was pre-Formica, the floor spread with some kind of linoleum. It peeled away at the corners, reminding Sylvia too much of the house where she grew up.

There was no stove, a toaster oven and microwave filled the bill. Sylvia wished they'd get rid of those, too, since it seemed no one here could fix a snack without burning it. A refrigerator constantly full of moldering left-overs and forgotten lunches bookended the counter. A wooden booth sat in a nook between the front lobby and the kitchen. Sylvia had never seen anyone use it.

The door to the backyard opened along the other wall. The whole room acted as a corridor to connect Sylvia's suite with the rest of the ramshackle building. From the window above the sink she could see the parking lot and road. The window in the back door showed an open space of scruffy lawn ending at a border of pines and shrubs. It could be nice with land-scaping and a gazebo, maybe a built-in fireplace and grill. But the staff at the Trust lacked vision.

Petal continued her sobbing. Nora kept treating her like a dog injured in traffic.

Mark's face glow red with anger. "Okay, enough of this," he said. "Stop wailing and tell us what's going on."

Face wet with tears and nose snotty and red, Petal slowly sat up from where she burrowed into Nora's lap. She hiccupped and drew in a shaky breath. She opened her mouth, presumably to explain the calamity, but let out another sob and dropped into Nora's lap again.

Nora patted her back, searching Mark's, then Sylvia's face for help. To be fair, Nora didn't know Petal's normal instability. But on her first day, she shouldn't interfere when she had no clue.

"Darla, Darla, Darla." Petal gasped between sobs.

Sylvia's stomach twisted. From Petal's first scream she'd felt a terrible foreboding.

Mark squatted in front of Petal, impatience written on his face. "What about Darla?"

Petal sat up again. This time she forced words. "She's dead." Petal blathered away, all her feelings and pain splattering everyone in hearing range.

What did this mean for Sylvia?

It didn't change anything. Whether Darla walked off in her Birkenstocks or whether she died, it didn't make much difference to Sylvia.

She needed to focus on Nora. Sure, she had a moment of hesitation about writing Sylvia a check. With Mark's urging—and Mark would do anything for Sylvia—Nora would be toeing the line in short order.

It had to happen immediately, though. The art dealer annoyingly demanded a down payment before she'd ship the Chihuly.

Petal's voice gained some strength, enough for Sylvia to understand. "Darla was just found in the trees by the road. They said she was shot close to the Trust and tried to make it to the highway for help."

The vision of the colorful glass vanished.

"She'd been there since Sunday night."

Sylvia stopped breathing. A flash flood of blood roared in her ears. No. That couldn't be. Even her brain, that wonderful and extraordinary tool, ground to a near halt.

That night. The night Sylvia found the glass. The night Darla threatened her.

"She was shot in the back. Who would want to shoot Darla?" Petal wailed again.

Sylvia's chest crushed with the weight of realization. Shot outside the Trust on Sunday night.

One shot fired out the door into the darkness last Sunday night.

7

Nora stood at her office window, heart pounding and her breath catching in her chest. She gently rubbed a smooth corn leaf between her thumb and forefinger. There was something definitely wonky about this place. Murder. *Murder!*

She squatted down and scratched Abbey behind the ears, letting his warmth calm her. Petal's pain had seeped through Nora's clothes and into her skin. Worse yet were Mark's and Sylvia's reactions to the news that someone they worked with had been shot. They hadn't seemed at all concerned and actually more annoyed that Petal disrupted the quiet morning.

"What sort of place is this?"

Abbey didn't answer her. He lay with his eyes half closed, wallowing in the attention.

The piles of paper and chaos of the office swamped her. "We ought to book it out of here."

Abbey rested his head on his paws.

"I'm not up for more murder."

He closed his eyes and let out a deep sigh of contentment.

"On the other hand, since you're the only one I talk to these days, maybe I ought to hang around for human contact."

He wasn't going to give her any advice; that much was plain.

A light knock on her door jamb startled her.

Fay stood in the doorway, her eyes wide in her round face. Her voice crackled softly. "So what happened? I heard Petal say Darla was killed."

Nora leaned back on her work surface. "I don't know."

Another head appeared over Fay's shoulder. The hairy guy working on air quality. Thomas. Score one for Nora remembering his name. "Did you get any details?"

Fay turned to him with her creaky voice. "I'll bet it was Mark."

Thomas shook his head. "Naw. He hired her. I think he liked her because he could control her."

Fay shook her head. "I can't believe she's dead. And that she was *shot*."

Thomas nodded. "Yeah. Right here." He scrutinized Nora's office and shuddered as if Darla had been shot in the room.

"Maybe it was Sylvia. She hated Darla. She hates everyone." Fay nodded at Thomas for confirmation.

"Freaky." Without any warning, they both wandered away.

Freaky, indeed.

Nora surveyed the paper orgy strewn across the work space. *A journey of a thousand miles begins with... filing.* She shuffled the pages into unruly stacks.

Interspersed among the spreadsheets, invoices and financial statements, Nora came across pages from a yellow legal pad. Like a child's scribbling on a blackboard as punishment, each page was filled with one line over and over. One page repeated, "I am smart." on all twenty-eight lines. Another said, "I will succeed." "I am beautiful." "I can do it." "I am rich." Nora's throat constricted with sympathy when she found the last one: "They DO like me." Over and over.

Nora picked up the picture of Darla and studied it. If Darla were thin or fat, cheerful or dour, the outwear concealed it all. One thing Nora knew for sure: Darla was not happy.

Nora replaced the photo and trudged along with the paperwork.

Well past lunch time, Mark stuck his head in her office. "Wow. You've made some headway." Snort. "Darla wasn't very organized."

He spoke casually, as if Darla—someone he'd worked with every day—hadn't just been found dead on a mountain. What a jerk.

Nora had slogged through much of the accounting fall-out on the desk. The documents consisted mostly of payroll spreadsheets and copies of paychecks, invoices—both paid and pending financial reports, and Post-it notes.

She'd found the reason for all the scribbled pages. Several self-help books occupied the closet shelf and a dog-eared self-esteem manual declared success through written affirmations. Darla was struggling to change.

Nora picked up a pile of handwritten accounting worksheets "I think Darla tracked grants and restricted donations by hand and allocated them monthly, then backed the totals out of the general fund."

He blanked.

"You can do it this way but it's a lot of work and there is a lag so that if checks were written early in the month, the actual fund allocation won't show up for a few weeks in the project budget."

He obviously had no idea what she was talking about. That gave her leeway to set up her own, more efficient system. "How's Petal?"

He waved his hand. "She's overly dramatic. I'm sorry you had to see one of her episodes on your first day."

Her friend and coworker was murdered. Nora knew what it felt like when someone you love is murdered. You can't get overly dramatic about that.

Mark's face reddened. He must have read Nora's expression. "It's terrible, of course. Unexpected and upsetting."

He stayed at the office door gazing at Nora. Not awkward at all.

To fill the void, Nora chatted. "I'll check to make sure all these invoices are entered and get them filed. I'll see about bank balances and check A/P."

Abruptly, he said, "Write Sylvia's check but everything else can wait until next week." Snort.

"Shouldn't she submit a reimbursement request and receipts?"

Mark waved that away. "She's a star scientist not an accounting clerk. She shouldn't waste her time with this trivia."

"The auditors..."

"Do it," he interrupted, and then seemed to catch himself. "Please."

She didn't commit. "I'm hoping to get this bookkeeping stuff out of the way by the end of the week so I can settle in and work on the funds and project worksheets and reports. I need to figure out how all this is organized."

Mark's eyebrows drew down and he snuffled, an even more nervous sound than his usual laugh. "That will come. But right now you need to pull some financials together for tomorrow's board meeting."

A mace, complete with spiked ball, swung straight from his hand with no wind up. It smacked into the side of her head. "A board meeting *tomorrow*?"

"Don't worry. I've got the financials Darla submitted two weeks ago for the board preview. You can just add a few expenses and a little income and they'll be good to go. I emailed them to you." His assurance felt as slimy as his dismissal of Darla's murder.

"It won't be accurate."

"No one expects them to be penny perfect. They only want an update from what they had previously. Just get through tomorrow and you'll have time to study everything in depth."

She doubted the board wanted or needed sketchy information. She didn't answer.

His face reddened as he became defensive. "We can't cancel the meeting. Daniel Cubrero fit it into his schedule. Bryson Bradshaw is over the Atlantic now and a few others won't want to cancel their flights and reschedule. These meetings are hell to arrange."

When she still didn't answer he said, "Do your best. But remember, we don't want to upset the board needlessly." He spun around and scurried away before she could respond.

She addressed Abbey. "Not a good situation." The Trust was an accounting nightmare. If someone didn't set it right, and soon, they wouldn't be able to continue to repair trails and maintain crucial habitats. The beetle kill research would take a hit.

Nora's guilt over almost spraying uranium-tainted water on the sacred peaks in Flagstaff drove her on a strange apologetic quest. She didn't make snow as she'd set out to do and the slopes were protected now, but she still felt she had a debt to pay. Maybe accounting wouldn't end global warming or save the whales, but straightening up this office could be her contribution.

Sour stew boiled in Nora's gut. How would she pull together financials to present to a board of directors when she had no notion of the organization?

8

The afternoon sun sent an uncertain ray through her window and Abbey lay in its weak beam in the middle of the room. Someone had overcooked popcorn in the microwave and the smell added to Nora's nausea.

An electronic beep sounded, startling Nora. A tinny voice invaded the room. "Nora?"

An old-school interoffice page. Must be coming from a phone. Nora raised her voice. "Hi. I'm here. Just let me find the phone." Nora pushed papers aside and finally found a beige Titanic of technology. She picked up the receiver. "Okay. I've got it."

"This is Sylvia. You haven't had a chance to tour my office suite. Why not you come down? I'm at a good break point."

Nothing like a summons from the queen. "Sure."

"I'm sending Petal to get you."

The queen and even a lady in waiting—rather, a Rasta-girl-in-waiting. A rustle caused Nora to turn to the door. Petal stood like a rag doll, all floppy and boneless, her eyes red-rimmed. Apparently, Sylvia had little doubt Nora would accept the command. "Here she is." Nora tried to sound pleased as she spoke to the intercom.

Sylvia must have already hung up.

"How are you?" Nora asked.

Petal shrugged. "Darla was my friend." Her voice sounded like a drop of water on a still lake.

"I'm sorry. Do you think you should go home?"

Petal shook her head, sending her dreads into a frantic dance. "Sylvia has work for me to do."

Nora couldn't say what she wanted to say, which was, "*Screw Sylvia.*" Could this really be her first few hours of her first day at the first shot of a job in a year?

"Well, let's go see the office, then."

Petal led the way down the narrow stairs through the kitchen. Someone had propped the back door open and a breeze blew away the scorched popcorn odor. Past the door, a few feet beyond the kitchen and an open storage area, Petal stopped in front of a closed door. She opened it and stepped back.

Nora hesitated before entering. The room was by far the largest in the building. It accommodated what appeared to be an antique banquet table in the center of the space, scattered with maps.

"Welcome!" Sylvia swept from behind a desk, graceful as a supermodel in her high heels. "What do you think?" She stepped back and displayed her kingdom as if she were a hostess at the White House.

"Impressive," Nora said, not lying.

Sylvia waved that away. "The Trust was too cheap to give me a separate office but I've adjusted to the constraints." She led Nora from the door, around the center table to the far side of the room.

The area Sylvia chose as her personal office occupied a whole corner. Her massive cherry wood desk nestled in the space created from two walls of the suite and one wall pieced together with file cabinets.

"I spent quite some time scrounging in antiques stores to find this book-case." She indicated an ornate wood bookshelf occupying the wall behind her desk. A Tiffany lamp on her desk cast a glow to reflect off the polished wood furniture. The bookshelf held her framed diplomas, a bronze of a nude, and volumes of expensive-looking hardcover books.

"But this is my real treasure." She swept her arm in front of her to showcase the antique dining table taking up the center of the room. Maps sprawled across the table. "I'm quite proud of that table. It was an amazing deal I found at a shop in Aspen. Darla questioned the expense and said a fifty dollar table from Costco would work just as well, but Mark backed me up."

Petal slinked away to another corner and folded herself into a chair. She rolled it close to a desk more like the humble discount office store kind the rest of the Trust staffers used. A small lamp sat on her desk, draped in a pink scarf. She hunched over a keyboard and began to type.

The addition felt tacked-on, without the charm of the turn-of-the-century farmhouse. Nora pointed to a stack of computer processing units. These weren't typical CPU towers to power a regular PC. Next to the tower stood a giant, high-tech scanner, almost as large as the antique table. "What is all this for?"

Sylvia seemed pleased to be asked. "The Cubrero Family Foundation paid for sophisticated modeling software and sufficient power to run it. We needed to have the tools so I could create the maps." Sylvia indicated the scanner. "This machine prints with the necessary detail and size."

Nora studied the 3X4 foot color maps tacked on the walls.

Sylvia spoke as though conducting a grade school field trip. "Mountain pine beetle is infecting the forests at a rate ten times any previous infestation. It's at about three point two million acres in Colorado and Wyoming alone. Common wisdom says the large beetle population is the result of climate change. But I'm suspecting the beetle is actually altering local weather patterns and air quality. There's a big difference between the effect of a living forest and a dead one on the environment. I'm studying the age old question: what comes first, the chicken or the egg." She laughed at her own cleverness

Nora stepped to the table and bent to the maps.

"You know," Sylvia explained. "Is the climate driving the beetles or are the beetles driving the climate?"

Tappity-tap, tap, tap. Petal worked away.

Nora lifted the corner of one of the maps and leaned on the table to scrutinize it.

Sylvia slid the map from Nora and thrust a finger on it. "You see? These overlay colors and shading indicate not only temperature and cloud cover but times and trends, followed by these stills." She pulled out another map from underneath and spread it on top of the first. "These indicate the spread of beetle kill. When I combine them in an animated digital process, I can illustrate the actual correlation between climatic factors and beetle spread."

"That's amazing. And you created this technology?"

Sylvia laughed. "Oh, not all of it. I used some of what I developed with my team at HAARP facility in Alaska."

"Isn't HAARP something like an array of towers that shoot energy into the atmosphere? People think it's some sort of weather altering thing or mind control or doomsday weapon?"

Sylvia laughed. "There are a hundred and eighty towers and they send out a ping but the energy used is much less than any sun burst. What happens is that the towers send a billion watts of energy into the atmosphere. That's about a hundred times a thunderbolt. It excites the ionosphere and creates a plume and then bounces back to the surface."

"What is the point of the research?"

Petal quit typing. She sat still as if listening.

"What does it matter? All major scientific breakthroughs have come about with research for pure knowledge sake. We don't know what we'll discover that will create real good. For instance, there is hope that some of the HAARP technology will actually facilitate ozone repair."

"You get information from HAARP for the beetle kill research?"

"Oh no. I've developed a tower using similar HAARP technologies. It's an advance on the work of Nikola Tesla. I've developed the technology to use only one small installation on Mount Evans, not far from here."

Oh. Where Nora met Petal.

Petal started tapping on the keyboard again.

"It's one of Colorado's tallest peaks. The highest electron density is on tall mountains because the negative charge is reaching for the positive charge in the atmosphere. My tower sends extremely low frequency waves, ELF, and the waves that bounce back create the raw data I use in the modeling software I created."

Didn't she say earlier she'd bought the software with donor funds? Maybe she worked with Al Gore when he invented the Internet, too.

"So it's a matter of tweaking the tower's angle of refraction to gather the matrices to compile the complicated 3D images."

Nora pulled another map from the bottom of the pile and slid it on top. A red Sharpie circle marked a map of South America. "Are you researching Ecuador?"

Sylvia shoved another map over the South America one. "No. Of course not."

Petal typed away, not appearing to pay any attention to their conversation.

Sylvia eyed Petal and placed a hand on Nora's arm. "It's a lovely fall day. Let me show you the friendship garden. A garden club donates their time to give us a place for reflection by the creek."

They walked through the kitchen, out the back door and into the yard. The brown grass crunched underfoot. "How are you settling in?"

My office looks like a volcano of paper erupted in it. The previous Finance Director was murdered. The star scientist is a prima donna. The Executive Director is a creepy loser from high school. The sanest person here is a dreadlock-wearing woman of indeterminate age.

"As well as can be expected for a first day," Nora said.

"That's good." Again, no mention of Darla. Sylvia stopped well short of the promised garden. "I'll need that check today."

Now we get to the point of the welcome tour.

"I won't be able to do that until next week." Firm. Competent. No nonsense. And if she kept her jaw clenched and hands clasped behind her back, Sylvia wouldn't notice how shaky she felt.

Sylvia's nostrils flared. "I don't need the entire amount right away. Just fifty thousand."

Just? Nora squinted into the sun. The soft breeze sending the scent of pine didn't make her feel as happy as it usually did. "The problem is I don't know if we have fifty thousand pennies, let alone fifty thousand dollars."

"My work is funded through the entire year."

Sure, make me feel unreasonable.

A voice traveled from the side of the house. "Yoo hoo!"

As if she heard the scream of an incoming bomb, Nora had the urge to dive for cover in the shrubs next to the house.

Sylvia gazed past Nora's head.

Nora held her breath and turned. "Mother. What are you doing here?"

Other people's mothers provided stability and support and the familiar comfort of home. Not so much with Abigail. When she dropped in unexpectedly, it usually meant drama. Lots of it.

Abigail waltzed toward them. A twelve hour drive from Flagstaff would mean she left at two in the morning, and yet, here she stood, after hours of being folded into her car, as fresh as if she'd just returned from a fundraising luncheon. Her slacks weren't even wrinkled.

She held out her arms for a dramatic embrace. "Nora! How is your first day?"

Nora didn't fall into the maternal hug. "I'm kind of busy, as you can imagine."

Abigail dropped her arms. "It's your first day, dear. You've barely started."

Says the woman who has never worked. "How did you even find this place?"

Abigail held up a phone. "This is my new toy. Isn't it fantastic? It has GPS and the Google and weather. It even has apps for shopping."

"Nice." Nora wanted to program the phone to send Abigail back to Flagstaff.

Abigail turned to Sylvia and extended her hand. What a pair of matching fabulousness they were. "I'm Abigail, Nora's mother."

Sylvia placed her manicured hand in Abigail's. "Sylvia LaFever. I'm a scientist here."

Abigail nodded in appreciation. "A scientist. How lovely. Do you live here in Boulder?"

Sylvia hesitated. "Temporarily."

"No denying Boulder is charming in its unique way. But a woman of your obvious sophistication must find the whole casual, hippie atmosphere somewhat provincial."

Pretentious much, Abigail?

Sylvia preened, obviously enjoying Abigail's keen perception. "I'm working hard for the Trust so I don't have time to miss the luxuries lacking here. But when I wrap this up, I'll be on a fast plane to Europe."

Abigail latched on to the conversation. She might disparage Boulder's outdoorsy attitude, but it beat the glamour of Abigail's life in the mountain cabin outside Flagstaff. "What's your favorite city?"

Nora let them bond over memories of escargot and wineries in the French countryside. Compared to Sylvia's suit practically cut from dollar bills, anyone might appear dumpy. But Abigail glittered like a gold brick, holding her own on the magnificence scale.

Nora needed to get back to her office. She'd scan the documents Mark said he'd emailed her. Then she'd boot up the Trust software and see what those financials revealed.

Now she had a plan, standing here in the afternoon sunshine made her skin itch. She started to back away from the delightful duo. Her feet crunched on the fall-withered grass. She stopped.

She blinked.

No. I don't see anything.

The flash of blue to the side of the farm house stole Nora's breath.

No. Not now. Not ever.

She had left Flagstaff. Fled the mountain with its real or imagined spirits. They wouldn't follow her here. But he had followed her, at least to Mount Evans, hadn't he? Unless she was crazy. And of course, Nora was crazy. Still, she was an ignorant white woman lacking in any spiritual quality that might appeal to a kachina.

"What is it you and Nora were talking about?" Abigail didn't seem to mind prying into Trust business.

Sylvia responded as if it were a simple request. "I need her to cut me a check."

I can hear you, Nora wanted to say.

"Good luck with that," Abigail said and they both laughed. They'd only known each other for a few minutes and already worked in tandem to torque off Nora. "She can be so tight-fisted and serious."

If by tight-fisted you mean set up a generous budget that doesn't include world cruises every six months, then yes, I'm a tightwad.

Sylvia seemed quite taken with Abigail. "I'm glad to know it's not just me."

"Oh heavens, no. She's been like this since she was a toddler. When she was six she begged me to get her a cash register. Not a toy, mind you. She settled for an adding machine. She spent days writing figures in columns and adding them up. It was cute, then."

Nora forced herself to stare at the side of the house where she'd imagined the kachina. Maybe a staffer was taking a smoke break and wore a blue shirt. Of course there was no kachina. Kachinas didn't exist.

"At least she's had lots of practice," Sylvia said. More of their instant-bestie twittering.

"We should have lunch soon," Abigail said.

Sylvia headed back to the house. "It's been delightful meeting you."

Nora faced her mother with a stern expression, folding her arms.

Abigail raised her eyebrows. "What? I just stopped by to get the key to your apartment. I'll go there and wait for you. I know you couldn't possibly take time from your first day to spend with your mother."

Nora dug in her jeans for her keys and started to pull off the apartment key. "How long are you staying?"

Abigail shrugged. "That depends, dear."

A hard fist formed in Nora's chest. She half-considered refusing to give her key to Abigail and insisting she turn the car around and head home.

She saw it again. The blue. It appeared, then disappeared. Damn it.

Abigail plucked the key from Nora's limp hand. "You don't look well, Nora. You need to take better care of yourself."

Nora watched as Abigail strode across the brown grass. Just as Abigail disappeared along the path to the parking lot, the kachina stepped around the side of the house, heading toward Nora.

Nope. I don't see you. You don't exist.

Nora fought the wave of panic cresting behind her eyes. She must hang on to reality. Besides, if she blinked the kachina would disappear.

So blink.

Damn! When she opened her eyes the vision remained. But the kachina, with his plug mouth and feathers, clutching the hatchet and wearing a bright blue sash, wasn't advancing on her. Instead, a slightly built Native American closed the last few feet to stand in front of her.

He wore a plaid shirt and jeans jacket. His jet black hair combed neatly and cut short, he could be a regular guy in a regular yard.

"Hi, Nora."

Part of her wanted to throw her arms around his neck and hug him as an old friend. Part of her wanted to turn tail and run. She pushed back the silly fear. "Benny!"

His serious face broke into a slight grin. For him, that was like bursting into song. "You are well."

She hugged him. He was shorter than Nora and small-framed, but his answering hug felt strong. "What are you doing here?" she asked.

He stepped back and tilted his head to scrutinize the huge farm house. For as long as he studied it, he might have been memorizing the architecture.

Nora waited out his sloth pace. Impatience jangled her nerves.

It was Benny's faith and loyalty to his friends that had saved Nora's life in Flagstaff. She'd been forced to his home on the Hopi rez and he'd given her refuge and wisdom, both at the speed of melting snow.

"Do you like it here?" He asked by way of response.

Good question. She liked being employed. Not only was she about to start sharing Alpo with Abbey, her isolation was grinding her to a nub of insecurity and craziness. Hadn't she been seeing the kachina and those damned blue flashes?

Blue flashes and now Benny.

His steady gaze seemed to read her doubts.

"I think I'm going to like it fine. Loving Earth Trust does some great environmental work."

He nodded but didn't act convinced. "What sort of work will you do?"

Why did he get to ask all the questions? He showed up out of the blue —literally. "What brings you from Hopiland to Boulder?"

"You." He said it simply.

Not weird at all. A little Hopi farmer, aged anywhere from thirty to fifty, who hated to leave the Mesas and his corn, traveling eight hundred miles to see someone he didn't know all that well was perfectly normal.

This was going to be trouble.

"How did you find me?" She dreaded the answer.

His eyes twinkled with humor. "It wasn't hard."

Whew. She feared he'd say something far worse—.

"Nakwaiyamtewa told me."

—like that.

She swiveled on her heels and ran to the back door of the house.

9

Nora pulled into the well-lit parking lot of her apartment complex long after sunset. She located a spot between a beat-up Honda and a rusted pickup.

The complex had the ambience of a dormitory. Several buildings snugged together in a maze of two-story units with worn shingle siding. A wrought-iron railing lined a balcony that ran along the second story with the apartments' front doors opening onto the concrete walkway. Each apartment had a deck on back and many held bikes and cheap grills. Cars and motorcycles drove in and out at all hours.

Two twenty-something girls with heavy backpacks carried giant Jamba Juice cups as they chatted on their way to a first floor unit. A young man whizzed behind them on a bike. He called to the girls and they hollered back.

Nora sat in her Jeep staring up at the porch light in front of her apartment. The Stress-O-Meter didn't go high enough to measure her first day of work and now she must face Abigail and try to be pleasant.

Fall's night time temperatures brought enough chill Nora's fingers and cheeks tingled as she clumped up the metal outside steps to the second floor. Abbey followed acting as if this were any ordinary trip home and not one sending them into a wasps' nest.

"With any luck, Abigail will be tucked into the spare bed." Abbey gazed at her but, as usual, didn't answer.

Earlier, the staffers of the Trust checked out one by one, Nora stayed glued to her computer screen, studying, searching, printing documents and trying to understand the different projects and their fund details. Each discovery made Nora's stomach churn more until it felt like a bucket of acid.

The third-quarter financials Mark sent her bore little resemblance to the numbers on her computer. The climate-modeling program headed by Sylvia LaFever showed the largest discrepancy. Its deficit tilted the entire organization into red.

No wonder Mark wanted Nora to present the financials he sent, since they showed a much rosier view of the Trust. But Nora couldn't lie. And when she told the board the truth, Mark would fire he.

She'd balanced up as much as possible, printed and collated the copies for the board, and said good bye to her office. Nora already calculated the salary she'd receive for just one day—and it would barely buy a bag of dog food.

She sent a fervid prayer to the universe that Abigail would not be in one of her nitpicky moods. Or one of her nagging moods.

Or, just please don't let her harp on me about what I wore today, and what food is in the apartment, my furniture, housecleaning ability, and just for tonight, let us not discuss her budget and why, as trustee of her accounts, I refuse to open up the checkbook and let her bleed it dry.

The board meeting started at the Bolderado Hotel at eight in the morning. She must present herself as professional and competent and a lover of the environment. Normally, none of this would be a stretch. Tonight, after a fourteen hour day, it all seemed impossible.

She tiptoed the last few feet to her doorstep. Abbey waited behind her. With a fortifying breath she turned the knob and stepped into the over-heated apartment.

Abigail stood in the middle of the living room, fully visible from the front door. She held her cell phone to her ear. She'd changed into black yoga pants and stylish tunic. Far from being ready for bed, her short blonde bob and makeup looked good enough for an evening out. "Oh, never mind.

She just walked in." She punched the screen and set the phone down. "Where have you been?"

Like everything in the complex, the apartment was nothing more than a glorified dorm room. Just two bedrooms in what served mainly as student housing for the University of Colorado, it suited her purposes. The main room consisted of a galley kitchen separated from the dining space by a counter bar. The living room continued about fifteen feet from the dining area and ended with a sliding door. The balcony had an excellent view of Devil's Thumb hitching its way off the Flatirons. The whole unit weighed in at less than 700 square feet. A kingdom fit for Nora's command.

The weekend parties and late-night noise reassured Nora. After the frightening summer on the isolated mountain in northern Arizona, she liked knowing other people surrounded her. Though furnished mostly from Ikea, everything in the apartment was new.

"Hi, Abigail." Nora hung her bag and coat on hooks she'd installed next to the front door. She stepped into the kitchen and opened the cabinet under the sink and scooped out dog food.

Wow. You know you're hungry when the smell of dog food makes your stomach growl. She poured it into Abbey's dish, sandwiched between the dishwasher on one side and a micro-pantry on the other.

Abigail watched her. "If you had a phone like mine I could have texted you. Or even sent you a picture. Why do you have that antique?"

"I like my phone." Nora felt no need for a smart phone to keep her plugged in.

"You're young and should be hip. It isn't right to have that rusty technology."

New topic. "Was that Charlie on the phone?" Charlie was one of Nora's best friends. That he was also her mother's most recent husband disturbed and delighted her in equal measure

"Yes. He was worried about you."

Good. Keep Abigail off the Nora Improvement tack. "Why didn't Charlie come with you? Are you fighting again?"

Abigail's face hardened. "Don't try to change the subject. Do you really think it's wise to stay out late on your first day of work?"

"Nine o'clock isn't late."

"Those circles under your eyes show you're exhausted."

Abbey crunched happily on his food.

Nora always felt like her apartment offered sanctuary. With Abigail here, it felt crowded. Although Nora liked the low, flat sofa in bright red and the contrasting deep green chair, Abigail would hate the bright colors and think them garish. She might approve of the no nonsense coffee table and TV stand. A smallish flat screen monitor faced the sofa.

It all reflected Nora's effort at a fresh start. With this job, the transition into the New and Improved Nora should be complete. Why then, did she still feel like the old, insecure, scared woman who left Flagstaff a year ago?

She'd be doing fine and then at random moments, like now, the memories would crash in on her. Nora's drive to save her marriage and business had led her to push for man-made snow on peaks sacred to the Hopi tribe. By the time she'd discovered the extent of the harm she'd bring to her mountain, it was too late. In the end, she'd managed to save the mountain but she held herself responsible for the death of her unfaithful husband, Scott, and that of Heather, a vibrant and passionate young girl.

Abigail stared at Nora as if expecting an answer. Oh yeah, work. "It's okay."

Abigail frowned. "That's all you have to say?"

Nora opened the refrigerator with the insane hope food had materialized since morning. "I'm hungry."

Abigail pursed her lips. "There's not much we can do about that. This pantry is nearly empty. Not even a can of soup."

"I think there's cereal."

Abigail frowned. "No milk."

Nora opened a cupboard and pulled out a box full of creamers in tiny plastic tubs. It was her one indulgence on camping and backpacking trips. "Voilá!" She picked up the cereal box and creamers.

"Don't neglect the pantry of your life and leave it barren as a looted grocery store."

Nora stated at Abigail. What?

Abigail stopped as if reviewing what she'd said. She pulled a small notebook from the pocket of her tunic and slid out a matching miniature pen. She scribbled on the pad and caught Nora's scrutiny. "I'm taking an online poetry class."

Nora congratulated herself on keeping a straight face.

Abigail dropped the notebook and pen back into her pocket and found a bowl and spoon and they retreated around the counter bar to the small dining room table. It consumed slightly more space than a card table but was big enough to hold a basket for Nora's mail and bills. Bright, Mexican woven placemats covered most of the pine top.

After setting the dishes on the table, Abigail pointed to the sliding glass door that opened onto the tiny deck. "What is with the plants?"

Nora tried not to wince. "Nothing. I like green things. The photosynthesis purifies the air."

Abigail raised an eyebrow in skepticism. "Houseplants are all well and good, but this goes beyond a little color."

Abigail was right, of course. Most people didn't have a dozen big pots of bushy plants in their living room. Like the smaller version Nora had dragged to work, these corn plants grew in terra cotta pots decorated with Hopi designs. Six of the largest plants lined the glass slider, leaving space for one person to slip through the door to the balcony. Smaller pots formed another row inching into the living room. Nora shrugged, a response more appropriate to a teenager being asked why she didn't turn in her homework.

"They have to do with the Hopi thing, don't they?" Abigail asked.

"Why would you say that?"

Abigail's hands rested on her hips. "Because I saw Benny give you a bunch of seeds when you left Flagstaff and ask you to plant them to help him out."

Busted. "Okay. Yes. They are Hopi corn. But I think they're pretty and Abbey and I like the outdoor feel." Except maybe growing the plants created a connection with more than nature. Maybe *that's* why Benny showed up at the Trust. That was a ridiculous notion, of course.

Here came that slow drip of guilt down the back of her throat. In all probability, Benny had saved her life in Flagstaff and now she repaid him by running from him. She'd buried herself in work trying to forget all about him. If he was smart, he'd give up on her and head home. Maybe he was already on his way. She hoped he understood why she couldn't see him.

Heck, why would he? She didn't understand it herself.

Abigail lowered herself to a chair opposite Nora. Abbey retreated to his bed tucked between the corn plants.

Nora peeled the tops from the little creamers and lined them up on the table. "How are you, Abigail?"

"Tell me what's going on with you. You aren't yourself and you've taken this job, which is obviously beneath you."

Abigail normally loved talking about herself why wasn't she jumping at the chance?

"I had a panic attack." Whoa. That popped out of nowhere.

"What do you mean?" Abigail opened a creamer.

Nora dumped the little cream buckets over her cereal. "Never mind. It's no big deal."

"While you were in the mountains?" Abigail sounded on the verge of an attack herself.

Nora shoveled Cheerios into her mouth. Stupid to bring it up.

"You could have been hurt. Why do you insist on these dangerous sports?"

Nora swallowed. "Abbey and I love to hike."

Abbey raised his head and flopped his tail against the floor.

Abigail leaned in, her eyes sharp. "What triggered it?"

The kachina sightings were like drug flashbacks from the worst time in her life, and she didn't want to talk about it. But Abigail pulled the confession from her as if she were five years old again and had picked all the tulips in the garden. "I keep seeing a flash of blue, like I did in Flagstaff during all that snow-making business. Then I thought I saw the kachina and all of it came flooding back. I thought of Scott and then—" her throat closed and she had to wait a beat to let it clear—"Heather. Then I sort of shut down."

It was easier to keep things to herself in phone conversations than when her mother sat in front of her.

Abigail sat back, a frown of concentration on her face.

Nora kept eating. When she swallowed, she felt a little more control.

"Have you had a panic attack before?" Abigail asked.

Nora shook her head.

"My friend, Charlotte—you know, she and her husband used to go on cruises with Beryl and me? But her husband, what a bore. He smoked these awful cigars and the smoke always drifted to our balcony. Surprising how even the sea air didn't—."

"Mother!"

Abigail startled. "Oh, well. Charlotte had these panic attacks. Not that anything terrible ever happened. She had a weak disposition—."

Nora raised her eyebrows in warning.

Abigail huffed. "Anyhoo, she said that once you have one attack, you're prone to have more. It's like one episode introduces the behavior to your brain and it knows it can do it again."

"Great."

Abigail picked up the cereal box and poured more in Nora's bowl. She started peeling tops off creamers. "You need to do something about it."

Nora peeled a few creamers. "I'm taking Tae Kwan Do classes."

Abigail started pouring the creamers on the cereal. "What for?"

Nora shoveled in a bite and talked around it. "Self-confidence."

Abigail studied Nora. "You're spending too much time alone. You should get in touch with Cole Huntsman. You two would make a great couple."

Nora choked on Cheerios. Why would Abigail mention him? Nora hadn't seen him in a year, if she didn't count ill-advised day dreams and a fantasy or two. Cole definitely did not belong in her life now. Maybe never. "I have Abbey."

"Solitude is fine. I know I'm steeped in it on that crazy mountain. But you need people to talk to, dear."

"Is that why you're here? Too much solitude? What's up with Charlie, anyway?"

Abigail's eyes widened and she tightened her lips.

Nora sat up straight. "What's wrong?"

"Nothing."

Nora leaned forward. "Tell me."

Abigail studied her for a moment, her eyes teared up. "I'm leaving Charlie."

Smack her in the head with a two-by-four. "What? Why?"

"He's having an affair."

10

Nora dropped her spoon into her bowl with a clink.

Kachinas dancing on mountaintops made more sense than Charlie having an affair. "But he *adores* you."

"Apparently, he adores someone else more."

"You need to explain..."

A soft tap at the front door made them both turn. Abbey let out a woof. Nora pushed back from the table and started for the door. "This conversation is not over."

"You aren't going to open that without seeing who's out there?"

Nora shook her head and reached for the knob. "It's a big apartment complex, no one is going to stand out there and gun us down."

She pulled the door open to a shivering Petal, wrapped in various layers of knit and gauze.

Petal? At her front door? Why? How did she even know where Nora lived? Weird ringed this girl like a wobbly Hoola Hoop.

Nora pulled her inside. "Come in. It's cold out there."

Petal huddled by the front door. Abbey sniffed her hand, accepted the distracted pat and retreated to his bed. He plopped down with a grunt.

While Nora waited for the strangeness of Petal to explain itself, she carried on with regular old politeness. "Abigail, this is Petal, a coworker. Petal, this is my mother."

Abigail hurried over. "Petal, how nice to meet you."

Petal's eyes showed panic. "I'm sorry. I didn't know you'd have company."

Abigail tried to draw her into the living room. "Nonsense. Come in and sit down."

There goes any chance of getting the Charlie story from Abigail tonight. Nora had a big meeting tomorrow, and couldn't stay up late. She'd never outlast whatever avoidance plan Abigail cooked up.

Petal allowed herself to be seated on the couch, still wrapped in all of her layers. "Can we get you some coffee? Or a beer? It's all Nora has in the house or I'd offer you something to eat."

Petal shook her head. "I just came over to, you know, see how you are and to talk or whatever."

Doesn't anyone think about sleep?

Abigail retreated to the kitchen and made coffee.

Petal curled up in one corner of the couch. She pulled off her Chacos and slipped her feet underneath her.

Nora sat beside her. "What's going on?" *And why am I the one you want to talk to, at my house, at night, when I want to get rested for a big day, and not play hostess?*

Petal drew her fingers inside the sleeves of her sweater. "I miss Darla so much." Her voice was little more than a squeak.

Abigail stepped around the counter from the kitchen. The coffee maker hummed behind her. "Was Darla your dog? I've had dogs before and losing them can tear your heart in two. I had an adorable Bischon named Fluffer—"

"Mother." Nora slammed the brakes on that run away train. "Darla was the Financial Director before me."

"Oh." There was a moment of silence Abigail probably couldn't stand. "People move on, dear. I'm sure she saw career advancement and is in a better place. I suppose the Trust is a temporary stop for anyone with any ambition. There doesn't seem to be a lot of growth potential."

Petal sniffed and rubbed her sleeve across her nose.

Nora kneaded the growing pain in her temple. "Darla was found shot to death. Is the coffee done?"

Abigail made a choking sound and a beat of silence followed. "Oh, my. I'm sorry, dear. There's nothing more painful than losing a loved one. I, myself, have buried three husbands."

Nora glared at her. "The coffee, Mother."

"Of course." Abigail retreated to the kitchen.

"Did you and Darla spend a lot of time together?" Nora asked.

Petal nodded while tears dribbled out the sides of her eyes. "We were roommates. I can't be in our space today. I see Darla everywhere."

Nora steeled herself from feeling Petal's pain. She slid an arm around Petal, smelling the wet wool of her wraps and let her cry. "I'm sorry."

Abigail returned with a coffee mug. Petal's hands were still mittened inside her sweater. Abigail lifted one hand and pressed the mug into it until Petal brought the other hand up and clamped the mug between them. "Here, dear. Drink this. It will warm you up."

Abigail sat on the other side of Petal. She seemed oblivious that her turquoise and orange print tunic clashed with the red fabric of the couch.

Petal dropped her head onto Abigail's shoulder. "Darla was special. She invited me in when I didn't have anywhere to go. She was friends with everyone, even Fay, who can be a terrible gossip. She was even nice to Mark when he was so mean to her."

Abigail patted Petal's back. "Let it out, dear. 'Grief is a bucket of pig slop to be splashed across the mire of life.'" Abigail slipped her notebook from her pocket and jotted in it.

Petal's description of Darla didn't match up with Fay's opinion of a weird accountant. "How was Mark mean to Darla?"

Petal hiccuped. "He forced her to make up reports for the board. Like he's tried to do with you. But you aren't afraid of him like Darla was. She did what he asked but she hated it. She wanted to quit and was going to. And then she died."

This sounded fishy. "How do you know Mark wanted me to falsify reports to the board?"

Petal dropped her head. "I'm sorry, Nora. I miss Darla."

"You said that."

Abigail flashed her that I-will-paddle-you–if-you-don't-shape-up expression she'd perfected when Nora was little. "Nora! Quit badgering Petal."

Petal set her mug on the coffee table. She stared at the corn plants and maybe through the plate glass door into the darkness. "No, that's all right. I didn't mean to spy, really. I used to hang out in Darla's office. She's got all those windows and it's warm. Darla said I could be there anytime I wanted."

Nora didn't mind people in her office but she'd like to know about it.

"The day she died I didn't know what to do or where to go. So I went to your office while you were in the bathroom. I hid in the coat closet. I heard Mark tell you to make good report."

This girl was a strange ranger. "Why would you hide in the coat closet?"

Petal curled into an even tighter ball. "I used to hide there from Sylvia."

"You hid from your boss in a coat closet?" Nora asked.

Abigail nodded, making the connection. "Sylvia is your boss. She has a wonderful sense of style and smells so nice."

Petal shrank into herself. "Yes. But when she's mad she yells at me and throws things. Sometimes I can't take it and then I hide in Darla's office. I mean, your office."

Abigail collected her and held her close. "You poor thing. You should tell the Executive Director."

Petal sent her dreds in a flurry. "Oh no. I couldn't tell Mark. Sylvia would fire me."

Abigail huffed. "It's not right."

Petal peeked out from Abigail's embrace. "No. It's okay. She is under a lot of pressure."

Nora felt drained by all the drama.

Petal jumped up. "I'm sorry. I know you're tired and you have the board meeting tomorrow. I wanted to come over and warn you." She faded out.

Nora bit. "Warn me?"

"Darla found something in the books. I don't know what it is. But she was really worried about it. Maybe that's why she died."

Nora stood, feeling crowded amid her sparse belongings. "You should probably tell the police."

Petal shook her head. "I shouldn't know about it. If someone killed her because of that and they find out I know, they might kill me, too."

Kill her? Petal's imagination might be even more active than Nora's. "What do you think Darla found?"

Petal shrugged and clamped her mouth shut. After a moment of silence, she scurried to the door. "I need to get back to the Trust. Sylvia is working late and expects me to be there."

Abigail sounded aghast. "It's nine-thirty!"

Petal pulled her wraps tighter. "She works really hard."

Nora and Abigail eased around the coffee table and walked Petal to the door. They watched as she hurried along the balcony and down the stairs, disappearing into the night.

Nora shut the door and Abigail slid the chain on to lock it.

Nora turned to Abigail. "Okay, what's going on with you and Charlie?"

"We'll talk about it later. We need to concentrate on you. What are you going to wear tomorrow?"

Abigail's topic-hopping could give anyone whiplash but Nora had grown up with it. She wouldn't get any more information from Abigail tonight. They walked back to Nora's bedroom and stood in front of the closet.

Nora stared at her clothes.

Abigail whisked hangers across the rod assessing the clothes. "Wear the black Tahari suit. It shows off your fitness and is professional."

"I don't think the meeting is that formal."

"Not for the board meeting."

Nora rubbed the spot of fatigue eating at her forehead. *Just let me get some sleep.*

Abigail pulled out the suit. "I set up an interview for you tomorrow."

Nora spun from the closet. "What?"

"United Amalgamated Financial."

Nora couldn't think of anything to say.

"Pearl Street Mall. That cute coffee shop with the weird name. It'll be a quick meeting and you can give him your resume. I'm sure he'll have you meet the other partners later in the week."

Little hammers of annoyance picked in her brain. "He who? Wait. No. I *have* a job."

"I won't let you trod on the shining crystal of new life."

Argh! "Stop writing poetry about my life."

"Adam Thompson. He's my dear friend Marilyn's son. I pulled some strings and he's very excited for you to join the firm. You'll be perfect."

11

Sylvia paced from Petal's junky desk and circled the antique table, running her fingers along the polished wood. She held the phone to her ear, fuming at Eduardo's rudeness in making her wait.

How odd that Darla was found murdered on the same night she'd confronted Sylvia. The gunshot must have drawn attention and someone found Darla out there alone and killed her. Life was full of strange coincidences.

Finally Eduardo came back on the line.

"I don't appreciate being on hold." Sylvia didn't care how important Eduardo thought he was, she would not be treated as a common solicitor.

"I am a busy man, *carina*, what is it you wish to discuss?" He might think his soft voice and Ecuadoran accent would spread her knees, but it didn't work on Sylvia. When she'd let him sample her honey, it had been on her terms.

"It's not a question of want, it's a matter of deserve. There's a mix-up at the Trust. Darla's gone missing and the nitwit Mark hired won't pay me. I need you to deposit fifty thousand into my Cayman account immediately." Sylvia collapsed in her office chair. She pulled her laptop in front of the PC monitor and opened it.

"First of all," he paused in that false lazy attitude of a Latin lover. "You haven't shown progress to warrant a bonus. Secondly, World Petro is under extreme scrutiny and I can't make unexplained expenditures."

"You expect me to continue working for nothing?" The Chihuly glimmered from her laptop screen.

He chuckled. "You must appeal to the board of directors."

She bristled at his insulting tone. "In the interim I'd appreciate something to bridge the gap."

His sigh sounded as though he was reasoning with a petulant child. "That is impossible at this time."

How dare he patronize her? She slammed the lid on her laptop and jumped up, striding around her desk. "Don't say *impossible* to me. Remember what I'm doing for you."

"A business transaction. Which is overdue and over budget."

Neither of which should bother him much. She tried a sweeter tact. He wouldn't resist her if she reminded him of her other benefits. "I know what a—creative—person you are. You're clever enough and rich enough to get cash to me."

Again the pause and sigh. "The board meeting is tomorrow. Use your considerable skills to make love to them."

She wouldn't go begging like some match girl freezing on the streets. "Tell your son to sway the board."

Eduardo's voice hardened like cooling lava. "Daniel is not to know about our understanding. To you, he is a board member and nothing else."

Sylvia's skin tingled with her rebellion. Nothing more than a board member? If Eduardo only knew. "Fine. But you used your influence with him to get me hired, you could use it again to get me paid."

"Danielcito is not your concern."

"My money is my concern," Sylvia insisted. She checked the thermostat on the wall. This damned office stayed perpetually cold.

"*Mi corazon*, wouldn't you say securing more funds would be easier if you had some success to show for the time and money you've spent so far?"

Whatever happened to deferred gratification? "I'm not Walmart churning out commodities made in China."

"I must go, *carina*." He hung up.

Eduardo hung up! How dare he try to scare her. Who did he think he was?

She hurled the iPhone and it banged against the office wall. She wouldn't be threatened. He didn't scare her. He. Didn't. Scare. Her.

The office around her faded and there she was, six year-old Sylvia huddled next to her older sister, Margery, on the cracked linoleum of the mold-infused shack.

Her stomach gnawed on emptiness as they sat sweating in the liquid air of Bucktown in New Orleans.

"I'm starving," she said.

Margery hugged her. At ten years-old, she took care of Sylvia. "They'll be home soon. They promised."

But soon turned out to be the next day when her parents crawled in smelling of booze and cigarettes.

Margery stood in front of her father, twisting her grungy t-shirt in her fist. "Did you bring us anything to eat?"

Her mother stumbled past them down the dark hallway toward the bedroom. She'd probably throw herself onto the unmade bed still in her shorts and halter top. Maybe she'd get up later today, maybe tomorrow.

Her father ignored Margery and trudged after her mother.

Margery considered Sylvia who had begun to cry.

"Please," Sylvia mouthed.

Margery tugged on her father's arm. "Do you have some money? I can get hamburger and cook it."

His glazed eyes flitted over Margery and with a flick of his arm, he sent her flying into the wall.

Sylvia ran to Margery and they clung to each other in silence until snores shook the shack. They crawled to the bedroom. Margery rifled the discarded trousers and purse for enough change to buy a jar of peanut butter.

In the quiet of her office, Sylvia spoke aloud. "No one will make me feel that helpless again."

She paced the office in her Manolos. The thud of the heels gradually brought her out of the red zone and she glanced down to see the perfection of leather on her delicate feet. She let her gaze travel up her shapely ankles to her well-formed legs. The Versace suit fit her perfectly. She was a fine woman. So much more than anyone had dreamed she'd be. Amazing, really, she'd achieved all that she had.

Beethoven's Fifth sounded from the floor between two file cabinets. Sylvia's phone.

Maybe Eduardo had second thoughts about treating her so abysmally.

Sylvia stalked to the phone, disappointed to see the name on the caller ID. She composed herself before answering. "Hello, Margery." She punched the speaker option and set the phone on her desk.

Margery's weak voice trickled through the phone. "I haven't heard from you in a long time and wanted to say hello."

Likely story. While Margery droned on about the weather and the other residents at the care facility, Sylvia drew a tree chart. She labeled the circles in her chart for her various credit cards and private donors who'd funded her research in the past. If she transferred her balances from these two cards to....

"I know it's a lot to ask but if you could help me out, I'd appreciate it."

So Margery wound down to the reason for the call. Money. It always came down to that.

Sylvia opened her laptop and gazed at the screen. "What did the doctor say?"

Margery sniffed. That annoying, constantly runny nose. "He said having it removed would be a good idea."

Of course he thought it would be a good idea. It's money in his pocket. Margery's gullibility always cost Sylvia.

Unless Sylvia got firm, this would never end. "I paid an extra thousand last month. I wish I could help but I can't afford any more."

"Oh." The peep of a response barely made it through the speaker.

A razor of anger sliced into her brain. "Last month the flu ran through the home and you needed a vaccine that insurance wouldn't pay for. And before that he recommended some experimental drug."

Sniff. "I'm sorry. You've done so much. I shouldn't have asked."

But she did ask. Every month. Over and over. Always trying to apply the scalding compress of guilt. Sylvia had never asked Margery to work three jobs to pay for Sylvia's tuition at Tulane. It certainly wasn't Sylvia's fault Margery got knocked up by a low-life trucker that never paid a dime of child support.

Enough was enough. Sylvia had bankrolled Margery far too long. She'd paid her debt.

The Chihuly stretched her thin enough. She shouldn't have to give it up. "I'm sorry. I just can't do it."

12

Despite Abigail's apoplectic fit, Nora opted for the black silk shirt and black jeans with cowboy boots. She'd parked several blocks from the Bolderado Hotel on the other end of the Pearl Street Mall in the hopes that the walk in the crisp fall morning would calm her nerves.

Pearl Street was closed to traffic for a few blocks to create an open-air mall. Interesting shops from designer clothing stores to outdoor gear, free-trade stores to tourist joints, and art galleries lined the street along with eateries of all kinds. The center space of the mall contained sculptures suitable for climbing and touching and raised flower beds that changed varieties along with the seasons. Right now, bright yellow chrysanthemums blasted their cheer in the brisk mountain air.

This early, Nora passed a few joggers and walkers. Later, when the stores opened, the place would buzz with Boulder's energy. Buskers would perform everything from magic and juggling to amazing feats of yoga or memory on all but the coldest days. With Boulder's eclectic mix of business people, affluent retirees and young families, students, street people, Rastafarians, and mystics, if the mall wasn't the best people-watching venue in the world, it ranked in the top ten.

Nora inhaled the fresh morning air. *Get through today. That's all. Present to the board and move on.*

Her phone rang. Of course. Abigail burst from the line. "You left early. I wanted to talk to you."

Slipping out before Abigail got up was no accident. "It's a big day."

"I see you didn't wear the Tahari."

When Nora didn't respond she continued. "I've been thinking about Petal. She's obviously a disturbed girl. This friend of hers, the accountant, you need to find out what happened to her so Petal can find closure."

The accountant. Darla. The girl had a name and a life, and Petal seemed like the only person who cared. Nora stepped back emotionally. "The cops will investigate. I can't help Petal with this."

Bulldog Abigail. "Her coming here supposedly to warn you is an obvious cry for help."

Nora turned north off the mall and glanced up. One block away the Boulderado loomed. Tall trees surrounded the historic hotel and their bright fall leaves accented the walk. Inviting smells of coffee and cinnamon baked goods wafted from the hotel's coffee shop. "Just because Scott was murdered doesn't mean I know anything about murder investigations."

She pictured Abigail leaning forward, getting serious. "It's not just for Petal. She's got a crazy notion that Sylvia is somehow involved and we know that's just not true."

Nora laughed. "And how do we know that?"

Abigail let out a puff of air. "Look at her! She's refined and intelligent and has taste. She's got no need to commit crimes."

No fighting Abigail logic. "I'm not investigating. I've got enough to do learning a new job."

"You're making excuses."

Absolutely. She couldn't face more death now. The thought of it spun her mind back over a year ago.

In the chill of the dark forest, Nora's nostrils filled the smell of Barrett McCreary's sweat as he crushed her to his side with an iron arm. She struggled to break his hold.

Charlie lay dying on the forest floor. With one hand pressed to his gushing gunshot wound, Abigail threw rocks at Barrett.

Someone crashed from the forest into the clearing.

Barrett jerked his head toward the intruder and crushed Nora even closer to his side.

The intruder wore a kachina mask and full costume. He carried a hatchet adorned with ribbons and feathers.

With his hatchet raised, the kachina rushed across the clearing toward Barrett and Nora. He swung his hatchet and hit Barrett in the throat with the dull edge. Barrett grunted.

The kachina darted in again, striking at Barrett's gun arm, ripping the shirt on Barrett's bicep.

Barrett swung Nora as he turned and tried to get a bead on the dancing kachina. Nora's feet slid along the ground and she lost her balance. Barrett's arm pinned her to his side and kept her from falling.

The kachina retreated across the clearing to Abigail and Charlie. He didn't slow his zigzagged dance but the masked face turned toward them, as if checking on them.

Barrett raised his arm and sighted in on Abigail.

The kachina circled back, hatchet raised.

Nora pitched and writhed and kicked, screaming in Barrett's ear.

With incredible force, he flung Nora toward the rock. The back of her head cracked on the granite and she flopped to the ground. Her knee struck a rock and her leg went numb.

Barrett stepped toward Abigail. He couldn't miss. At that range, he'd rip a hole into Abigail that would tear her in two.

Nora dragged herself, fighting to stop Barrett.

Suddenly, the kachina flew from the forest straight at Barrett.

Barrett didn't alter his aim at Abigail. The third shot exploded from Barrett's gun.

And seventeen year-old Heather lay dead.

The courageous girl had saved Abigail's life by dressing up as a kachina.

Abigail's chatter grounded Nora in front of the Boulderado. "The clues are in the bookkeeping. I suspect once you dig into the finances of the Trust you'll find it's not the place for you. You will be helping clear Sylvia, give Petal closure, and get your career on track. Win, win, win."

A jogger in black spandex tights, warm-up jacket and headphones plodded past, chugging white puffs of breath.

Nora slowed as she neared the hotel. She inhaled to give herself courage.

"Do it for Petal if not for yourself. She's not like you. You're confident and smart and beautiful."

That's right, Abigail, lay it on nice and thick.

"She's a fragile wisp of a soul searching for an anchor in a world of storms."

"Poetry?"

"I think that's a good line, don't you?"

Dog tags clinked behind Nora and a woman in a ski coat passed her with two Westies on leashes.

Nora inhaled competence and professionalism. She hoped. "I've got to go."

"See you at three. At Laughing Goat Cafe."

Nora forced herself to step up to the hotel door.

"Next to the book store."

She shut her phone off and dropped it in her bag.

In the likely event Mark fired her after her report, agreeing to attend Abigail's bizarre job interview might not be such a stupid thing.

13

Nora pulled her shoulders back, raised her head, and entered the Boulderado. Victorian elegance steeped the lobby with its dark polished wood and opulent furnishings. A stained glass copula completed the rich mood. A series of balconies viewed the lobby from two separate levels.

The meeting rooms were on the second floor. Nora climbed the thickly carpeted stairs, located the conference room and stepped through the double doors.

The conference room echoed the elegance of the lobby but with a business feel. Carpeted with a pattern of red squares and pink swirls, moldings painted tasteful beige. Striped wallpaper in more beige shades covered the walls. The twenty foot ceilings and elongated windows gave the room the feel of a historic, upper-class venue.

A breakfast buffet spread out on a couple of tables along the far wall. White draped tables in a u-shape filled the center of the room. Several chairs lined the wall.

Mark balanced a plate of pastries and chatted with a tall, thin man in jeans and corduroy blazer. Mark shoved in a bite and flakes of pastry stuck to his soft lips.

Fay sat at the conference table with a middle-aged woman, eating fruit and yogurt. They seemed in the throes of an earnest conversation.

A few knots of two or three people milled around or sat at the table to bring the total to about a dozen attendees.

Nora had read the board bios and knew the group consisted of an interesting and illustrious collection of investment bankers, trust-funders, attorneys, and college professors. Ten people in all, but she didn't know how many would attend today's meeting.

She tried to appear casual as she studied them. Which one was Mark's father?

Nora set her folder containing copies of the financials for the board on a chair along the wall. She placed the messenger bag she used for a purse on top and, with her back to the room, gazed out the high-reaching windows at the sun shining on the Flatirons. A wisp of clouds flirted with the sheer rock face.

"Good morning" a man's voice spoke behind her.

She twisted her neck to greet him. How she'd missed him when she walked in was a mystery. Gorgeous. Tall, chiseled-featured, dark-skinned, lean and Hollywood handsome. She managed not to gasp in admiration and introduced herself. "Nora Abbott, the new Finance Director."

He smiled with even, white teeth. "Daniel Cubrero. Mere board member."

There was nothing "mere" about this man.

"Daniel!" Mark inserted himself between Nora and Daniel. "How was your flight?"

Daniel barely noticed Mark. "Unremarkable. Now tell me, Nora." His Latino accent sounded like satin sheets. "How long have you been at the Trust?"

Mark snorted. "We'll get to introductions at the meeting. Right now, I need to speak with Nora, so if you'll excuse us."

"Oh, no," Daniel linked Nora's arm and headed her toward the buffet. "She has not eaten. Come, Nora, you must try the pastries."

Whew. The last thing Nora wanted to do was talk to Mark. He'd ask her for her report and she'd never get a chance to present to the board.

Mark's strangled expression converted to a wet smile instead.

They left him and headed for the food. Daniel reached for a coffee cup and filled it at the silver urn. "Have you been in Boulder long?" Nora picked up a plate and plopped a scone on it.

Before she could answer, a man about sixty years-old with a pot belly and a white beard and hair like Santa Claus approached and started talking to Daniel. "Did you see that report estimating the oil reserves in Ecuador? Now I know your father…"

Nora stepped away but when she peeked up, Mark bore down on her. She switched directions and nearly bumped into a thin Native American woman in a business suit. Straight black hair hung down her back and turquoise jewelry accented the formal business attire.

The woman held out her hand to steady Nora. "I was on my way over to say hello. I'm Alberta Standing Bear. Fay says you're replacing Darla. Welcome to the Trust."

Nora felt as though she ought to offer condolences to Alberta for the loss but had no idea what to say. "Thank you." For the welcome and for saving her from Mark.

"Maybe we can visit at lunch. Excuse me." Alberta scooted off to talk to Daniel.

Fay marched toward Nora with a heaping plate of fruit. She stuffed a strawberry into her mouth and spoke in her creaky voice. "Sylvia did it. I know she did."

Thomas appeared behind Fay. He'd covered his hairy legs in khakis but still wore a Life Is Good t-shirt, this time blue. "I think it's Mark. He embezzled and Darla found out."

A short, balding man in faded jeans, blue Oxford cloth button-down, and Chacos joined them. Fay tilted her head to Nora then to the man. "Bill, this is Nora. Nora, Bill's our resident asshole," she croaked.

Bill shook her hand. "Attorney." He glared at Fay. "*I* think it's Petal."

Thomas and Fay laughed. He joined them. "Don't you know it's always the last person you'd suspect."

Where was the grief for a dead colleague? Nora's heart twisted at the thought of the yellow pages: *I am smart. I will succeed. They DO like me.*

Fay poked Nora's arm. "Don't be so shocked. We're joking."

Thomas's eyes suddenly watered. "Darla was a loner but she was okay. I can't imagine why anyone would kill her."

Bill shook his bald head. "A random act. Some wingnut with a violent streak found a lone woman at night and BAM, it's all over."

A hand on her arm made Nora jump.

Mark whispered. "I need to talk to you. Outside."

A woman on the downhill side of fifty, with thinning gray hair and a body twice her healthy size boomed a command. "Let's get started. We've got a lot to cover." This must be Etta Jackson who served as chairman. She'd inherited a fortune her father made in banking. Her trust fund allowed her to contribute a couple of million dollars a year to causes in which she believed.

A moan of frustration escaped from Mark. He straightened his shoulders and a fake smile appeared on his face. While everyone settled in he spoke. "Welcome to Boulder dear, dear friends of the Trust."

The staffers arranged themselves on the row of chairs along the wall while the board members sat at their places at the conference table. Nora sat next to Fay.

Fay leaned close and whispered. "I saw you talking to him, isn't he one big ball of hotness?"

Nora acted innocent. "Who?"

Fay laughed.

She whispered to Fay. "Which one is Mark's father?"

The room quieted. "Stepfather." Fay's voice dropped to a breath. "He never comes. I think he can't stand Mark and avoids him."

Nora didn't blame him. "Where is the rest of the staff?" she whispered.

Fay shrugged. "They say they're out in the field. Anyone's guess where they really are. Sylvia will blow in for her personal appearance. That's about it."

From where Nora sat she had a full-face view of Daniel, Alberta, the Santa man, a Birkenstock-clad woman with long, curly gray hair and Etta Jackson. From the bios she knew a college professor of ecology who'd written several important books, two attorneys, a man retired from the auto industry, a retired advertising exec, and professional do-gooders also sat on the board. She might spend the rest of the meeting playing match with the faces and the bios.

Mark held his hands up. "We're lucky to have this golden Colorado weather to greet you here. You never know with October in the Rockies. It might have been a blizzard." He laughed and most everyone responded with polite tolerance.

"As you can see by your agendas," Mark said, "we'll start with open space and Fay. Thomas will update his air quality work, followed by Bill with his report on litigation. In the interest of time, we aren't hearing from everyone today. We'll have the financial spotlight right before lunch. We've ordered an amazing buffet downstairs. When we reconvene, Sylvia LeFever will give us her exciting update about her climate change modeling work." He stepped back. "Etta, would you like to conduct the meeting?"

Through the first two hours of the meeting, Mark groveled before the board, nearly kowtowing to them, giggling nervously, and belittling the staffers.

As the seconds ticked into minutes and hours, Nora tried to pay attention and learn about the Trust. Instead, she silently rehearsed the disaster report she'd deliver soon. The agenda called for her next, right before they broke for lunch. If her job security teetered on the brink yesterday, she headed for a real swan dive in a few minutes.

"Thank you, Bill." Etta said. "I think I speak for the board when I say we're impressed with the work you've done. Your ability to juggle our various interests is truly amazing."

Mark nodded and grinned. "Bill's been out on the front line, that's for sure. He spent Tuesday in the Colorado legislature talking to our reps about legislation to fund Sylvia LaFever's amazing study of climate change with regard to the beetle kill."

Fay leaned in. "Get a plug in for your little pet. Disgusting."

Etta kept her eyes on her agenda, crossing off items with a pen. "Yes. As Bill said. Thank you, Mark."

"It's cutting edge." His eyes glittered as if placing a delectable feast in front of the board. "We're incredibly fortunate to have her at the Trust."

Etta didn't respond.

Fay stood up. "Excuse me. If there's nothing else you need from us, Bill, Thomas and I will head back to work."

"By all means." Mark dismissed them.

Etta pushed back from the table. She and Fay embraced and agreed to meet at seven the following morning.

Amid thanks and good byes, the three walked out, abandoning Nora.

Nora's heart jumped into her throat. One more moment to remain employed before she landed back on the streets.

"Excuse me, Etta," Daniel Cubrero said.

They all turned to him.

"If I might, I'd like to bring up a topic not on the agenda but one that is dearest to my heart."

Not a woman alive could say no to that man. Etta was no exception. "Of course."

He paused and surveyed the board members in turn. "*El Oriente,* or the Amazon basin in Ecuador, as you know it." He smiled at them. "It is under attack. The region of tropical rain forest is home to the most diverse collections of plant and animals in the world. A half-million indigenous peoples live there."

No one moved. His voice caressed them and they loved it. Nora included.

"The big oil companies have discovered that the world's last great oil field lies underneath this crucial environmental area. I would like the Trust to consider joining a coalition to save the rainforest from these marauders."

The way he said *marauders* made Nora want to be overrun.

The Birkenstock woman, obviously the trust-funder named Marion Dempsey, interrupted. "Didn't the UN pay Ecuador billions to stop development of the rainforest?"

Daniel nodded. "Yes. But it isn't enough. What if there is a disaster in Ecuador? If suddenly they have tragedy like Haiti after the earthquake there in 2009? The government will acquiesce and allow the oil companies to drill and the rainforest will suffer."

One of the back of heads—Nora guessed it belonged to the advertising exec, Bryson Bradshaw—said, "Doesn't your family own World Petro? What do they think of you working on this initiative?"

Daniel's smile would bring even a serious man like a banker to his knees. "We have held very...lively...discussions about this. But my father ultimately agrees that this area must remain pristine. He is willing to donate one million dollars to set up a foundation for the rainforest protection."

Etta must be a woman of steel because she sounded as if she might turn Daniel down. "We're more of a local operation. Getting involved in Ecuador seems out of our league."

He conceded. "Perhaps."

The Santa man—he must be the college prof named Willard Been—said, "If your father is donating a million dollars, why do we need to join?"

"Mostly to add prestige to the group. The more organizations joining the coalition, the more who will want to be a part of it. It can create a snowball, yes?"

Mark held up his hand, smiling like a stray dog in the pound, hoping someone would love him. "We're running a little late. Why don't we break for lunch before the finance report and come back refreshed?"

Etta cast a slight frown in his direction. She addressed the group. "What do you say? Shall we add this to the agenda for the next meeting?"

The guy in the corduroy blazer—he was either an attorney or a philanthropist, Martin or Stanzio—consulted his watch. "I'd agree to that. What about a working lunch?"

Marion Dempsey said, "I need to catch a flight so I'd like to keep forging ahead."

Etta leaned back in her chair. "I'm going up to Silverthorne to do some hiking tomorrow and wouldn't mind wrapping up early, as well."

Daniel Cubrero addressed Mark. "Perhaps you could ask the kitchen to bring our food in here for a working lunch." Not only did Nora like his idea of sending Mark out of the room while she spoke, she nearly melted at his South American accent.

Mark dipped his head, never losing his grin. "I'm not sure they'll do that. They're planning for us downstairs."

Professor Santa's voice sounded like a mallet. "We'd appreciate it if you'd do what you can. Cancel the lunch and bring us deli sandwiches if you need to."

Mark jumped up as if hit with an electric prod. "Of course. I'll take care of it."

Daniel Cubrero nodded, satisfied. "*Bueno.* Now, let's see how our finances are sitting." He smiled at Nora and her legs went wobbly.

Mark pushed back from the table. He walked past Nora on the way out of the room and when his back was to the board, he widened his eyes in what she assumed was a warning.

Etta cleared her throat. "We're deeply sorry to hear about Darla Barrows. She served as Finance Director competently and thoroughly for three years. She was always willing to help and ready to answer our questions. She'll be missed." Etta leaned over and pulled a tissue from a canvas bag. She honked her nose in tribute.

Bradshaw cleared his throat. "Is there any news on the investigation?"

Etta shook her head. "As I understand it, there are no leads and the detectives will be questioning staff."

"Perhaps we should hire a private investigator?" Daniel said.

Marion Dempsey shook her gray hair. "We're here to save the environment, not track down murderers."

At least they had their priorities straight.

Etta allowed the minute or two of murmurings about the sadness and waste of Darla's murder and then cleared her throat. "At this time, I'd like to welcome Nora Abbott. Yesterday was her first day so we'll muddle through this together as best we can."

The members turned pages in their board reports to settle on the financials. Nora stood and hefted her stack of pages. "I studied the financials in the board packet. Unfortunately, they don't match up to what is currently in our system, so I prepared another P&L. I'm sorry I haven't had time to work up a cash flow, but I printed out a balance sheet."

She handed out the reports and gave the board a second to digest the new information. These were professional board members and business people used to cruising financial statements like NASCAR drivers ran a track.

Corduroy guy, Martin/Stanzio, frowned. "What happened to the cash balance in the general fund?"

Bradshaw frowned. "The long-term investment asset balance is substantially down, too."

After they'd mumbled among themselves for several minutes, Nora spoke. "As you can see, there are some differences from the previous report and generally, they show the Trust is in a worse financial position. I assume December will bring an influx of donations, but until then we're in for a dry spell as far as cash flow."

Etta's double chin wobbled. "Can you give us a quick overview?"

Nora skimmed through, surprised her voice sounded strong and confident because inside, she was a sickening swamp of anxiety. Somewhere in the middle of the report, where Nora kept reminding herself to breathe and speak clearly instead of racing along and mumbling, the door behind her opened and closed. It had to be Mark. If he had an ax in his hand, he'd swing and her head would roll onto the plush hotel carpeting, blood clashing with the tasteful reds.

When Nora paused, Etta spoke. "What I'm hearing is that the open space and air quality are on budget, forest restoration and trail maintenance are slightly over, but climate modeling has already surpassed the entire budget for the year."

Nora nodded.

"If this is accurate," Professor Santa said, "We won't have the funds to fight oil exploration in the Amazon basin."

Daniel Cubrero frowned. "We can't allow that situation to continue in Ecuador. We must do something to protect the delicate eco-system."

While Nora stood with her face burning—her palms a puddle of sweat and her heart banging in her chest—the board erupted in concern over the careless oil companies denuding the rainforest. It was a topic that concerned Nora as well, but hardly relevant to this meeting.

Etta raised her arms to quiet the table. "First things first. We obviously need to deal with these disturbing financials." She waved a come-in motion to the person behind Nora. "Can you explain this, Mark?"

He walked past her, the smell of nervous sweat wafting from him. Of course he began with a laugh. "Obviously Nora hasn't had time to get to know our system." Mark lasered such murderous intent at Nora she almost dove for the carpet.

Etta drew in a deep breath. "Mark, Nora, would you mind stepping out for a few minutes while we discuss this among ourselves?"

"Of course." Nora walked past Mark on her way to the door. She was pretty sure she could outrun him once the conference room doors closed.

"Lunch is on its way. They'll bring it any second." Mark's shrill voice rose.

Etta sounded strained. "Thank you."

As the door clicked closed behind Nora, Mark said something else. It probably irritated them that Mark didn't leave as instructed but it suited Nora fine to have a few minutes to escape.

She strode down the hall, heading for sanctuary in the rest room.

A light touch on her arm set her off like a rocket "Agggh!"

Benny stood beside her. He'd made no sound when he approached, like his mysterious ancestor that haunted Nora's imagination.

"Maybe you should cut back on the coffee," he said, his face expressionless.

It was too much to hope that he'd returned to Arizona. Tenacious little guy. If she didn't listen to what he had to say he'd never leave. She glanced down the hall and saw no sign of Mark. She slipped into an empty conference room and pulled Benny after her. "What are you doing here?"

"I came to talk to you."

He had all the time in the world. After all, the Hopi had been promised over a thousand years ago they'd be the longest surviving tribe of all. Nora didn't have time to spare. In a matter of minutes she'd have to face Mark. "What is going on, Benny?"

He paused. "I was sent to warn you."

14

If she thought it would stop her from hearing she'd ram her fingers in her ears. Warnings, threats, messages from long-dead Native Americans. She'd left Flagstaff to get away from this.

She stood in the darkened conference room. The red patterned carpet, tall windows and striped wallpaper decorated this room but with the lights off and no tables or refreshments set up, it felt cold and dead. "Go away, Benny. I don't want to hear it."

"You need to stay watchful and do what you can to protect the Mother." His unfathomable eyes watched her in endless serenity.

"You know this message is going to make me crazy, right? I want to ask you what is going to happen and what to watch for and what I'm supposed to do. But you'd only tell me the balance depends on me and you can't tell me what to do because that's not the Hopi way."

Her words brought the ghost of a smile. "You can learn. That's good."

She thought back to the time she'd spent with him at his shack on the mesa in northern Arizona. Hopiland. She'd been sent there by Cole. *Kidnapped* was the technical term.

Cole...

.   .   .

The heat of the Arizona summer that morning seared the top of her head. Benny walked between bushy corn plants in the blazing desert sun below Second Mesa. He caressed their leaves. "Hopi have a respect for life and trust in the Creator."

"Seems like you could grow more corn if you used a tractor or irrigation sprinkler. Why would your spirits want you to do everything the hard way?" Nora asked.

Benny straightened and brushed his hands together. "Making things hard prepares us for what may happen. Like a runner practices every day, building strength and endurance so he can run the marathon, we Hopi live a meager and hard life so we're ready to survive when the time comes."

He handed her a stick about a foot long and thick as a broom handle. He reached into his pocket and brought out a small plastic bag of corn seeds. "You stay here and plant these seeds over there." He pointed to a sandy spot next to the outer corn plants.

Planting corn was a stupid idea and she didn't want to do it. She squatted down and thrust the stick into the ground. She dropped in a few seeds and packed the earth around them.

She straightened and stepped sideways, falling on her knees to dig a new hole, dropped in the seeds and scooped dirt.

After a while, Nora rose from the ground, feeling deep connection with the seeds. The earth gave life to the corn which nourished the people here in Hopiland. It was this way all over the world. Abigail had given life to Nora and loved her, teaching her and protecting her. And if she were lucky, someday Nora would be able to do the same with a child of her own.

Words wouldn't form but rhythm and sound grew naturally, boiling up her throat and erupting from her mouth in a song. She danced, tears falling from her face, her voice loud and deep with love for the corn and the earth that would nurture it.

Now, she felt her boots firmly rooted on the conference room carpet. She focused on the Hopi man in front of her. He believed his tribe held responsibility to keep the entire planet in balance. If they didn't perform their ceremonies in the ancient way, the two brothers who sat on the serpent on the Earth's poles, would let the serpent lose.

It had happened before. The Hopi said it was when the Third World ended due to man's wickedness and the good people had climbed to this world, the Fourth.

Modern scientists had an explanation that sounded similar. They speculated the earth had shifted on its axis maybe sending the dinosaurs into extinction. Some said it could happen again.

Nora knew this and more but she didn't want to let Benny know how many hours she'd spent online reading about Hopi, studying their thousand year-old prophesies, trying to follow the instructions for living a simple life. If she believed everything she read, she'd be crazy. She found it interesting, that's all.

Nora ran a hand through her hair. "I suppose Nakwaiyamtewa" —she stumbled over the pronunciation— "thinks that me working for the Trust positions me to protect or restore something. Maybe he's worried about the Amazon rainforest. But I'm having a hard time believing a chief from the 1800s—."

"*Kikmongwi*," Benny interrupted.

"Okay, what you said." Nakwaiyamtewa was a *kikmongwi* who lived on the rez nearly a hundred and fifty years ago. When Nora had been stressed to the breaking point because enviros tried to kill her, she'd imagined she saw him in the form of a helpful little man. Again, if she believed that, she'd be crazy.

Not believing, not crazy. "Anyway, I'm a white woman and I don't understand Hopi so Nakwaiyamtewa can choose one of you spiritual Native Americans to work for him."

Benny shrugged. "I can't answer for him. I only know what he told me."

"And he didn't tell you much."

He shook his head. "He never does."

"I've had about enough of kachinas coming and going in my life. He shows up, tells me I've got to do something then disappears without helping. In the meantime people die. Heather died."

Benny lowered his head, the sorrow evident.

"Why me? Is it because I planted the corn you gave me? Or that I've read a little about the Hopi Instructions and I'm trying to live a more balanced life?"

His face remained inscrutable. "The Hopi life is for Hopi. It's not for everyone."

"Right. So that means, since I'm not Hopi, you and your *kikmongwi* can leave me alone."

"The hardest thing in the world is to be Hopi. We must constantly be vigilant. I see things. Signs the Fourth World is coming to an end and we will enter the Fifth World."

Every religion thought the end was near, pal. "I don't believe that, Benny."

He spoke with his usual speed of a snail on sedatives. "The prophesies call for us to act, to lessen the violence of the end of the Fourth World."

Mark stomped past the open door without glancing in. He hunted her.

"What I have been told to tell you is this: 'the whole world will shake and turn red and turn against those hindering the Hopi.'"

Nora could make a run for it, get out of the building before Mark found her. "I'm sorry, Benny. I don't understand this."

He inhaled and waited. "You will learn things moment to moment as you need to understand."

She calculated the distance to the stairs.

"The message I have to give you says the prophesy is being fulfilled and if you stop it, all will be well. If not...." Again he shrugged.

"You need to conference with Nakwaiyamtewa. Let him know I'm not up for the role of Enviro Girl."

Mark pounded by the other way and this time, his head swiveled toward her and he stopped dead. "Are you hiding from me?"

Nora shook her head. "No. I saw an old friend we wanted to catch up."

Mark's eyebrows shot up. "Really? And where is she?"

Startled, Nora spun around. She hadn't noticed a door on the other side of the room. Apparently, Benny had. He must have slipped through it before Mark saw him. "I'm not sure where he went. I'd better go find him."

Nora whipped from the dark conference room into the hallway.

"Stop." Mark caught up to her and stood too close. His stomach must be a boiling mass of anxiety because it came out in sour breath. "What did you tell them?"

Gulp. "Just that the finances aren't as rosy as their last reports indicate."

He sucked in his flabby lips. "We've got money coming in any day now that will make those reports accurate. God, what a mess."

Nora almost felt sorry for him. "We could create a projected revenue report for the board."

His face looked like an angry tomato. "You didn't tell them that Sylvia's work is over budget?"

The overhead glare of the hallway lights felt like a heat lamp. "They need to know the truth."

"Sylvia is brilliant. She's amazing. If you've done anything to hurt her…"

The hallway was closing in on Nora.

Mark held his hands to his head. He seemed to be talking to himself. "I need to think. How can I save her? We can't let her go."

"Maybe we—."

"You did this." You don't understand. Don't know how special she is."

"If we—."

"No." He shook his head. "You can't be here. You're fired."

15

Even though Christmas was a few months away, they resembled a human candy cane standing in the hallway outside the conference room. Mark's bright red face contrasted with Nora's pasty complexion.

Sylvia expected to see Nora Abbott in a business suit, not a jeans and cowboy boots. Such an interesting choice to wear something so earthy to the board meeting. Nora had that annoyingly fresh and healthy appearance. Her copper hair bounced around a face alive with interest and blue eyes that seemed ready to smile. That easy beauty and confidence annoyed Sylvia, who'd had to fight for every ounce of her own sophistication.

Someone should tell Mark to tuck his shirt in. Actually, someone should tell Mark to quit dressing like a Mormon boy on mission.

Mark sputtered in Nora's face. Another crises he obviously couldn't handle. Sylvia would talk him down from this one, as usual. She sighed and considered the diamond-encrusted watch on her slender wrist. She'd hoped to get to the board meeting early enough to schmooze them over lunch.

Damn Eduardo. She shouldn't have to do any of this.

She approached Mark and Nora. "What is the problem here?" Her voice sounded like cool spring water.

Mark jumped as if swatted from behind. He verged on tears. "She told the board your project is over budget. That all of the Trust is running in the red."

Damn.

Sylvia smiled warmly. "I wasn't aware of any overages. But the board understands the importance of the work. It'll be all right."

"All right?" His voice raised two octaves. "She ruined everything."

Despite her bloodless appearance, Nora managed dignity and calm amid Mark's breakdown.

Sylvia forced herself to touch Mark's shoulder, knowing contact with her would soothe him. "Stay calm. I'll take care of this. Etta is a dear friend, and Bryson Bradshaw and I attended a world environmental conference together last year. Over lunch I'll explain the situation and why it's taking time. They'll approve the increased budget."

Mark shook his head as a sweat rained from his temple toward his pudgy chin. "They're taking a working lunch." He pointed to the closed conference room doors. "The caterers just delivered their food and we aren't allowed in. Even to eat."

Why was everything going against her? "I'm on the agenda right after lunch. I'll work my magic and we'll be running smoothly again. Please don't worry."

"I'm sorry, Sylvia," Mark said, his voice cracking slightly. "I thought she'd be good. At least grateful for a job in this economy. I didn't know she'd turn on us. But she's gone. I swear. I fired her."

Still, Nora didn't say a word. She could pass for a marble statue, all chalky and cold.

Sylvia displayed the exact amount of disappointment and sympathy in her beatific smile. If she weren't such a brilliant scientist, she could have been another Julia Roberts because inside, she flared with anger. "Let's not over-react Mark. She's new and hasn't learned how to manage the board." Sylvia addressed Nora. "They don't want to be alarmed with hiccups in cash flow. They're busy and important. Your job is to ease their minds. Unless, of course, there is real cause for concern. But there isn't, so you see, you've worried them needlessly."

Nora opened her mouth but Mark rushed ahead. "I told her that. I told Nora we're getting a donation next week that will right everything."

Sylvia nodded. "See? It's all okay. I'll make it good with the board."

"She's still fired." Mark set his moist lips in a pout.

"You're the executive director. Do what you think is right."

The door of the conference room swung open. Daniel Cubrero leaned out. What a perfect specimen of male sexuality. "We're ready for the next agenda item. Has Sylvia LeFever arrived?"

Mark swallowed, obviously grappling for control.

Glad she opted for the four-and-a-half-inch heels and the shorter skirt, Sylvia imagined the glow of her skin and her inviting full lips. She stepped forward and extended her hand as if she didn't know Daniel as intimately as she did. "How good to see you again, Daniel."

He wrapped his hand around hers, with his long, tapered fingers. "Ah, Sylvia. I did not see you there."

A shiver of anticipation ran through Sylvia. Sometimes the old cliché about men's fingers held true. At least in Daniel's case it did. She had no qualms about mixing business and pleasure.

Later, though. Now it was show time.

As Sylvia strode into the room, taking command of the situation, Daniel said, "Mark, please join us. You, too, Nora."

How annoying. Really though, what did it matter to Sylvia who sat in the meeting? As usual, she would have them begging to do her bidding. She sat opposite Etta. Amid the scattered detritus of lunch, Sylvia would shimmer like a diamond. She smiled at Etta. "How are you, dear?"

"Thanks for joining us. Can you give us a brief update?" Etta must be ignoring their friendship in an effort to be professional.

Nora sat to the side of the room in one of a dozen chairs along the wall. Mark plopped next to Etta.

"Most of you are familiar with my research but I'll brush over the basics to remind you." Ordinary people needed a refresher on this complicated science. "HAARP stands for High Frequency Active Aurora Ionospheric Research Program. This is the government's program located in Alaska that includes dozens of aluminum dipole antennae towers that send out high frequency signals."

The board members stared like drugged bunnies.

Sylvia chuckled. "It's technology difficult to discuss with non-scientists."

Again, Etta must be struggling to mask her affection for Sylvia and said with a straight face, "You're no longer with HAARP so we don't need to know this."

The old bag. "I developed much of the HAARP technology and am using the principles in my modeling work here at the Trust."

Etta frowned. "We'd appreciate it if you could be brief."

"Of course." Sylvia nodded in Daniel's direction, letting her eyes connect in a subtle, seductive signal. "Before I left HAARP, I worked on developing a tower that uses ELF, extremely-low-frequency, waves and I've taken the technology further to create a single tower that sends concentrated beams of particles into the atmosphere."

Etta frowned at her, probably because she was too dull-witted to understand.

Sylvia tried to dummy it down. "The key Tesla discovery was that the earth reverberates with a pulsing electrical current in the low ELF range. I discovered the exact frequency at which the earth normally pulsates. Of course, HAARP takes credit for that breakthrough."

Bryson Bradshaw interrupted. "Isn't what you're talking about—the ELF waves and ionosphere and all that—isn't that linked with weapons of mass destruction?"

Sylvia shrugged. "HAARP is a government program. It's not inconceivable a classified study works on weaponry."

Marion Dempsey gasped. "You're not working on weapons, are you?"

"Of course not. The tower I've installed is for climate study only."

Bryson Bradshaw leaned forward. "How does that work?"

"Extremely-low-frequency waves are much shorter than short waves." She paused to let them digest that. "ELF waves are focused into the ionosphere to a specific location, creating a bulge in the atmosphere. The waves are then bounced back and can be sent beyond the horizon."

She surveyed the board, her kingdom of the moment. They appeared dull-eyed, probably struggling to absorb the simplistic explanation of a concept far more complicated than their normal minds could grasp.

Etta waved to indicate Sylvia should continue. "You're using those waves to gather data for climate-change modeling. You've told us this already."

Although Sylvia enjoyed imparting some of her vast knowledge to the uneducated, they didn't want to learn. "Exactly. We know that warming temperatures have allowed the pine beetle an extra breeding cycle each year, but what we don't know is how their destructive habits might be affecting the climate and perhaps exacerbating temperature increases. By using ELF waves in the ionosphere I'll be able to chart that and create models predicting future trends."

Silence fell on the room. Once again, Sylvia had wowed them with her brilliance. Most of the board studied their papers or stared at Etta.

Etta cleared her throat. "Your progress report is nearly verbatim from our last meeting four months ago. Is it that you didn't take the time to write a new report or has there been no progress?"

Progress? She'd solved a particularly difficult question regarding wave intensity and direction. She'd pinpointed several possible locations for targeting the waves to achieve Eduardo's goal. She'd researched long-term weather patterns and was far into a computer modeling program the likes of which the world had never seen. But none of it had a thing to do with the mountain pine beetle. "Much of my time in the last months was spent struggling with insufficient software. Too much of the data needs manual input and my assistant, Petal, and I can only work so many hours. As you can see, I've added upgrades into my budget for next year."

Again, silence. A few members shuffled papers, perhaps considering the budget. Then Etta spoke, "You're proposing an increase of four hundred thousand dollars."

Sylvia eyed Daniel. A mere pittance for his family, especially when she delivered on her promise. "That's correct. I realize this is a non-profit organization run with donations and I'm operating on a shoestring."

"I see," Etta said.

Alberta raised her finger. "I have a question. I've heard that with HAARP technology it will be possible to alter the weather. Is that true?"

Etta interrupted. "Sylvia isn't working on HAARP."

"But I want to make sure her tower can't do any damage to the mountains," Alberta said.

Finally, they were moving away from money. But the direction wasn't much better. Sylvia laughed. "Conspiracy alarmists are out there cruising the Internet for anything to feed their paranoid minds. HAARP is located in the Alaskan wilderness because it is an auroral region but they see it as 'hidden' and shrouded in secrecy. The technology is difficult to understand and therefore, scary. Ronald Regan funded it as part of his Star Wars defense and suddenly nefarious intent is suspected."

Face cold as stone, Alberta said, "So, can it alter weather?"

Who was Alberta to ask for a follow up when Sylvia had given her all she needed to know? "The HAARP facility will not affect the weather. Transmitted energy in the frequency ranges used by HAARP is not absorbed in either the troposphere or the stratosphere—the two levels of the atmosphere that produce the Earth's weather. No association between natural ionospheric variability and surface weather has been found, even at the extraordinarily high levels of ionospheric turbulence that the sun can produce. If the ionospheric storms caused by the sun don't affect the surface weather, there is no chance that HAARP can do so either."

There, you simpleton.

Etta didn't have anything to say, she must acknowledge Sylvia's superiority. "Okay."

Still Alberta wouldn't quit. She shuffled papers. "I found this quote from a Russian journalist about HAARP." She read from the paper. "Ionospheric testing can trigger a cascade of electrons that could flip the Earth's magnetic poles."

Sylvia laughed. "Preposterous. This is what I mean by crazy theories."

Etta bowed her head briefly toward Alberta to politely end the tangent. She didn't give Sylvia the same respectful expression. "We understand that despite your efforts at economy, you're way over budget."

Sylvia avoided Nora. "The financials might technically show a deficit. But there is obviously a mistake. Our new Finance Director is top-notch but she only joined the Trust yesterday. Darla had a great deal more insight."

Etta stiffened as if bracing to eat a plate of worms. "We started funding your research three years ago with high hopes for achieving important and lasting environmental restoration. We're not a large organization and can't afford this kind of fiscal drain. This" —Etta picked up a packet of stapled pages that must be Nora's financial reports— "drives the nails in the coffin."

I'll pound some nails in a coffin and it won't belong to my project. The

Chihuly chandelier retreated from her grasp. She wouldn't let that happen, even if this two-bit board pulled her funding.

"We're asking you to wrap up your research and do a final report by the end of the year."

Sylvia had the power to smile like a queen. She inclined her head in grace.

The door behind her opened and the entire board suddenly became more alert as if threatened by attack.

Sylvia spun around.

A hotel employee, in her company blazer and polyester slacks stood just inside the doors, a strained expression lining her young face. Behind her, two uniformed police officers walked into the room. Their waists weighted down with guns, handcuffs and who knew what sort of hardware, their clothes crisp, black shoes sturdy. One officer stood several inches taller than his partner. The shorter, darker man stood akimbo. They both surveyed the room with serious expressions.

Etta stood. "May I help you?"

The taller of the two addressed Etta while the other focused on Sylvia. "We're here to see Sylvia LaFever."

What?

The room fell silent and all eyes rested on Sylvia.

The cops zeroed in on her. "You're Ms. LaFever?"

Sylvia forced a smile. "Yes. What can I do for you?"

"We'd like you to come down to the station for questioning in the death of Darla Barrows."

Cool, collected, Sylvia chuckled. They didn't know anything. "Don't be ridiculous."

The taller one with blond hair spoke again. "I'd advise you to get a lawyer before saying anything else."

She allowed her indignation to surface and stepped close enough to scrutinize their name tags. She addressed the tall one, A. Langston. "What's this all about?"

"We understand you own a Smith and Wesson 638 Airweight Revolver," Langston said.

Everyone stared at her.

Ice picks bit into Sylvia's skin, yet her voice remained calm. "It's a popular model."

The shorter officer, B. Kirby, smirked. "It happens to be the caliber that killed Darla Barrows."

"Not a hundred yards from your office," Langston said.

Sylvia sounded unconcerned. "I haven't even seen my gun in ages. It's probably on a shelf in my bedroom closet."

Kirby's smirk deepened. "Actually, it's in evidence at the station" Pause. "Seized from your office." Pause. "Showing a shot was fired recently. We're having it tested for rifling right now."

Her gun! "How dare you go to my office. That's breaking and entering. What gives you the right?"

"A search warrant," Kirby said.

"Issued on the strong suspicion from a tip," Langston said.

"Whoever gave you that tip lied."

Kirby held his palms up. "And yet, we found the gun just where they suggested it would be."

Every eye in the overheated conference room focused on Sylvia. She must show them her steel. "It was planted. It's not my gun."

Kirby raised his eyebrows. "It's covered with your fingerprints."

Langston studied her. "We understand you have a trip planned to South America. We'd like to have you cancel that and stick around."

What were they talking about? Her silk blouse acted like a greenhouse to direct scorching heat on her skin. "I have no trip planned."

They exchanged smirks and Kirby said, "You didn't book a flight on your credit card this morning?"

"I suppose the same person who planted the gun and put your fingerprints all over it charged the ticket to your credit card." Langston laughed.

Even her scalp felt on fire. "You have no proof."

Langston nodded agreement. "Not until the test fire results come back, anyway."

Kirby raised his arm to indicate the people watching. "Wouldn't you like to come down to the station to discuss this?"

16

The thrill of victory and the agony of defeat in less than forty-eight hours. Okay, maybe she hadn't been so thrilled with Loving Earth Trust on the first day, but the agony of finding a new job felt crushing. Maybe getting free of the cornucopia of dysfunction at the Trust might be a good thing. Oh well, as Charlie would say, she was looking for a job when this one came along.

Nora trudged down the stairs of the Hotel Boulderado, glad she hadn't bothered to dress up. She strode across the Victorian lobby toward the outside doors. Laughter erupted from Q's, the bar on the ground floor. Maybe an unhappy pre-happy hour cocktail would ease the sting. Or maybe not.

Nora peeked in the door of Q's and wasn't surprised to see Thomas, Bill, and Fay. No doubt they saw Sylvia escorted out by the police.

Sylvia might be the only person who had a worse day than Nora. Being accused of murder trumped getting fired. No matter how awful Sylvia seemed, she couldn't really be a murderer. No one liked Sylvia but did anyone hate her enough to set her up?

Nora stepped into the brilliant sunshine. The morning's chill turned to a perfect fall afternoon. She'd need to walk several blocks to meet Abigail at the coffee shop on the Pearl Street mall. All old brick interior with a menu featuring organic and healthy food, it opened the busy pedestrian mall. Maybe the sunshine, the beautiful, rugged surface of the Flatirons, and the dazzling air would work their magic and Nora's mood would bounce back.

Nora fell in behind two young mothers pushing strollers and herding a toddler. She wasn't in a big hurry. Yes, she needed a job. Yes, an investment firm might be a great job. No, she didn't covet corporate games and daily dress-up.

Her boots found their way onto Pearl Street, now bustling with Boulder's eclectic population mix. The pizzeria's aromas faded into the burger joint and then Thai as Nora made her way with heavy steps toward the coffee shop. She stopped to gaze at rock climbing gear in a women's-specific sporting goods store window. Next year, she vowed, she'd overcome her fear of the mountains and start rock climbing again.

It was possible. She could do it. She could make her life new and exciting. She would. Yes.

In fact, tomorrow she'd take Abbey back up to Mount Evans and try again. The kachina could go take a hike—not the hike she planned, but one somewhere in Arizona.

Nora noticed her watch. What kind of supernatural powers did Abigail possess? She'd scheduled the meeting with Adam for three o'clock. She didn't know when Nora would present to the board, let alone plan for the hoopla that ensued and she certainly didn't predict Sylvia being led away by two cops. Yet, if Nora hurried, she'd make it to the coffee shop just in time.

"Nora." Her name spoken in a hushed but commanding voice paralyzed her. She knew who owned that voice. Waves of warring emotions crashed inside her. Happy, apprehensive, fearful, excited—one rolled into the next in a powerful tsunami.

Cole. Ah, damn. Cole.

She froze and lowered her head, closing her eyes.

Cole's hiking boots made no sound on the concrete as he walked around to stand before her. How could she isolate the feel of him amid the group of college kids, shoppers and the few homeless hanging out on the mall?

Nora struggled to appear unrattled. She might have turned tail and run but her limbs refused to move. So she forced open her eyes and straightened her neck.

He hadn't changed in the year since she'd last seen him on the mountain in Flagstaff. He still had the soft, sandy hair falling across his forehead, the deep blue eyes, the long legs lanky frame. He wore a flannel shirt with rolled sleeves, jeans, and hiking boots. But instead of the warm smile she remembered, he looked nervous.

"Hi, Nora."

She forced words. "What do you want?" It sounded mean. Too late to take it back.

He studied the ground in front of them then caught her eye. "I was hoping... I thought maybe...Oh hell. How are you?"

Finally the shell hardened around her heart. She stepped around him. "Best day of my life. See ya."

His hand shot out as if to grab her but thought better of it. He let it drop. "Wait. Please."

She stopped. Couldn't help it.

He strode around and faced her again. "I know this is a shock and not exactly the way I wanted to make contact again. But..."

"But what?" She didn't want to hear him speak... She wanted to hear everything he had to say... She wanted to run away... She wanted to step into his arms.

What had he been doing for the last year? Did he think about her? Did he care about her now as much as he had in Flagstaff? Should she have cut him out of her life before they even had a chance to know each other?

Pink tinged Cole's ears. That happened when he was embarrassed. Gaa! Nora didn't want to know these details about him. She spun away and bumped into a white-haired man wheeling a cart full of silly hats.

Cole steadied her. "Abigail called."

She should have known. "Holy mother of dog. What did she tell you?"

A high school-aged-boy and girl approached with clipboards. One said, "We're with Greenpeace and wondered if you'd sign this petition."

Nora snatched the clipboard and scribbled her name. She must seem like a lunatic because as soon as she handed it back to them, they scurried away.

"Are you okay?" Cole asked.

Okay? For a year she'd struggled to get solid footing. Cole had a way of slicing her heart open and she couldn't risk that exposure now. "I'm fine."

He squinted at her. "Abigail didn't say much but she said you needed help."

Cole liked to show up when she needed saving. If she had any idea of being whole and sound again, she needed to work out her own life. "I don't know why she'd say that. I have an appointment so I've got to go."

He smiled tentatively. "Maybe we can get together later? I'm in town and I'd love to catch up."

Catch up on a whole lifetime of not knowing each other, punctuated by a few weeks together in mortal danger? "I'm not interested." She started to walk away again.

He fell in beside her. A mom-and-dad-visiting-their-college-daughter group separated Nora and Cole. After they passed he closed the gap between them. "Benny called too."

Her jaw tightened. "Are you and Benny planning to kidnap me again?"

Cole ran a hand through his hair. "We've been through this before. It kept you alive, didn't it?"

"I don't know what Benny is doing in Boulder. He's got ideas about the Fourth World ending, or maybe wants to ease the transition into the Fifth. Whatever. Why don't you and Benny have a night on the town and leave me alone? In fact, invite Abigail." She sounded angry. But she wasn't angry. Cole scared her in a completely different way than the kachina did.

"Benny's already on his way back to the mesas. You know he hates leaving the rez."

She stomped down the mall, weaving in and out of meandering shoppers and gawkers. A breeze rustled the dying leaves on the trees and it sounded like they whispered, telling her run.

His hand closed on her arm. "Can't we just go someplace and talk?"

"I have legitimate reasons for not going out with you." Because she found him attractive and had from the beginning? Because she craved his strength even as she fought against it? Or because she felt too fragile to allow herself to be vulnerable? "The first of which is that you remind me of a terrible time in my life I'd like to forget. Second, I don't trust you. And third—maybe most important—my *mother* thinks you're a hot fudge sundae with a cherry on top."

"Maybe you should listen to Abigail. She was right about your first husband."

Silence grew between them. "Oh, you must mean the dead one." She glared at him, daring him to make light of the situation.

He bent his head again. "I'm sorry. I'm really nervous and I'm not saying anything right. Will you have dinner with me? Or drinks? Or even coffee?"

She shook her head.

His face almost glowed red. "You know I was raised on a ranch in Wyoming?"

She nodded. "So?"

"So, spilling my feelings doesn't come naturally to me. It's been bred out of us macho rancher types."

"You wear hiking boots and eat tofu. You're no rancher."

"It's hard to overcome your raising."

Arguing with Cole on the Pearl Street Mall while leaves sifted to the ground in the brilliant afternoon sunshine felt almost natural. Time to stop it. "I've had a terrible day so far. You aren't making it any better."

"I'm sorry. The truth is, Abigail and Benny aren't the reason I'm here."

His tone was way too serious. "I've got to go."

She peeled off from him and skirted around a raised flower bed, rushing down the mall.

The coffee shop nestled between a headshop and a new age bookstore. Several café tables sat in front filled with normal folks enjoying a normal break. Abigail must be inside. Nora stopped several feet from the shop to pull herself together. Beyond the windows Abigail sat across from a dapper young man with thinning hair. She had that absorbed expression she usually wore when she wanted to impress someone. Dear Abigail was doing all she could to help Nora.

Here I go, girding my loins or whatever it is women warriors do. I'll make a hella investment banker. Abigail will be so proud.

Nora stepped toward the shop and noticed pile of garbage in the niche between the coffee shop and a display for tarot cards and crystals. Wait. Not garbage.

Petal curled into the crevice, not more than a pale face amid a jumble of fabric and dreds.

Nora hurried over and held her hand out to pull Petal up. "What are you doing here?"

Petal didn't meet her eyes. "Waiting for Abigail."

"Does she know you're here?"

Petal focused on the ground. "No. Everyone at the Trust was at the board meeting and I got scared and didn't want to be alone. I went to see Abigail and she said she was meeting you here."

"Nora!" Her shouted name startled her. Daniel Cubrero jogged down the mall, dodging people.

She patted Petal's arm. "Wait here." She stepped toward Daniel.

"I'm glad I found you," he said, catching his breath from the short run. His white shirt must be tailored to cling to his muscular chest and arms in just the right way without looking too tight. His short dark curls absorbed the sunshine and his brown face glistened slightly from exertion.

Over Daniel's shoulder, Nora spotted Cole. He watched the scene as he made slow progress behind a family of shoppers.

It seemed extreme that a board member would make such an effort into wishing a fired staffer well, but maybe Ecuadorans were ultra-polite. Besides, whatever Daniel Cubrero had to say, Nora would listen, just to watch his gorgeous face and hear that liquid accent.

Nora pulled out the professional persona, the one who graduated top of her class in business school and was offered enviable positions with New York's best financial institutions. She didn't need Loving Earth's measly finance director position.

Well, maybe she did, but she wouldn't let Daniel Cubrero know that.

"It was good meeting you today," she said.

His Latin accent sounded like melted chocolate. "The board is impressed with you, Nora Abbott." His brown eyes warmed her as she fought to be professionally cool.

"I'm not sure the board liked what I had to say. I know several project directors at the Trust won't be happy."

"The board did not have much faith in the previous Finance Director. We suspected the picture wasn't so rosy as Darla painted. We discussed hiring an auditor."

Interesting, but not her problem. "I hope you can find someone to help figure it all out."

He gave her a puzzled expression. "You think we should hire an auditor to help you?"

From a short distance Cole stopped and studied them. Petal watched them from beneath her dreds.

"You might not need an auditor if you can find a competent accountant for your Finance Director," Nora said.

Daniel shrugged and held his arms out. The flamboyant gesture suited him. "What do you mean? We have a Finance Director. Surely our meeting didn't scare you off? We were tough, admittedly, but we are concerned for the Trust and you were giving us information that has been lacking in recent years."

"I'm not scared," Nora said. "I was fired."

Daniel laughed. Oh my, if she thought his accent, his dark handsomeness, and smoldering masculinity were intoxicating, this cheerful abandon nearly did her in. "You are definitely not fired. The board begs you to stay."

They wanted her? But did she want them? "I don't know. I'm not sure I'm such a good fit at the Trust."

He considered that. "I understand the atmosphere around there might not be, shall we say, warm and fuzzy. But stay, please. We are serious about getting the Trust back on track. Our first priority is the finances."

Nora studied the sophisticated and, no doubt wealthy, investment banker sitting with Abigail.

Petal's eyes pleaded with her.

Daniel murmured, "Please join us, Nora Abbott. I am begging you. You will have total autonomy and report directly to the board, to me."

Talk about employment benefits. She still hesitated.

"May I be frank with you?" Daniel said. He seemed earnest and his eyes focused on hers.

She nodded.

"I am a wealthy man."

No surprise.

"It is family money. I am ashamed to say I have not always been responsible and wise. But it is time for me to grow up. I chose to serve on the board of the Trust and to raise money for them because I am passionate about this planet. But my father?" When American's shrug it's usually a simple movement of the shoulders. Daniel's shrug seemed to come from his whole body. "My father indulges me because he thinks I am a child. I want to show him I chose a good organization and I can make it successful."

Nora peeked into the coffee shop. Abigail hadn't spotted her, yet. "The Trust's work on open space is a model for cities all over the country. That's got to say something for the Trust."

Daniel agreed. "But that was before my time. I am eager to see the work move ahead in the Ecuador rainforest."

Nora tried to inch out of Abigail's sight line. "Sylvia's research has potential to be very press-worthy."

He shifted uncomfortably. "However, when my father discovered I was on the Trust board, he used his influence and money to bring Sylvia here. He did it out of goodness, to prove to the board I could bring in world class scientists. I did not ask him to do this."

Cole watched them from several yards away. Yes, Nora knew what it felt like to have someone else always saving you.

Abigail spotted Nora. She waved.

Nora pretended not to see her. "What do you have in mind?"

"I will work here with you and together we will find the financial discrepancies and grow the Trust into an international environmental protector."

Petal shivered even though the afternoon felt warm to Nora.

Abigail rose as if to hurry out to get Nora.

Nora looked from Petal to Abigail and back again.

17

Sylvia sat on a hard plastic chair in a tacky lobby. The drafty space with muted colors and linoleum smelled of commercial room freshener punctuated by the odor of the unwashed as they came through the doors. Body odor, cheap perfume, clothes steeped in grease from fast food restaurants—low class.

A uniformed woman cop, nothing more than a clerk, stood behind the counter tapping on a computer screen and pretending to ignore Sylvia. A few other uninteresting drones worked away on their dull jobs sitting behind their metal desks. Boulder's police station wasn't like the gritty TV shows where cops dragged in perps, and hookers and pimps wandered around. This was just a hard office with Sylvia endlessly waiting.

Sylvia had been here for hours at the mercy of these imbeciles. She had refused to talk to them, of course. She insisted they wait for her attorney and they'd allowed her a phone call. She contacted Daniel, who had dispatched a lawyer.

The Cubreros always had connections and this lawyer was some whip-smart savant from Denver who wasted no time freeing Sylvia from custody, if not suspicion. Without the results from the test fire to match the bullet rifling, they had no hard evidence. In their fear Sylvia was a flight risk, they'd overplayed their hand. The hard-nosed young woman Daniel sent had no trouble springing Sylvia from their clutches. The attorney had double-timed it back to Denver leaving Sylvia waiting for Daniel to pick her up from the station.

Finally, Daniel sauntered into the station. As usual, he created a ripple of admiration when he appeared in the station. The clerk behind the counter perked up and smiled eagerly. At forty-five, Sylvia had a few years on Daniel but she was every bit his equal. Together they were a couple worth noting.

Sylvia jumped up and hurried to him, her heels clacking on the cheesy linoleum. She met him halfway through the lobby, fuming. "How nice of you to grace me with your presence."

He lifted her hand and kissed it. "At your service."

She scurried to the door and waited for him to open it for her. "You should have been here twenty minutes ago."

"*Carina*, I arrived as soon as I could. Did the attorney not get here in good time?"

Daniel and his father used the same endearments for her. If only they each knew where the other had whispered those names.

She pushed the glass lobby doors open herself and stomped to the parking lot, only to slow down for Daniel to show her where he parked. She'd been waiting so long that the afternoon had drifted into evening and the sun dropped below the Flatirons. She scanned the lot filled with Subarus, economy cars, rugged SUVs , and the collection of various sedans and minivans. She didn't see a sports car she'd expect of Daniel. She glared at him, waiting for his direction. "The attorney made it here from Denver."

He strode down a row of cars with easy elegance. "She's very good, I'm told."

"She made it to the Boulder Police Department before you could drag yourself away from whatever consumed you." Sylvia's short legs worked double time to keep up with his saunter.

That smile of unconcern burned her. "Your charms are difficult to resist, *carina,* but I have other business to attend to. See? You are not so injured. Let me take you home and we will see what can be done to erase your troubles."

Did he think to appease her with a roll in the hay? If Daniel knew the riches she was about to provide for him, he'd treat her with more respect.

At least Eduardo knew her value. She hoped he wouldn't find out about her being accused of murder. Still if this hotshot attorney didn't get her off, Nora would have to call Eduardo. He'd take care of it because he needed Sylvia.

David pulled a key from his pocket and hit a button. The taillights on the car in front of her lit up.

She laughed. "A Prius? Taking this environmentalist image a little too far, aren't you?"

He raised his eyebrows and gave her an amused smile. He pressed another button on his key and the door unlocked. She waited for him to open it and she slid inside. With the smoothness of a jaguar—the brand of car he should be driving—Daniel eased himself into his own seat.

Sylvia anticipated their tryst in a few minutes between the silky sheets of her exquisite antique bed.

"So," he said, as if starting a casual conversation. "Why did you feel it necessary to kill our little Darla?"

"Don't be ridiculous." *I couldn't have killed Darla. A shot in the dark couldn't be that lucky—or unlucky.*

She folded her arms and viewed the city park outside her window. As usual, grungy college students and leftovers from the hippie days of Boulder's glory sprawled on the grass. The cops should be out rounding them up and carting them off the streets instead of chasing Sylvia.

Sylvia tried to calm down and think of something pleasant. She would wear the new lace bustier with the black garter belt and the spiked leopard print sling-backs Daniel favored.

Daniel switched lanes and turned right on Broadway. "A charge of murder is serious. Even if you did not kill Darla, you will have to devote much time and expense to defend yourself."

A flare of panic flashed inside her before she thought about it. No. Eduardo wouldn't let her go to prison. "My work is very important. Perhaps the Trust can pay for my legal defense."

They drove in silence and Daniel hummed tunelessly while maneuvering through traffic. After several minutes he pulled into her exclusive

neighborhood directly underneath the Flatirons and stopped in front of
her house. The 5,500-square-foot home with its cathedral ceilings, thick
pile carpets and polished wood floors and, what the realtor described as
"spectacular Flatirons view" always made Sylvia cringe. It seemed so pedestrian and ordinary. But she didn't have the time to devote to building something more suitable. When she finished her work here, she'd pick the
perfect location—maybe several locations—and build something more
fitting. For now, she could tolerate this, as long as she obtained the Chihuly.

Daniel's gaze flitted to the cement porch. It really should be much larger
with a few columns. Stone lions might be too much.

"I did not know you were an animal lover."

Sylvia spun around to see the scruffy calico cat on her porch. "I'll need
to call the HOA again. She turns up every few days and begs for food.
Someone in the neighborhood must feed her."

Daniel raised his eyebrows in dismissal. He waited a moment. "And
how do you propose the Trust find the money for your defense?"

She thought he'd dropped the subject.

"You haven't given the board much progress to make them inclined to
pay for expensive lawyers."

What had gotten into everyone all of the sudden? The board and
Eduardo, all of them thought she did nothing all day except dance to their
tune.

Only her dignity kept her from slapping him. "What about your family
foundation? Can't you get it from your father?"

Daniel eyed her as if gauging her mood.

Sylvia opened her car door and a rush of cold air invaded them. "Are
you saying you won't support me in this?"

His eyes focused on her cleavage in obvious desire. "I did not mean to
upset you. I am only wanting you to think about the problems you've
created for the Trust and my family."

His family. As if Daniel had the slightest clue what his father felt about
anything. "Ask Eduardo. He'll make sure I don't go to prison."

Daniel's eyebrows jumped up. "How is it you and my father met?"

In her anger she'd made a wrong step. Eduardo wouldn't want his name brought up to Daniel. "He admires my work. That's why he brought me to the Trust."

Daniel digested that. "He brought you to the Trust, where I sit on the board, so your groundbreaking study would reflect well on the organization. And he so generously allows the family trust to donate to your research."

Careful now. She ran a fingernail along the base of his throat and watched the goose bumps rise. "Eduardo wants you to be happy."

He caught her hand and pulled it away from his neck. "Is that why he sent you? Because I can't find my own importance in the world? Because I can't find my own women?"

"You couldn't be suggesting Eduardo is pimping me out to you, either personally or professionally?"

Daniel studied her. "Did he?"

How dare he? She flew out of the car. "Eduardo doesn't control my research or who I sleep with."

He narrowed his eyes. "Are you on his payroll to keep an eye on me?"

Intolerable. She slammed the door and started up the walk.

The damned calico cat twined herself between Sylvia's legs nearly bringing her to the pavement. She kicked it into the grass. The cat yowled and sped away.

18

The old farmhouse creaked every few minutes. Nora thought ghosts probably wandered the dark hallways and empty offices. If they didn't, they should. This building seemed strange enough in the daytime but at night, when she was the only one here, it felt like the House of Dracula.

Darkness filled her window, casting a reflection on her office and the light she'd turned on to dispel the creeps. *Thank dog no wind howled down Boulder Canyon to rattle the window and shriek against the siding or I wouldn't have been able to stay here this long.*

After her escape from Pearl Street and Abigail's dreams of a corporate career, Nora had hurried home to get Abbey. Then she met Daniel at the Trust. They'd tried to sift through the various activities and funds, bank statements and grants. Daniel said he had something to do and left for about an hour, then came back and insisted he take her to dinner.

They'd eaten at a Mediterranean place downtown. He was as charming as he was handsome, and the food was delicious. They'd chatted about childhood and exchanged details of colleges and highlights of their lives. Nora passed over her marriage, the snow-making scheme in Flagstaff, and the drama associated with it.

She'd been fascinated by Daniel's self-deprecating humor as he told of growing up in excess. He'd spent his youth chasing excitement from skiing in the Alps to scuba diving on the Barrier Reef to misadventures in Europe and the Middle East. Nora was sure he had enough stories to keep talking for months. But after all that running around, he said he finally understood his wealth could be used for something besides his own pleasure and he planned to spend it protecting the Ecuadoran rainforest.

Nora felt an urge to get back to the office and he'd obliged. He tried to talk her into going home but she wanted to get a few things organized before she called it quits for the night.

She'd been building the mother of all spreadsheets. Tomorrow she'd populate the columns and rows with the data from bank statements and financial statements and then she'd be able to analyze where the money came from and where it went.

Her eyes burned and she leaned back for a break. "That's enough for tonight," she said to Abbey.

He opened his eyes and thumped his tail.

Nora's eye caught the empty box she'd used to bring some of her personal things to the Trust. "She's not coming back." This time Abbey didn't bother to open his eyes. Nora stood and stacked the self-help books into the box and placed the porcelain animals on top. She carried the stack of Darla's affirmations she'd collected and added them to the box. Finally, she picked up Darla's picture.

A heavy blanket of sadness fell on Nora. She couldn't imagine someone so overlooked in life would be remembered long after death. It seemed a terrible waste.

She placed the picture in the box and contemplated the top yellow sheet. "I will confront Sylvia." It was copied the length of the page. Nora picked up the stack of sheets and paged through until she found what she searched for. "I am strong enough to stand up to her." Nora assumed the *her* was Sylvia.

"What do you suppose she wanted to confront her about?" Abbey lifted his head and yawned. The other staffers and now the police suspected Sylvia of killing Darla. Maybe Sylvia had something to do with whatever it was Darla supposedly found in the books. And maybe the moon is made of green cheese, as Abigail used to say whenever Nora's imagination got the best of her—which happened often.

Nora winked at Abbey. "I agree. Time to call it a night." She donned her coat and picked up her bag. Abbey followed her as they descended the narrow stairs to the kitchen. They turned toward the lobby and Nora stopped.

She hesitated. "It wouldn't hurt to check it out."

Abbey didn't protest as Nora tiptoed through the kitchen to Sylvia's office. The kitchen floor creaked and Abbey's toenails clicked on the linoleum. Nora slowed as she approached Sylvia's office door. She shouldn't snoop.

She whispered to Abbey. "I won't touch anything. Just look around a little. No going through drawers or anything like that." She pushed open the door, the sound like thunder in the quiet house. Nora stepped into the room and felt for the light. She flicked it on.

Someone screamed.

Nora screamed.

Abbey barked.

Nora jumped back, ready to retreat.

Her eyes finally focused. She clamped a hand to her chest and sucked in air. "Petal! What are you doing here?"

Petal sat in a nest of her own clothes close to her desk. The pink glow of her scarf-draped lamp faded in the overhead light. She blinked in the sudden brightness. "I'm—uh—I'm—sometimes Sylvia can't sleep and works at night. I thought maybe she'd be up tonight because of the, uh, the —because of the trouble."

"This is crazy," Nora said. Abbey sat in the doorway.

Petal rose and pulled out her desk chair. She huddled into it. "She doesn't ask me to do it. It's okay."

With Darla gone Petal had no one to go home to, no one to keep tabs on her.

Even if Abigail was furious about Nora's no-show earlier, at least she knew her mother loved her and would care if she never came home. "I think I saw some hot chocolate mix in the kitchen cupboard. Why don't I make us some?"

Petal jumped up with a grin on her face. "I can do it." She scurried from the office and Nora heard banging in the kitchen.

She tilted her head at Abbey. "As long as we're here..." She wandered casually to Sylvia's desk. A 24 inch monitor dominated the desk and a laptop sat on the edge. The wood gleamed with only one lone sheet of notebook paper shoved half under the laptop.

The microwave hummed in the kitchen. Nora gingerly slid the sheet of paper from under the laptop. A tree graph with several circles showed a confusing jumble. It looked like Darla's idea of fund accounting. In other words, chaos. Nora bent closer. Credit card and bank names labeled the circles along with various names of people. Dollar amounts in the thousands were inked on arrows going from circle to circle.

What a financial juggling act. Sylvia was either a genius or heading for a big crash.

The ding of the microwave warned of Petal's return. Nora shoved the paper back and headed for the kitchen.

"That smells good," Nora said when Petal handed her a chipped mug of hot chocolate. Actually, it smelled sickening sweet. "Let's sit at the booth."

Petal acted surprised. "Okay. I don't think I've ever sat there before."

They settled themselves in the booth with the glow of an overhead light casting their reflection in the darkened window.

"Can I ask you something?" Petal said. "What's your mother's story?"

"Her story?" Nora thought a moment. "Well, she grew up in Nebraska and went to school here in Boulder at CU. I guess she met my father there, but he apparently left us when I was a baby."

"Where does he live?" Petal asked.

Nora shrugged. "I don't know and don't care. He didn't want us, so why should I want him?"

Petal frowned and sipped her hot chocolate. "What happened to your mother after he left?"

Nora held her palm over the steaming cup. "She married Berl when I was about five. He had a lot of money and that suited her."

Petal sipped and set her mug down. "I thought so."

"What do you mean?" The hot chocolate tasted too sweet for Nora.

"Well, she's got all this high society class and taste and stuff, but she's too nice to have been raised with money."

Nora wrapped her hands around her warm mug. "I hadn't thought about it but maybe Abigail's coming full circle. She started out humble, lived large for a while and now she's back to humble."

"With Charlie?" The pinks and oranges of Petal's layers became flowers in the window's reflection.

"Well, there was another husband between Berl and Charlie, but he died of a heart attack when they'd only been married a couple of years."

Petal finished her hot chocolate and curled her feet under her. "Do you like Charlie?"

The house had been growing steadily colder since the heater's timer set it on nighttime temperature.

Nora couldn't stop her grin. "Charlie's my best friend. Or he was when I lived in Flagstaff. He's a real character. Vietnam vet, true environmentalist. Loyal and completely devoted to Abigail." No matter what she said about an alleged affair.

Petal sighed.

"What about you? Where is your mother?" Nora asked.

Petal swirled her cup. "Oh. My mother lives in New Orleans. She's got some medical problems. That's why I need this job. I help her out."

A boom sounded from the front door. Nora and Petal both jumped and Petal let out a squeak of alarm. Abbey lifted his head and woofed.

The building sighed as the front door opened.

Nora's heart nearly burst. Petal flew out of the booth and raced toward Sylvia's office.

"Boulder County Police," a low-pitched woman's voice called.

Nora rose on shaky legs and stepped around the kitchen wall into the lobby. Abbey followed her.

A uniformed police officer stood by the door, her belt weighing her down with all manner of tools or weapons. She held a flashlight but hadn't turned it on.

Nora hurried to her. "I'm Nora Abbott. Can I help you?"

The officer studied her. "Officer Garcia." She introduced herself. "Do you work here?"

"I just started yesterday." Nora's heart still thudded.

Officer Garcia surveyed the room and let her gaze travel up the stairs. "Are you here alone?"

Nora pointed toward the kitchen. "My colleague is here."

Garcia nodded. "Working late?"

"Yes. Trying to catch up." Nora adopted the spare speaking style of the officer.

Garcia's voice bordered on masculine and she sounded almost angry. "You know a woman was murdered out here a few days ago."

Fear spiked Nora's flesh. If Garcia were here to reassure Nora, she failed.

"I'd suggest you wrap up your work for tonight and head home."

"I was just leaving."

"Good. I'll wait in the parking lot and follow you out." Garcia swept her gaze over the lobby and she walked out the door.

Petal crept around the corner. "Is she gone?"

Nora watched Garcia out the front window. "Guess she's checking up on us. Probably a good thing."

Petal hung her head and retreated to the kitchen.

Nora followed feeling suddenly felt exhausted. "Can I give you a ride?"

Petal shook her head. "No. I've got my bike."

Nora carried their cups to the sink. Petal scuttled to Sylvia's office.

Nora shrugged into her coat. She hollered to Petal. "I'll wait for you and lock up."

Petal stuck her head out of the office. "Go ahead. I'm going to leave Sylvia a note in case she comes in."

Nora held the door open for Abbey and closed it after he stepped out on the porch. Cold mountain air chilled Nora's fingers and nose. The deep silence closed around her.

Darla died on a night like this. Not a hundred yards from where Nora stood.

Someone killed her.

On a night like this.

19

The furnace rumbled to life in the drafty farmhouse. Nora reached under her desk and turned off the ceramic heater that had made her office tolerable for the past two hours. She scoped out at the clock on her computer. Seven o'clock. Weak light sneaked from her western-facing window announcing another day.

She'd been here late last night with Petal; late enough that Abigail had given up waiting for her and gone to bed. Nora returned hours before dawn, cutting her night short. Whenever something creaked or bumped—which happened often in the rambling old building, Nora had to talk herself into staying calm and ignoring her urge to leave.

As creepy as the Trust was, it seemed a good alternative to facing Abigail's wrath. She'd endured one raging phone call about missing the interview yesterday and would probably be in for a few more. But if she could delay it, Abigail might lose steam. She could hope, anyway.

She scratched Abbey behind his ears and he didn't bother to open his eyes. "Another hour before anyone comes to work." At least, Mark said they were supposed to show up at eight.

Her green banker's lamp illuminated the work space around her computer and she hadn't bothered turning on any other lights. She'd focused organizing and familiarizing herself with the inner workings of the

Trust. The $4 million budget divided into eight distinct projects with their own budgets, each funded with grants and donations, some shared, some specific with restricted and unrestricted funds coming in and going out of five different bank accounts and tied to several investment accounts. She'd need to simplify the system. No one could monitor of this financial maze. Tracking the grants alone might be a full time job.

Nora could usually drill into a problem and block out any distractions. It's how she'd been so successful in school and able to run a ski resort on her own. But this morning, her brain was like a kindergartener with ADHD.

One moment she thought about Cole standing amid the colorful fall leaves on the mall yesterday. The Cole slideshow flipped to him on her ski mountain in Flagstaff, defending her at Scott's funeral. Next slide: Cole fighting off an attacker who tried to strangle Nora to keep her from making snow on the sacred peaks. Flip: Cole grinning and catching her in his arms when she'd discovered he hadn't been killed. He'd risked his life to save hers.

Stop this!

As soon as she forced her mind from Cole, it bounced back to Benny and worse still, Nakwaiyamtewa. She was never sure if he and the kachina were one and the same. The kachina wore colorful clothes and feathers, his mask fierce and frightening.

Nakwaiyamtewa stood no taller than five feet and appeared and disappeared like Whac-a-Mole. Nora had only seen him a few times in quiet moments. He was a man of few words and those were usually some kind of annoying riddle.

Turns out, Nakwaiyamtewa died in the 1880s. His descendent, Benny, carried on the Hopi traditions. No doubt they had coffee together every morning and discussed the local corn harvest and state of the world they claimed responsibility for.

Another reason Nora had climbed from her bed so early was the dreaming. The kachina had crashed through the forest every time she drifted off last night. He chased someone, maybe her, she couldn't tell in the dream. The fear bursting through her sleep into her bedroom left her panting and unwilling to go back to sleep. Now a low grade headache banged behind her eyes.

Focus.

The Trust staffers should be showing up soon. Would they find out she'd spilled her guts to the board and revealed whose work was in the red or black? If so, they might treat her like a squealer. Good bye to the notion of friends.

Mark must hate her. Thinking about him gave her the creeps.

Footsteps on the stairs made Nora stiffen. She couldn't hear the front door from here and someone was already on their way up.

"Don't think you can avoid me forever." It wasn't what she expected.

"Good morning, Abigail."

Anger wafted from Abigail in waves but it didn't affect her appearance. She wore wool slacks, turtleneck and boots, all coordinated with a car coat that carried the chilly fall morning into Nora's office. "Don't 'good morning' me. I set up an appointment with a very busy man on your behalf and you embarrassed me in front of him. I can't imagine what he'll tell his mother."

"I'm sorry." She'd repeat it as often as necessary. It would do no good to shut Abigail down. Might as well let her spew.

With the Abigail white noise, Nora was finally able to concentrate. She stared at the screen. What was this? Wasn't the balance of Sylvia's restricted account much higher in August than the balance the computer showed for September?

Abigail slapped the desktop. "Are you listening to me?"

Nora pulled her gaze from the screen. Ignoring Abigail wouldn't work. She noted the time and gave Abigail ten minutes to rant. The headache gained momentum.

"'Casting away radiance in pursuit of mediocrity in a flight of fear.'" Abigail reached into her slender leather handbag and pulled out a tiny notepad. It sparkled with gold glitter adorning Michelangelo's cherubs and had a matching, miniature pen. She paused and slid the pad back into the bag. "Something not right about that. I'll work on it."

The morning lightened enough Nora snapped off her desk lamp. "Poetry aside, Abigail, I'm trying to work. Can we talk at home?"

Undaunted, Abigail continued. "You're making a big mistake. Even Cole agrees with me on that."

Nora sat back in her chair with a creak of springs. "You discussed me with Cole?"

Abigail's tone softened, as it always did when she talked about Cole. "He's concerned about you working at the Trust and frankly, after hearing what he had to say, so am I."

"What, do you have him on speed dial?" She rubbed at a knot on her neck, hoping to ease the knocking in her brain. Maybe she needed coffee.

And here it came again. The speech Abigail worked herself into every time Cole's name came up. "Why do you have such a problem with that man? He's strong and capable, certainly not hard on the eyes. And he cares about you."

Easy lob to Nora's court. "Let's talk about you and Charlie."

Abigail stiffened. "Nothing to talk about."

"You don't really think he's having an affair?"

Abigail clamped her lips and spun toward the door.

Victory! Sometime soon she'd have to dig into the details of the Charlie mess, but not now.

Abigail walked back in. Drat. She'd called the match too soon. "I saw it with my own two eyes. Some woman your age."

Nora's eyes wandered to the screen but she swiveled her chair to give Abigail her full attention. "Did you ask Charlie about it?"

Abigail set her bag on the desk and slipped out of her coat, dashing Nora's hopes for her hasty departure. "Why would I give him the opportunity to make up a lie? I won't allow myself to be mocked and humiliated."

Nora wanted to rush Abigail to the finish line. She definitely needed caffeine to battle the headache. "Charlie's a good man. There's probably an explanation."

Abigail perched on the edge of the wicker chair. The burnt orange and browns of her fall ensemble clashed with the lavender and mint motif. "I wasn't surprised when I caught him. All the signs were there."

"What kind of signs?"

Abigail straightened her shoulders in sturdy dignity. "He started cleaning up and wearing nice clothes every day. Or rather, what he considers nice clothes. He refused to wear the chinos and golf shirts I bought him. I know they'd be more comfortable than his old button-down flannel shirts and Nora, his jeans were a nightmare of faded and frayed."

Coffee might save Nora's life. The rickety heater chugged warm air through the floor vents pushing aside the abandon feel of the night.

"He left the house every day, as usual, but he wasn't going into the woods."

"How do you know?"

Abigail's despairing expression stabbed at Nora. "I can't believe I sank so low. I actually sniffed his clothes. They didn't smell the same as when he wandered the trails with the fresh air and pines."

Nora stood and stretched. "Why didn't you talk to him instead of building resentment?"

"That's the most telling part. His personality changed. With me, anyway." Abigail's gaze traveled toward the window. "You know how charming and solicitous he usually is with me."

Abigail always appreciated goddess worship.

"He became moody. Sometimes he ignored me. And once, he even snapped at me."

Abigail made Nora want to snap like a feral Chihuahua, but Charlie had endless patience.

"The real clue though, is that he wasn't interested in," she lowered her voice, "the bedroom."

"Really, Abigail? This is what you want to tell your daughter?"

"It's natural. Do you think your desire goes away when you hit forty?"

"I don't want to think about it." Nora paced to the door and scanned the hallway to see if anyone else had made it to work.

"Well, it doesn't. I'm a healthy woman with healthy needs like any other woman. I notice when my lover loses interest."

"Stop talking now."

Abigail sat back. "You can't hide from the realities of life, dear."

Nora wandered back to her desk and propped against the work surface. "We're going to have to talk about this later. I've got a raging headache. Probably because I haven't been sleeping."

Abigail hurried over to Nora and placed a cold hand on Nora's forehead. "Are you sick? Why haven't you been sleeping?"

Nora brushed Abigail's hand away. "I'm fine. Just having dreams."

"Nightmares?"

Maybe it would help exorcise them if Nora talked about it. "Kachina dreams. It's probably new job stress."

Abigail acted overly concerned about Nora's lack of sleep.

Nora rubbed her forehead. "From what I know, kachinas are supposed to stay on the sacred mountain in Flagstaff or on the mesas in Hopiland. They don't travel all over the place like goblins with frequent flyer miles."

Abigail frowned and stared out the window.

"I know that November starts a new season for the kachinas. So they leave the mesa where they've spent the summer and go back to the mountain for the winter. Maybe Nakwaiyamtewa thinks a visit to Colorado would be nice before he goes home."

Abigail put on her coat. "You're over-thinking things. It's just a dream."

"Maybe it is just a dream about Hopis. But I saw the kachina on Mount Evans and then Benny showed up here. Why?" Nora waited for her mother's dismissal of kachina sightings as signs of Nora's overactive imagination.

Abigail seemed distracted and in a hurry to leave. "Why wouldn't Benny visit? He likes you."

Nora shook her head. "No, it's more than that. He hates leaving the mesa for anything." Nora leaned back and mused. "What is my connection to Hopi?"

Abigail grabbed her bag and scurried to the door.

This didn't seem right. "Mother?"

"I've got to go, dear. Talk to you later."

Nora's radar kicked in. "Hang on, Abigail. What are you hiding. You've got that secretive look on your face."

Abigail's smiled looked strained. "I don't know what you're talking about."

The hairs on Nora's neck jumped to attention. "What?"

"I try to live in the present. I don't like to dwell on unpleasant things in the past," Abigail stammered.

As much as it sounded like more of Abigail's bad poetry, Nora thought

she might be serious. This wouldn't be good. "You're going to tell me something you should have told me a long time ago, aren't you?"

Abigail huffed. "You don't need to know everything about me. I'm enti-
tled to a few secrets."

It only got worse. "But this secret involves me, doesn't it?"

"Maybe." Abigail's eyes traveled from the coat closet up to the ceiling,
over to the shelves and to the window. Then she focused on Nora's light-
weight hiking boots.

"Spill it, Mother."

Abigail glanced down the empty hall and stepped back into the office.
"Did you ever wonder how I met Berle?"

Berle was Abigail's second husband. The man who raised Nora.

We're going to take the long way. "This train has a caboose, right? And
when we get there it's going to tell me something I need to know, right?"

Abigail sat in the wicker chair. "I met Berle in Flagstaff. He was there on
business with Kachina Ski."

Nora's stepfather had given her the ski resort in Flagstaff as insurance
for Abigail. He was afraid if he died before Abigail, she'd run through his
money. Which is what happened. Nora promised him she'd take care of
Abigail. Which she did.

Nora would die of old age or frustration before Abigail made her point.

"I never told you the reason I was in Flagstaff. It had to do with your
father."

"My biological father?" Nora didn't remember Abigail ever voluntarily
mentioning him.

"Yes."

Nora plopped into her chair.

"Your father was from the Flagstaff area. He grew up there. Had a bunch
of family."

Abigail paused. Nora wanted to scream at her. *More. More!*

"He didn't really run away from us, you know." Abigail said it softly. "He
died. And I took him home and let him be buried by his family."

Nora's throat felt too dry to speak. "My father died? Why didn't you tell me?"

Abigail stared ahead, her eyes misty with tears. "I thought if I told you he died, you'd go looking for his family but if I told you he abandoned us, you'd hate him and not ever try to contact him."

"That makes no sense."

Abigail raised her eyebrows. "It worked, didn't it?"

"Yeah, but I've spent my whole life angry at a man who didn't deserve it."

Abigail considered that and then went on. "We were so young. We met in college and married within a month. Neither of us ever finished. So in love. We didn't have any money and we didn't care. Oh, I know you won't believe me when I say that. But your father was... he was special."

Nora couldn't speak; she struggled to breathe.

"It was a car wreck. The sort of thing that happens to other people. And suddenly... our dream ended. He was gone and I was a few weeks pregnant."

"I'm sorry." Nora wanted to cry for her mother's loss. "Why didn't you tell me this?"

A father and family she didn't know. How could her mother not tell her? When could she meet them and begin to understand her past? Thoughts flew at her like hailstones battering against a window.

Abigail fought tears. "I wanted what was best for you. Maybe I was wrong. I don't know. You turned out so well and you're successful and educated. But it's coming full circle."

Chills snaked through Nora.

Abigail's eyes pleaded for understanding. "Your father was Hopi."

After so much tension, Nora laughed. "He was not. I've got red hair."

Instant anger burn Abigail's words. "He most certainly was Hopi. Maybe there was an indiscretion in his ancestry. There's also red hair in my family."

Could that be true? Maybe that's why she could see Nakwaiyamtewa. "Am I related to Benny?"

Abigail waved her hand. "I imagine so."

"Does he know?"

"I don't know. He seems to know a lot of things."

Hopi heritage. This wasn't true. It couldn't be true.

Nora rubbed her forehead. "Why didn't you tell me my father was dead?"

The fire went out of Abigail. "I was afraid. I was young and alone with a baby. The Hopi have very strong family attachments and I thought they might take you from me. I would have shared you with them but I didn't know them and I didn't trust they would give you back."

"And they're destitute. You couldn't stand the thought of me not having all those cute Urban Outfitters clothes and going on spring break."

"I am not a monster!" Abigail sounded hurt. "I wanted the best for you. And you got the best."

Nora tilted her head to stretch her neck. "I'm sorry. Can you…" She couldn't think what she wanted to ask.

Abigail stood and backed toward the door. "You need some time to think about this."

The world faded, leaving her isolated on her desk chair, floating in dense fog. Nora nodded. "Yes."

Nora sat still. If she moved, she might crumble.

Hopi.

She had family.

20

Nora sat at her desk, struggling with the idea of a father. A Hopi father. Did he love peaches and hate liver as she did? Was he a Rolling Stones fan or did he tend more toward Elvis. Or maybe he didn't like music at all.

"Good morning."

Nora gasped at the greeting. Mark stood at her doorway. "Sorry. I didn't mean to startle you."

Nora brought herself back to reality. Bright light shone from her window.

Last time she saw Mark he had fired her. Now he stood in her doorway. She scanned his hands for the giant butcher knife he probably brought to ram into her ribs. Instead, she saw two tall compostable paper cups with a Mr. Green Beans logo. "Hi, Mark." She tried for casual but it came out a croak.

He held out one of the cups. "I saw your Jeep out front so I turned around and went back for coffee."

She accepted the cup. This would help with her colossal headache. "Thanks."

"I got you a double shot skinny latte. Next time, you can tell me your favorite." He sniggered.

Mark's one-eighty in attitude made her more than a little jumpy. Abbey stood, stretched and wagged his tail as he ambled to Mark. When Mark didn't pet him, Abbey plopped down. Mornings exhausted him.

Nora sipped. Yuck. Mr. Green Beans over-roasted their beans or grew their own in the back yard. The coffee had a sickening, super-bitter taste. She smiled. "That's really nice of you."

He sipped his own coffee. "I need to apologize for my behavior yesterday. I'm only glad the board prevailed with their calmer heads." He snorted.

What a freak. "It's okay. I understand how stressful a board meeting can be. Sort of like a college final when your whole grade depends on one essay question." What had her father studied in college?

"I want us to be friends. We're on the same team—Team Earth." He raised a fist.

Everything he needed to know about life he learned in kindergarten and he must have been absent for half the lesson. "Thanks, Mark. I'm really happy to be a part of the Trust." Was her father short, like a lot of Hopis?

Mark studied her office as if he'd like to know what each carefully stacked pile of papers signified. "Have you been here long this morning?" He sounded more probing than friendly.

Long enough for my whole life to get tipped over.

Time to compartmentalize. She shook off her shattering news and concentrated on Mark. New job. Loving Earth Trust. Here. Now. "I wanted to get an early start. It's a complicated system and the sooner I get it conquered, the sooner I can write checks and pay bills."

The friendly slipped from his face. "The sooner the better. Sylvia needs that money."

Would it be poor form to ask about Sylvia and the police?

He pointed to her coffee. "How do you like the latte?" He seemed to expect her to drink more.

She took another awful sip and swallowed down the nasty brew. "It's great."

He nodded and watched her closely. *Again: freak.* "Okay, then. I'll let you get back to work."

She sipped just to be a good sport. "Thanks for the coffee."

He scrutinized her once more and left.

Nora set the coffee down and typed in the August dates on Sylvia's restricted account. The fund showed $1,295,672.56. She entered the dates for September. $895,672.56.

$400,000 difference. Exactly. Where did it go? It shouldn't be hard to spot.

Fay poked her head in Nora's office. She wore jeans and a fleece pullover, her thin blonde hair tangled down her back. Her voice crackled. "Some drama yesterday, huh?"

Abbey stood and offered himself for a pat from the newcomer.

Fay obliged. She spoke in comforting baby-talk. "What a sweetie you are."

Nora braced for harsh words. After all, she'd announced to the board that several projects at the Trust were over budget. That would probably mean cuts and someone might even lose a job to save money.

Receiving his fair share of welcome, Abbey made his way back to lie at Nora's feet.

Fay stepped into the office holding a Mr. Green Beans travel mug. She lowered her voice. "Did you get a chance to tell the board about Sylvia? They ought to know she doesn't do anything."

Nora didn't know what to say to that. "I only reported the financial situation." Which just worsened with a $400,000 disappearance.

Bill stopped outside her door. He hadn't shaved since yesterday and his shirt had more wrinkles than Harrison Ford's face. He also sipped from a Mr. Green Beans mug. He gave her a thumbs up and said, "Did you turn Sylvia in for embezzling?"

"What?" Nora gulped. "No. I..."

Bill grinned. "Just joking. They think she killed Darla."

Fay cackled. "Why would they think that?"

His tone dripped sarcasm. "Ballistic evidence? Flight risk? I wouldn't know."

Bill winked at Fay and they laughed.

Had they set Sylvia up? *Yes, they probably did and they're going to take her Ferrari and run away to Mexico. Sheesh, Nora.*

Darla's murder probably had more to do with the missing $400,000. But maybe it wasn't really missing. Nora needed to check out all the statements before she assumed it was stolen.

Fay nodded sagely. "I have no doubt she killed Darla."

"If she killed Darla, who do you think is next on her list?" Thomas walked up behind Fay. He unzipped his parka and gulped his coffee from Mr. Green Beans. The Trust ought to get a volume discount.

They stood in her doorway discussing motives and future victims of Sylvia's murder spree.

How could they joke about this? Further, how could they stand that coffee? Thinking about hers, Nora's stomach gave a twist.

"Petal and Darla, they're both strange if you ask me," Bill said.

The three of them carried on their gossip fest without including Nora. She didn't know how to shoo them out of her office without being rude.

"I don't know how she can work for Sylvia. Do you know how many grad students I could get into the field on that bitch's budget?" Thomas said.

"Maybe you'll get your chance now that she's going to prison on murder charges." Fay said.

An unmistakable Latino accent floated over Bill's shoulder. "I do not think Sylvia is going to prison." Whatever Daniel Cubrero said sounded like silk on skin.

Bill flushed. Thomas disappeared. Guilt settled on Fay's features.

"A police officer is downstairs now ready to conduct interviews. Perhaps you should make yourselves available to him." Daniel spoke to Fay and Bill as he slipped into Nora's office and removed the black sport coat he wore over a white shirt. His jeans snugged to his body like they were custom tailored. It occurred to Nora that they might be. That must be the finest Italian leather on his feet, the shoes probably felt more comfortable than her slippers and cost more than her Jeep.

Fay's eyes glazed slightly and her jaw slackened. Nora knew how she felt.

Daniel raised Nora's hand to his lips. Kissing her hand? Nora could never remember anyone kissing her hand before. Such an affectation and yet, it seemed natural for Daniel. "How are you this morning, *mi bonitacita*?"

Bill's eyes widened.

In an effort to appear more grounded than the gapers in the doorway, Nora pulled her hand from Daniel's and gestured to the wide work counter full of neat stacks. "I'm making progress." Nora didn't think she allowed herself to be undone by total handsomeness, but her stomach roiled and bile rose in her throat. Maybe the milk in the latte was spoiled.

"Point me in a direction and I will do your bidding."

His accent sent a little shiver through her. Or was it the nausea from the latte? She burped a little, the taste of the bitter coffee revisited made her feel sicker.

Daniel turned toward Fay and Bill. "The officer downstairs?"

"Oh, certainly," Bill said.

"Nice of you to get so involved." Fay blushed and blinked rapidly. "I hope we'll see you again."

"*Bueno.*" He turned back to Nora leaving the others to slink away.

"I'm not really sure what we're searching for. I'm starting with the most recent bank statements and working backward." Oh. Her stomach whooshed up and turned over. She held a hand to her mouth.

"Are you feeling okay?"

Nora waited for the wave of nausea to pass. "I think so." Another wave hit her.

Daniel grasped her arm. "You must sit down."

She let him lead her to the desk. She leaned against it and spotted a swirl of pinks and oranges outside her door. The fact it wasn't blue made her want to sing. But it might be Petal, alone and afraid, wanting to hang out in a safe office or maybe hide in her closet.

Nora plopped into her chair. She opened her mouth to call Petal into her office but what came gushing out wasn't words. Nora didn't have time to feel aghast at the stream of vomit coating the fine Italian leather of Daniel's shoes.

She swayed to one side of her chair, slid off and passed out on the floor.

21

The emergency room beyond Nora's curtained cubicle bustled with activity. The ER didn't smell quite as hospital-ly as she'd expect, but enough antiseptic and chemical lingered to remind Nora where she was. Wheels, feet, voices, clanking, urgency—it all seeped under the drape to add to Nora's anxiety.

Nora watched the IV drip into the tubing attached to the back of her hand. It looked pale resting on the white thermal blanket. She got up enough nerve to peek at Daniel. "I'm so sorry."

He grinned, showing white, even teeth and inviting lips. "You've already apologized."

She'd emptied her guts and wasn't sure her hair was always out of the way. She had sweated and then chilled. She must be gorgeous.

Nora wanted to hide under the blanket and yet she had to make conversation after she'd puked on his shoes. "Thank you for bringing me here." She had a sudden thought. "What about Abbey?"

Daniel raised an eyebrow. "Abbey?"

"My dog. I left him at the office."

The curtain around her bed swiped back. Cole burst in wearing his typical flannel shirt and jeans topped off with a navy blue down vest. He pushed his hair from his forehead and scanned her from head to feet

"Abbey's in my pickup. Are you okay? What happened? Are you sick? Did you break anything?"

Daniel's eyebrows popped up in surprise. "Nora, you did not tell me you were married."

"I'm not." To Cole she said, "Why do you have Abbey?"

Daniel's mouth formed a slight smirk. "My mistake."

Cole scowled at Daniel. "I didn't think you'd want him shut up in your office when you weren't there. What happened?"

"I got sick. Threw up. I'm feeling better."

A doctor with a lab coat over a simple brown paisley wrap dress stepped into the curtained space. She held a tablet computer in one hand and planted her other on her hip, staring down the two men. "One person allowed at a time. One of you will have to leave." She shook Nora's hand. "I'm Dr. Taylor."

Could Nora get a prescription for that attitude? Dr. Taylor had no trouble asserting her control.

Cole glared at Daniel.

Daniel raised one eyebrow in response and spoke to Nora. "If your... friend... will see you home, I need to attend to a few chores." Daniel bent over and kissed Nora's forehead. Maybe he did it to annoy Cole in some testosterone standoff. But his familiarity startled Nora. They might slobber all over each other in Ecuador but Nora preferred her nice, roomy American personal space. Especially since she suspected she might smell a little "off."

Cole frowned.

Dr. Taylor snapped the IV drip with her thumb and forefinger. "How are you feeling?"

"Much better."

Dr. Taylor studied her. "The nausea gone?"

Nora nodded. "It didn't last long."

"I'd guess you got it out of your system with all that vomiting."

Cole butted in, as if it were any of his business. "What made her sick?"

Dr. Taylor swiped her finger across her computer screen. "Could be any number of things. Her symptoms suggest food poisoning."

"Can you run some test? Is this normal?" He sounded insistent.

Dr. Taylor glanced from the screen. "We could. Yes. We could spend a lot of time and money and not come up with anything definitive. Nora is feeling better."

"When can I go home?" Nora asked.

Dr. Taylor tapped the drip again. "This is your second bag?"

Nora nodded.

"As soon as you empty this—unless you feel the nausea returning. If that happens," she turned to Cole, "bring her back immediately and we'll run those tests."

With that, she spun on her toes and zipped away.

Nora stared at the bag, three fourths drained into her veins. "You can go. I'll call Abigail to come get me."

"Call Abigail if you want but I'm not going anywhere."

"What are you even doing here?" Not that she cared what Cole thought but she'd rather he didn't see her this vulnerable.

"I stopped by the Trust to talk you and they told me you'd gone to the emergency room."

Could she poke a hole in the bag and make it drain quicker? "We don't have anything to talk about."

"Benny called and..."

Would that be Benny, her long lost cousin? She dropped her head on the pillow. "I don't care what Benny said. He's just a guy living out on a mesa in the desert having delusional episodes."

Cole's mouth tipped up in a half smile and his eyes danced. "Keep telling yourself that. You know better. You've seen it."

A year ago the kachina had directed her to the save the mountain, but he hadn't helped her save Heather. Nora saw the headstrong, passionate sixteen-year-old flipping her blue-back hair over her shoulder, courageous and foolish in her fight for her Hopi heritage.

Did Nora blame the kachina or herself more?

Nora felt tempted to tell Cole about her new-found heritage. She had the strangest urge to know what he thought of it. But she wanted to get used to it before she shared it.

Nora tried to reach up to tap the bag and force it to empty. Her efforts failed. If Cole would just leave she could relax and let her body rehydrate. "How is it you can just show up? Don't you have a life?"

He paused. "I've been in Wyoming on my family's ranch. It's slow season so they can spare me for a few days."

"I don't need you to babysit me. Go home."

His ears turned red. "There are more pleasant things to do than be rejected by you."

"Okay then. We agree. You need to go home."

"I can't do that."

"Why not?"

He shook his head as if it were obvious. "Because you need someone to protect you."

Now he was really dancing on her nerves. "And since you think you saved my life once you have the responsibility to keep saving me."

"It's not a case of responsibility," he said quietly.

Time to stop the conversation before he said something she didn't want to hear. She turned her head away.

He didn't leave. "You need to get away from the Trust."

She whipped her head around. "Why would I do that?"

"Because someone tried to kill you."

"I got food poisoning."

"What did you eat this morning?"

Nothing. When she got to the apartment last night she'd eaten handfuls of Cheerios from the box. The thought of Abigail's annoyance almost made her smile. That was the last food she'd had.

Until the coffee Mark brought.

The coffee she couldn't stand even though Fay and Thomas guzzled theirs.

22

Sylvia stood with her arms crossed assessing her dining room. The expensive original oil paintings and the thick hand-woven rug over the shining rosewood floor pleased her. The chandelier glittered, throwing sparkles into the dark cathedral windows. An ordinary person would think it adequate, maybe even like it. But it didn't suit Sylvia in the least.

The Chihuly should hang directly over the wrought iron and glass dining table she'd commissioned from an artist in Jackson Hole last year. A hard knot of frustration hit her gut as Sylvia adjusted one of the dining chairs. Until she had her glass, the room would be incomplete.

Sylvia's heels sank into the deep pile of the rug and the folds of her negligee swished softly against her legs as she paraded down the hall. She paused in front of a full-length mirror, the designer frame setting off her image. Daniel would appreciate the view. Too bad they'd had that spat after the police station yesterday. She'd expected him all day but he hadn't shown up. Sooner or later he would return to her.

The doorbell rang. The grandfather clock showed it was after nine. It could be Daniel, or maybe not. Her heart thudded against her ribs.

She descended two stairs to the foyer and tiptoed to the door to peek out the side window.

Daniel stood under the porch light. He oozed sex in his black blazer and jeans. He held a bottle of Courvoisier.

Sylvia smiled in satisfaction. She adjusted the neckline on the slinky black negligee, patted her hair, then unlocked the door and swung it wide.

"*Buenos noches.*" So much like his father; but he replaced the confidence of the mature man with the raw sexuality of a younger man.

"Please come in." She stepped back and her vision dropped to his shapely backside as he walked past her.

A splash of fur zipped by her, hurtling into the foyer. The damned calico cat slowed to a trot and wound around Daniel's legs.

"Oh, that pest!" Sylvia lunged for it.

Daniel bent down and picked it up. He handed the bottle to Sylvia. He stroked the cat's fur as he walked back to the door. "*Mi gato bonito.*" He murmured as if he actually liked the fur ball. He set it on the porch and gave it a gentle shove then stepped back inside.

His focus slid around the oversized vases with their exotic dried grasses that had cost Sylvia a fortune. He looked up the stairs. "Very nice." Whether he meant the house or her didn't much matter. He wasn't here for words.

Clever Sylvia hadn't wasted any time seducing Daniel three years earlier when she started at the Trust. The complicated twists of who used whom—between Daniel and his environmental sensibilities, Eduardo with his eyes on a most lucrative venture, and Sylvia with the expertise to pull it off—landed Sylvia at the Trust with a multi-million dollar budget funded almost entirely by the Cubrero fortune.

Daniel believed she researched climate change and he'd convinced his father to donate enormous funds. Eduardo knew he was paying for something entirely different than global warming research and that Sylvia and Daniel were colleagues, nothing more. Sylvia played one side against the other, hedging bets with her body and her brain. Why not? She had the skills.

Catering to Daniel's desires had more benefits than as simply life insurance against Eduardo. "I have a fire in the living room. Why don't we enjoy our drinks in there?"

He inclined his head, willing to let the evening unfold as it would. He chose a sofa in the glow of the fire. Sylvia would look irresistible in the dim light.

After she'd poured the cognac into the snifters and settled next to him on the imported white leather sofa, she said, "I regret our harsh words yesterday. I know you provided me with the lawyer and you did your best. Please, can we forget our tiff?"

He reached out and trailed a long, slender finger along her jaw. "I do not wish to fight you."

She made her eyes smolder with desire. "We fit together so well. It's as if we recognize that spark that makes us different from other people."

He leaned closer and the scent of warm skin and subtle spice of his cologne wafted around her, spreading moisture between her thighs. "Let me show you how we fit together."

She unfolded herself from the sofa and held her hand out to him. He took it and stood. She led him from the room. "Let's discuss this upstairs."

"Excellent idea."

He stepped close behind and slipped his arm around her, cupping a breast beneath the silk of her negligee. "We have found another area of agreement, no?"

She swayed her hips climbing the stairs, giving him a preview of what would follow. They ambled down the long hall to her bedroom. It might be her favorite room in the house, decorated in black and white with splashes of red. The duvet highlighted the room with massive scarlet orchids covering the white satin.

She pushed him gently onto the bed and stepped back. His body settled on the giant four poster she'd found at a Southerby's auction. She slipped her feet from the delicate mules. One spaghetti strap slid from her shoulders as she stared into his hungry eyes.

He rose and pulled the other strap down, letting the silky fabric puddle around her ankles. He paused for only a moment. She found men loved to gaze on her exquisite beauty. He pulled her to him, bending to kiss and nip at her breasts.

Like most men she'd allowed to touch her, he relished her physical artistry and she enjoyed his worship. It didn't take him but a moment to shed his clothes and lay her back on the bed. Sylvia went into her routine. What man could resist her?

She let him climb on her, wild in his desire. She'd learned to moan in the right places and move beneath him in a way that excited him. After an appropriate interval, she increased the volume and frequency and raw tones of her moans, faked her orgasm, and let him finish his own journey.

It wasn't that she didn't enjoy sex. All the foreplay and excitement of watching her partner get aroused created a deep pleasure in her. But the final act, the sweating body and heaving need, the squirt—all seemed sordid. There was a point when men quit seeing her as a priceless work of art and sought their own release that made it impossible for her to climax. She'd take care of that later, alone in her masterpiece of a bed.

Daniel rolled off. "You were right, *querida*. We have a special connection."

She watched as his fingers traced her areola.

She toyed with the black hair on his chest, enjoying the steady beat of his heart beneath well-formed pecs. It thrilled her that she'd had both father and son as lovers. "What kept you busy all day?"

He raised his jet black eyebrows. "I was at the Trust being a dutiful trustee and keeping an eye on Nora Abbott."

Sylvia didn't like the idea of him spending time anywhere near that troublemaker. "Isn't a non-profit trust beneath your talents?"

"I'm helping out temporarily. The finances are not what they should be. The budget is over projections. You don't happen to know anything about that, do you?"

The warmth of their lovemaking dissipated. "I haven't done anything. Nora said I exceeded my budget but it shouldn't be. Darla must have made a mistake."

He nodded, a quirk of a smile on his face. "Nora will find out, assuredly."

He obviously suspected Sylvia stole money from the Trust, just as Darla had accused her. She could tell by his smirk. "Why are you the one to keep an eye on her, anyway? Mark is there."

"I find her fascinating. And, as it turns out," he pulled his head back and studied her, "Nora might need protecting. She ended up in the ER this morning."

So what? Apparently she didn't die. "That girl can take of herself, believe me."

He lifted her hand from his chest and sat up. "Perhaps. At any rate I did not come here to discuss Nora."

She ran the tip of her tongue around his lips with the slightest touch. "I didn't think you came to discuss anything."

He grabbed her, kissing her with desire, thrusting his tongue past her lips. He let her go. "I have enjoyed you very much and now I must go." He rose.

She let the sheet fall just below her satiny breast. "Do you have to leave so soon?"

He dressed quickly, almost as if he couldn't wait to leave.

Of course she was being sensitive. He'd just made love to her and obviously couldn't resist the sexual spell she had over him. Maybe he wanted to give her time to recover from her awful experience with the police.

He didn't turn back before he sauntered out the door and down the stairs.

She waited until the front door clicked shut. Then she rose and showered. She padded down the stairs to finish her glass of cognac in front of the fire.

Her cell phone chirped and she considered not answering. She recognized the number and changed her mind. "How lovely to hear from you, Eduardo. Have you made my deposit?"

He didn't take the time to hear what she said. "You have murdered the accountant? For money? Are you insane?"

She stood in front of the fire but it wasn't responsible for the sweat that broke out under her negligee. "I didn't—."

"The police arrested you."

How did he find out? Did Daniel tell him? "They brought me in for questioning."

"And you have involved Danielcito, as I asked you not to do."

She trembled at the rage in his voice. "I was set up. It was Nora Abbott's fault. That conniving little climber."

"She was not at the Trust when this happened."

"I can't explain it. She's jealous." Sylvia paced away from the fire. "It's like at HAARP". Someone always tried to stand in Sylvia's path to greatness. "Bruce Franklin wanted my job and he spread lies about me. He stole the credit for my work." Of course she delegated the more tedious aspects of her job. That didn't mean she wasn't responsible for the work her department accomplished. He'd gone behind her back and got her fired.

"Enough of your jabber, *carina*." The endearment sounded like a curse. "I grow impatient."

"I need more time. And money. If you deposit—."

"No more money. But in case you need incentive to work, I've sent Juan to watch over you. Time is running out."

"Juan—." He severed the connection.

Sylvia ran to the control panel and slapped off the great room lights. She tiptoed to the dining room and snaked her arm around the corner to douse the chandelier. Then she ran up the stairs to her bedroom in the dark and slipped to the window facing the street.

A Lincoln Town Car sat on the opposite side of her street one house down, facing her way. She couldn't see inside the car so could only assume someone named Juan sat there watching her house.

Her hands shook as she dressed in black leggings and turtleneck. She pulled on the black riding boots she'd bought last week.

She wouldn't tolerate Eduardo's bullying. She didn't know where she would go but her Ferrari 430 could outrun a Town Car and she'd lose Juan in a hurry. That would show Eduardo she couldn't be intimidated.

Sylvia hurried down the stairs, through the kitchen to the garage. Who did he think he was treating her like some kind of minion?

She stomped to the Ferrari and slid inside. With one hand she hit the garage door opener and the other she pressed the start button.

She twisted to view over her shoulder. An unusual lump at the passenger window startled her and she caught her breath. Her eyes focused on it.

Snakes of fear slithered across her skin. A scream of terror built in her gut and exploded with echoes in the small car.

Her foot slipped off the clutch. Her hands flew in spastic flutters and she kept screaming.

The calico cat struggled against the passenger side window. Its head was trapped inside, the window rolled up just to where it trapped the cat, the body dangling outside, claws scrabbling to free itself. Its mouth gaped in a ghastly snarl, the sharp teeth bared and white, while it wheezed in a scant air supply. The cat hung with her neck suspended between the top of the window and door.

Sylvia's shaking fingers barely found the window toggle and she didn't wait to see if the cat survived after it fell from the side of her car.

23

The key twisted in the ignition and Nora's old Jeep fell silent.

Thankfully Abigail had been out somewhere when Nora and Abbey returned home in the early afternoon. Cole had driven her to the Trust to get her Jeep and made her promise she'd stay home all afternoon. But after a shower she'd headed back to the office.

Now she scanned her apartment, dreading another round with Abigail. She wasn't ready to discuss her father. She needed time and solitude. Instead, she had Abigail.

What a day. The Trust was a crazy place and Nora weighed whether saving the earth was worth sorting through the problems. Okay, maybe working as Finance Director didn't rise to the status of saving the earth.

She didn't hold with Cole's conviction Mark had tried to kill her. For all her wild imagination and despite the events in Flagstaff, she believed murder and mayhem occurred in movies and novels, not in real life.

Not usually.

Cold seeped into the Jeep. Much as she'd like to start it up and drive away and not have to deal with Abigail tonight, she could use a bucket of Abbey-love.

A group of students walked by chatting and laughing. They passed under the parking lot light and continued into the night. Nora smiled remembering the feeling of a new fall semester with all the hope and possi-bilities and freedom of youth. She climbed out of the Jeep and headed to the stairs.

Without warning, her mind flashed to an image of Cole at the hospital this afternoon. Maybe she'd thought of him more than she'd like to admit in the last year. It didn't matter that sometimes when she saw couples walking hand in hand along Boulder Creek, she'd imagined what it would be like to walk with Cole. But she'd trained herself to shove those sorts of thoughts far away.

She inhaled the crisp fall air. With every step she drilled more determi-nation into her brain. She would not discuss her father with Abigail tonight. Nora was bound to say something hurtful. She needed to process it on her time, whenever that might be.

I will be nice to Abigail.

She opened the door and stepped from the chill into a cozy apartment. In that tuned-in way of dogs, Abbey already stood by the door, tail wagging, tongue lolling, smile ready. Of course, in the micro-apartment, Abbey would only have to hear her hand on the door knob to get up from his bed under the corn plants and meet her at the front door.

Nora dropped her bag and squatted next to him, burying her face in his fur. "How're you doin'?"

Abigail's voice cut through Nora's closed eyes and the haze of comfort coming from Abbey. She stood in the galley kitchen, which opened into the four-foot square entry area. "I'm so glad you didn't work any later. Dinner would have been spoiled."

Nora realized she'd been inhaling a savory aroma, just like a real dinner. Meat with onions and garlic undertones and bread. Bread? Man, it smelled wonderful

Who thought she'd be hungry after her terrible morning in the ER, but her stomach growled. Guess she was emptied out pretty thoroughly. "You cooked dinner? That's great. I'm starving."

Nora surveyed the small dining room table. Instead of the colorful Mexican placemats and bright Fiestaware Nora furnished for herself, a white lace cloth draped over the table. Two places set with china sporting a sweet rose pattern. Wine glasses and candles added to the decidedly un-Nora table.

Forcing her lips into what she hoped passed for a smile of pleased surprise, Nora said, "Very nice, Mother. You really went all out."

Abigail picked up Nora's bag and thrust it onto a hook. "You only have those garish dishes. I thought you needed something more formal so I bought you a set of china and some stemware."

Abigail couldn't afford this. Neither could Nora. "I don't do much entertaining. Maybe we can box it up before we use it and take it back."

Abigail frowned. "You'll thank me. Believe me, you'll use these more than you think. Besides, I didn't spend a fortune. I bought all of this at the outlet mall. Of course it's not Wedgewood."

Hold the snark. She's only trying to be nice.

Abigail threw back her shoulders and lifted her chin. "Life is made more full by the simple joy of beauty. The red of the rose, the kiss of a lover."

Nora struggled with a response "Is that something you wrote?"

Abigail pulled the cherub notebook from her pocket. "I just thought of it. When you tune your subconscious to poetry, it springs forth." She paused. "Oh, that's good, too."

Poetry and spending. Her mother's talents never ceased. *Be nice, be nice, be nice.* "So what's for dinner?"

Abigail beamed. "We'll start with a butternut squash soup. The entrée is pork tenderloin medallions with garlic mashed potatoes and steamed green beans almandine, followed by apple pie."

Nora noted the clean kitchen. "You slaved all day on this?"

Abigail laughed. "That wonderful deli just off Broadway closed since I lived here. But I Googled around on my phone and found a great new place. I sampled them at lunch yesterday and they're excellent."

Dollar figures rolled in front of Nora's eyes like cherries and oranges on a slot machine. New dishes, stemware, and now a catered dinner for two. Nora bit down on the lecture forcing itself from her lips. Tomorrow. She'd sit Abigail down and explain about budgets and frugality and of living within her means—again.

With a nod of satisfaction, Abigail stepped back. "It's been a long day and I've got a novel I'm dying to sink into." She yawned. "I'll see you tomorrow."

"Wait. What?"

"Good night."

Nora spun around, fighting the rising horror of what she suspected.

Yep. Cole opened the sliding door and stepped into her mini-living room from the balcony.

"Mother!"

Abigail's back retreated down the hall. "It's like the china, Nora. You'll thank me."

Molten lava of indignation erupted in Nora. "This is asinine. My life is not some clichéd romance novel."

Abigail paused outside her bedroom door. "The pages of the novel that is life bursts with the genres of the soul." She reached into her pocket. "Oh, that's good."

"That doesn't even make sense," Nora shouted after the closing door. In the game of stubborn, Abigail had the upper hand. Nora studied Cole standing awkwardly in her apartment. "Hiding on the deck, huh? The Queen of Darkness pulled you into her black web of deceit." Gaa! Now Nora was creating awful poetry, too.

Cole's eyes twinkled. "I wasn't hiding, just planning an entrance. Abigail tricked me, too. She said you asked her to call me because you lost your phone."

"You weren't suspicious?" Nora's stomach growled. She pulled out a dining chair and sat. The simple cotton napkin revealed another of Abigail's penny-pinching ways. In the old days, the napkin would have been brocaded linen with a monogram.

"Of course I didn't believe her." He bent to rub Abbey's ears. "But when I found out you went back to work after you promised you wouldn't, I decided to come over. I knew it would annoy you as much as you annoyed me."

"Very funny."

He grinned. "You'd never lose your phone."

"What's that mean?" She tore off a piece of dinner roll and popped it into her mouth. Warm and buttery with just enough sweet to set off the yeast. Abigail knew her caterers.

Cole walked to the front door and reached for his down jacket on the hooks. Why hadn't she noticed it hanging there when she came in? "Come on, Nora. When was the last time you lost anything? I'll wager you've never even had a sock go missing in the dryer. It wouldn't dare."

She fought a smile. "Are you saying I'm controlling?"

He stood at the front door, about fifteen feet from Nora. "Well, if Abigail is the Atlantic Ocean, you're Lake Superior."

She lifted an eyebrow in question.

"You're land locked; only want to control your own shores."

She piled mashed potatoes on her plate, the garlic tickling her nose. "Abigail's tides are epic."

He watched her. "I never picked you for a cruel woman."

She spooned out green beans and slivered almonds. "Huh?"

Cole hadn't donned his jacket. "I've been sitting here for a half hour smelling this gourmet meal and you're helping yourself while sending a starving man into the wilderness to pick up a greasy burger and fries at the nearest drive-through."

She served herself some tenderloin and gravy. "I didn't concoct this romantic farce, but I'm going to end up paying for it. You're on your own, buddy."

He addressed Abbey. "Heartless."

Nora forked in pork and rolled her eyes at the savory goodness. "Let this be a lesson: Don't trust Abigail."

He surveyed the table. "That's an awful lot of food."

She regarded Cole and the table and imagined her empty apartment after he left. But it wouldn't be empty. Abigail would swoop out of her room and harangue Nora.

Cole might make a good Abigail buffer. "Fine. Come enjoy the bounty of Abigail's non-existent fortune. But no talking about... anything I don't want to talk about."

He tossed his jacket back on the hook. "Agreed. So, nice plants. Is that Benny's corn?"

"I don't want to talk about it."

He nodded. "Is that wine I see?"

Nora poured while he seated himself. "This will probably be a bad idea."

He flapped out his napkin and placed it on his lap, reached for his glass and sipped Cabernet. "Why is that?"

"Because I like you. But I don't trust you. So the best thing is for me to steer clear of you. I've had enough of untrustworthy men in my life."

He heaped food onto his plate. "Just let me have my last meal. Abigail went to so much trouble."

"I don't know why she's obsessed with you."

He shrugged. "I think Charlie's behind it. He's in love with me. Always has been."

She laughed and the weight of the day slid off, crashing to the floor and disappearing into dust.

Tomorrow she'd deal with The Abigail Ocean of Control and all the mess at the Trust. For just this one dinner, she'd let herself relax. No Lake Superior, just a free flowing Boulder Creek.

24

Sylvia whipped the Ferrari onto the turnoff, across the rickety wood bridge, and into the Trust parking lot. She shut the lights off and held her breath.

Headlights passed the turn and continued up Boulder Canyon. She sat another five minutes watching the highway. No one followed her.

After she'd calmed down enough from the cat prank, Sylvia had released the creature from her window and sped off from her neighborhood. She'd zipped through town and out Highway 36 to Denver. It hadn't taken her long to lose Juan in Denver's streets and then she'd backtracked to the Trust.

Sylvia slipped into the old farmhouse and locked the door after herself. She hurried to her office and snapped on the lights.

Fear fluttered like bats' wings in Sylvia's belly. Damn Nora, damn Eduardo. Damn them all! They didn't understand the way genius worked. She couldn't be forced to a timeline like an hourly drone. But if she didn't deliver something, Eduardo might just cut off his nose to spite that aristocratic face.

Alone, she paced the office. All the common people were home with their droll spouses and their stupid children, watching reality TV and eating cheap dinners. She could have been just like them. Even that would have been a step up from her childhood.

Sylvia sank into her office chair and gripped the side of her cherry wood desk as the office faded.

"Come and get your supper." She smelled her father before she saw his bare feet with the thick, yellowed toenails and dirt caked in black crescents. He stood on the linoleum in front of the torn and faded sofa with one of the legs replaced by a cinder block.

Margery lay next to her, eyes wide, breath only the merest whisper. If he found them under the sofa it would be bad. Her sister grabbed Sylvia's hand and squeezed.

"I slaved over this meal so you git your ass out here and eat it." He shuffled away, shouting into the room. He was leaving. In a few minutes he'd drink another glass of whiskey and he'd forget.

Suddenly the heavy plate, something his mother had stolen from the last diner where she'd worked, crashed against the wall. Two slabs of the plate hit the floor amid the mush of canned tuna fish, white bread and mayonnaise.

The crusty feet lurched across the room and he was on his knees, reaching under the sofa.

Sylvia screamed. She and her sister scrunched as far back as possible but his meaty fist stabbed after them. His hand closed around Sylvia's arm.

"No!" She cried and fought but her skinny little girl's body was no match for him, even if he was on his knees. Margery clamped onto Sylvia's ankle as their father yanked her from safety.

"You little shit! I made you supper and you're goddamned gonna eat it!" He pulled her with him as he stood up, dangling her by her arm, wrenching it from the socket.

She screamed again. And again. And kept screaming as his fist full of the tuna he'd scooped off the floor rammed into her face.

Suddenly he dropped her. She hit the floor on her tailbone and scuttled like a crab to the corner.

Margery hit him again in the arm with her small fist.

Her father clamped his hand on Margery's shoulder and drew his arm back.

"No. Oh, please." She couldn't say anything else as she watched her father slam his fists into her sister's face.

. . .

Sylvia jumped up from her desk to halt the images. She'd successfully blocked them from her mind for decades. With all this stress they were coming back.

The door of the lab squeaked open and Petal peeked in.

Sylvia motioned her in. She wanted to scream at Petal for taking so long to get here. "Hurry. You're letting out the heat."

Petal slunk in like a stray dog, a mess of hair atop a rag basket. She rubbed her hands against the cold. "It feels like a front is coming in."

What did Sylvia care about the weather in Boulder tonight?

She stomped around the map table to a wall of filing cabinets. "I don't know why you've been dragging your feet. We need to have the tower positioned to refract the ELF wave. Let's get that done tonight."

Petal showed all the reaction of an office chair.

Sylvia's hand shook when she raised it to push her hair from her forehead. "Why are you standing there? You haven't given me the angle of refraction. Why not? Are you too busy making friends with Nora Abbott?"

Petal flushed and stared at the floor in front of Sylvia. "It's Mother. She's been ill and I've been trying to get Medicaid figured out. They say her treatments aren't covered."

Such mundane matters. Sylvia opened a file drawer and slammed it closed. "Are you blackmailing me into giving you money?"

Petal's voice cracked. "No! It's the truth. She's sick."

"Tell you what, if all goes well here I'll give you a bonus and you can help your mother out."

Petal's eyes glimmered with gratitude. "Thank you."

So Eduardo sent Juan to watch her. Would he order Juan to kill her if she didn't deliver? Sylvia paced around the opposite side of the map table and stopped at her desk chair. "I need that angle measurement tonight. I don't care if you stay here all night. The beam will go out tomorrow."

Instead of running to her desk to start working, Petal gazed at her from under the disaster on top of her head. "I can help you. But the coordinates you've given me don't make sense. Why Ecuador? I thought we needed to measure the soil and air temperatures in sector 43. That's where the field crew is monitoring beetle kill."

She wanted to slap Petal. Of course she didn't do that. She inhaled and composed herself. Sylvia chuckled to show she was a good sport. "You give me the details I ask for and I'll do the strategic thinking."

Why had she let herself get so upset? She'd handled the situation, as she always did. Petal should have delivered the refractory angle earlier, but Sylvia hadn't stayed on top of her flakey assistant. All Sylvia had to do was be a good manager. After Petal provided the corrections, Sylvia would adjust the tower's angle and she'd send the beam tomorrow night.

Sylvia waited until Petal hunched over her computer then she left her office and hurried through the kitchen. She paused at a sink window to survey the Trust parking lot.

Petal's silly bike leaned against the front steps and Sylvia's Ferrari sat close to the front door.

A Lincoln Town Car sat at the side of the road, just across the wood bridge.

25

Nora opened her eyes to the dark bedroom. She should get up and head to work. But she rolled onto her back and stretched, enjoying one moment to think about last night. Because as soon as her feet hit the floor she'd grab hold of reality and force Cole out of her thoughts. She knew better than to spend time with him. It was sort of like going to the Humane Society and saying you were only going to look. Pretty soon, your heart mutinied and you ended up with a dog.

Abigail would say Nora should take a risk on love. But Nora already had her fragile heart and ego out there with this new job. And the whole suddenly-you-have-a-Hopi-father thing she would have to examine.

After a year of isolation, she needed to pace herself on total life immersion

Nora threw back the covers and planted her feet on the rug. She showered and dressed as stealthily as possible so as not to wake Abigail. She didn't want to discuss her dinner with Cole and she definitely didn't want to get into daddy issues.

"I will be nice to Abigail," she said to herself in the mirror. "And maybe I'll work on not talking to myself."

Nora tiptoed out of her bedroom and down the hall. She whispered to

Abbey and grabbed her coat and a plastic bag and slipped out to take him for his morning routine.

Fifteen minutes later, she snuck back inside and slid his leash over a hook.

"Good morning!" Abigail chirped from the kitchen.

Drat. "Morning." The smell of fresh brewed coffee hung in the air.

Abigail set a mug on the counter bar. She wore a white robe with embroidered pink roses on the lapels and pink slippers. "I made coffee. It's that hazelnut kind with the nonfat creamer."

Don't tell her you hate flavored coffee. Keep your mouth shut about artificial creamers. "I'm kind of in a hurry to get to work. Thanks anyway."

"Oh nonsense." Abigail filled her own cup. "I want you to sit down and tell me everything about last night."

Nora pulled her messenger bag from the coat hooks. "Dinner was delicious. Thanks."

Abigail patted the table to invite Nora. "You hit it off with Cole, didn't you? You two are perfect for each other."

"Yeah. I've got to go."

"Don't be silly. Come over here and have a cup of coffee."

Don't do it. Walk out the door. Really, DO NOT DO IT. "Can you leave me alone? Please just back off."

Abigail's face fell.

Damn it. What happened to that resolve to be nice to her? "I'm sorry. I didn't mean to hurt your feelings. The best thing I can do is to go to work."

"Oh, honey. You didn't hurt my feelings." That martyr tone always guilted Nora. "I'm only concerned for you."

"I really should get to work."

"It's not even six o'clock."

"I have a lot to do."

Abigail set her coffee on the table, and reached for Nora's bag. She hung it up. "I'm serious, dear. You need to talk about your father."

"I'm not ready."

"Ready or not—."

A soft thump on the front door stopped Abigail. They stared at the door. The noise came again but this time it sounded like a light tapping.

Nora walked past Abigail and unlocked the door.

"Wait!" Abigail whispered. "It's not safe. We need a weapon."

Nora rolled her eyes as Abigail searched for something dangerous. She opened the door.

Petal huddled on the welcome mat, shrouded with layers of wraps, probably from some sweatshop-less, free-trade market. Heavy hiking socks covered feet stuffed in her Chaco sandals. Her breath puffed from a cloud of dreds.

"Come in." Nora reached out, pulled her inside and shut the door. "What are you doing here—and so early?"

Petal shivered by the entryway. "I don't know where else to go."

Blurgh. Nora didn't need any more trouble. If she had any brains in her head, she'd shove Petal back outside and slam the door. Instead, she helped unwrap the first layer, a blanket it seemed, from Petal's shoulders and draped it on the coat hooks.

Abigail grasped Petal's frozen fingers. "Why, you're an ice cube. Let me get you some coffee."

Petal curled up in the same couch corner she'd sat in before.

Nora sat beside her. "What's going on?"

Petal's puffy eyes implored Abigail. "I can't go home. Darla is everywhere."

Abigail pushed dreds back from Petal's face. "I know, honey. It hurts."

Petal hiccupped. "I open a cupboard and see the coffee mug I bought her with the happy face on it. I tried to move on, but when I reached for the tea it was the special blend of coconut and white tea she loved."

Abigail nodded. "I know."

"So I went to lie down and the pillows smell like her."

Nora wanted to help but Petal's words brought sharp images slicing through her. The empty spot next to her in bed after Scott died. Cleaning out his closet, touching his bike gloves, knowing his fingers would never fill them again.

Abigail patted Petal's hand. "It's okay. You can stay here today. I'll bet you haven't slept. We can make you a bed on the couch."

Sure, Abigail invited Petal to camp out on Nora's sofa, but when Scott died, she'd insisted they go shopping. Petal could whimper and cry; Nora had to get on with life.

"Thank you so much, Abigail." Petal turned hopeful eyes to Nora. "You don't mind, do you? It won't be for long. Maybe just until after the funeral today?."

In the olden days—72 hours ago—Nora's small apartment felt like a quiet haven she shared with Abbey. They took walks and Nora read or watched TV or searched for jobs while Abbey napped in his warm bed. Suddenly her apartment transformed into a circus with Abigail as ring master.

"Sure. Let me round up some sheets." That was another problem. Nora owned the sheets on her bed and a second set on the guest room bed. She never imagined she'd need more than that. Maybe she could take the top sheet from her own bed. She mulled over the unacceptable possibilities on the short walk down the hall. At least she had a sleeping bag Petal could use. Nora pulled open the flimsy linen closet door to retrieve the sleeping bag she stored on the bottom shelf.

Abigail kept cheerful patter going in the living room. No doubt distracting Petal from her grief. Either that or numbing her into a false calm.

What?

Nora faced two shelves of new housewares. A set of sheets bordered with delicate eyelet embroidery and several fluffy pink towels stacked neatly next to an electric roaster pan and—what was that? A fondue pot?

"Mother?"

Abigail's chatter stopped. "Yes, Nora."

"Could you come here, please?"

Abigail swept down the short hall in her robe and slippers.

Nora indicated the closet. "What is all this and where did it come from?"

Abigail checked the closet. "Oh, that. Honey, a woman needs to have things to feather her nest. If you don't have beauty and comfort to surround you, you'll feel prickly."

"I hate pink. I've always hated pink. I like my home the way it is."

"You say that now, but you'll be surprised at how much comfort a little luxury and a well-supplied home can give you."

The evil Abigail troll climbed behind Nora's eyes, pulled herself on her little trampoline, and jumped, throwing her body against the inside of Nora's forehead. "I don't want towels and china, with matching stemware. I'd rather strap on my backpack, whistle for Abbey, and go to the mountains."

Abigail raised her eyebrows. "You won't be able to do that forever. You aren't getting younger."

Nora bit back a retort. "And what is this?" She pointed to the roaster pan.

"You don't have one, do you?" Abigail sounded concerned.

"Why would I have something that would feed a dormitory? It's only me and Abbey here."

Abigail placed her hands on her hips. "You have no vision for the future. Every woman should have an electric roaster. Someday you'll have children and they'll bring their baseball team over for sloppy joes or you'll need to supply chili for the gymnastics fund raiser, and then you'll thank me."

"How do you even know these words? When did you ever cook for my friends or volunteer at any of my functions?"

Abigail sucked in her lips and held her breath as if holding back tears. "There you go again, heaping blame on me for not being the perfect mother. I tried, Nora. I was a single mother focusing all my energy on keeping food on the table and clothes on your back."

"What alternative universe did you live in?" Nora managed not the fling the towels from the shelves. "We lived in a four-thousand-square-foot house with a crystal chandelier in the entryway. You hosted catered cocktail parties on a regular basis."

Fire lit Abigail's eyes. "I'm sorry, dear. I didn't have the luxury of going to college and business school. When I married your father we had no money and I worked at a department store. When I married Berle, my job was being his wife. You enjoyed the nice things and a wonderful education because I kept Berle happy."

Nora exploded. "I don't know anything about your life with my father. You told me he abandoned me!"

Abigail grew still. "Now we're getting to the real problem. You hate me for protecting you."

Nora pulled the one-thousand-thread count sheets from the closet and marched down the hallway. "I don't hate you."

Abigail jerked the pillow from the closet and followed her. "There you go, running away from the truth like you always do."

The hallway wasn't long enough. Nora had to pull up or she'd be in the living room with Petal. "Stop trying to run my life."

Abigail stood too close. "Someone has to because you're creating a disaster."

"And now we're talking about Cole again, right?"

"If you weren't so stubborn you'd see I'm right."

"If you weren't so controlling you'd see I can manage my own life."

They walked into the living room to find Petal dissolved in tears. She curled into the couch, head in her arms, sobbing silently.

Abigail hurried to sit next to Petal and gathered her in her arms. "Now, now. It's going to be okay."

"I can't do it." Petal choked out the words.

"Do what, honey?"

Nora deposited the sheets on the couch and stood above Abigail and Petal. Hard fingers of sympathy squeezed her heart; she knew what it felt like when someone close was murdered. If only she could lift Petal's pain and toss it into the chilly morning. But part of her, a large part, wanted Petal to take her drama and all the memories it stirred up and find another friend. Nora had only known Petal a few days, why did she have to hold the unraveling ball of nerves together?

Nora sat on the arm of the couch and patted Petal's back. Why, indeed? The least she could do was let Petal cry.

"The funeral," Petal squeaked.

"What about the funeral?" Abigail had to draw every word from Petal.

"It's later this morning. I can't go."

"Of course you can go, dear."

Petal pushed herself up and swiped a sleeve across her nose again. "Whoever killed Darla will be there."

Abigail gave Nora a helpless expression. "You don't know that."

Tears continued to run down Petal's face. "If they killed Darla they might kill me."

"Oh, posh." It appeared Abigail would only cotton to so much drama, even from Petal. "No one wants to hurt you."

Petal sobbed again and dropped her head onto Abigail's lap.

Abigail patted Petal's shoulders. "I think you're being paranoid but if you'd like, Nora and I will go to the funeral with you."

Funeral? No way. Nora didn't do funerals any more. Heather's funeral following so closely after Scott's had cured Nora from going to another funeral. Ever. She hadn't even known Darla. Abigail could go. She could hold Petal's hand and feel needed and like a hero for rescuing an unfortunate waif.

Not Nora. Uh-uh. Nope.

26

Cold, dry air sent shivers down Nora's arms and raised goose bumps on her legs as she hurried along the sidewalk with Petal and Abigail. The church occupied a whole city block just south of the Pearl Street Mall in downtown Boulder. Because snow threatened, they'd parked in a covered public garage several blocks away and now suffered the winds of the cold front as they hurried toward the church. The heavy clouds snuffed out the sight of the Flatirons. Nora could have used a sunny day and mountain view to balance the dread of the funeral.

Despite the foul weather, cyclists buzzed by on the streets and an occasional runner dodged them. Students bundled in ski coats and Uggs hurried by with their heads down.

In the cozy warmth of her apartment, her mother's disapproval of pants versus a dress didn't seem important. Today, she should have worn the slacks and let Abigail stew. Abigail appeared regal in her appropriate black pencil skirt, pumps and wool coat. At least Nora wore boots and a long skirt against the gusts coming off the mountains.

In their traditional and tasteful funeral wear, Nora and Abigail flanked Petal, dreds a wild mass flowing around her shoulders, her eyes and nose tomato-red and puffy. Petal huddled under layers of everything from yoga pants, an unhemmed denim skirt and the perennial gauze, t-shirts, sweaters, scarves and wraps. Abigail didn't seem fazed at accompanying Petal in her disheveled homeless fashion.

A tall, black metal fence outlined the church property. The red-brick structure loomed ahead of them, with a bricked courtyard in front, a well-equipped playground to the side, and what was probably a school, attached to the create a block-long building. They crossed the courtyard and headed for the massive double doors of the chapel. Nora fought the urge to run. So far, Darla's death felt more like a movie or novel. Attending a funeral made it as real as Scott's murder. As horrific as Heather's violent passing.

You can't hide from death forever. Now is the time to face it down.

Her hands closed on the cold metal handle and she pulled the door open. They entered a posh narthex. Carpeted in muted rust and browns, spotless and perfect in the way of affluence, the room could accommodate a crowd of Sunday worshippers on their way from the chapel. Nora inhaled the heat and underlying candle wax and furniture polish, relieved to be out of the coming storm. "It doesn't seem like anyone is here. Are you sure this is the right place?" she asked Petal.

Petal swiped a sleeve across her nose and sniffed. "Darla didn't have much family. She didn't have many friends. Just me."

Abigail marched across the narthex to more double doors that must lead to the chapel. These stood open. She poked her head inside and hurried back to them. She whispered, "I think this is the place."

Petal threaded her arm through Nora's and attached herself to Nora's side. They made awkward progress through the doors and several steps down the aisle. An older woman sat behind an organ at the back of the altar. She played what sounded like a succession of chords but was probably a standard hymn, the elevator music of a conservative church.

Petal raised her head and must have caught her first sight of the simple casket on the altar. She froze, her mouth open in silent despair.

The light wood of the closed casket blended with the pulpit and altar railings. It looked lonely with few flowers surrounding it. Petal trembled and sucked closer to Nora.

Together they followed Abigail down the aisle. "Do you want to view the casket, dear?" Abigail whispered to Petal.

She answered with a whimper.

A handful of people spread out in the pews about five rows down from the front. Abigail headed toward the altar. Petal reached out and grabbed Abigail's arm to stop her. Her hand gripped a back pew. As usual, Petal tried to be invisible.

Nora slid into the pew and Abigail let Petal in next to sandwich her.

Nora shrugged out of her coat and surveyed the sparse crowd. She recognized Fay's blonde tangle next to Bill's slightly balding pate. Three others sat between Bill and Thomas, with his bushy brown hair. They must be staffers she hadn't met.

Daniel sat in a middle pew across from Nora. He glanced back and tipped his head in greeting, then sat straight. Nora wouldn't think he'd be required to attend the funeral of a staffer, but it showed a certain decency.

The organ music droned into the chapel. A couple of people picked away on their phones. Apparently, they weren't close with Darla.

With a jolt, Nora realized she had more than passing familiarity with one of heads two rows back and to the outside of Daniel. She knew the sandy hair and laugh lines around the side of the mouth visible to her.

Cole. What was he doing here?

Nora glared at Abigail. It must be more of her mischief.

A ruckus at the back of the chapel caused several heads to turn. Mark and Sylvia entered amid a flurry of urgent whispers. Their argument stopped when they realized people watched them. Sylvia straightened her spine. Her high-heeled black boots and long coat gave her the sleek appearance of a panther, despite her petite frame.

Petal squeaked and sank into herself.

Mark guided Sylvia to a front pew and they sat, staring ahead.

Finally a middle-aged woman in a dark suit, thick calves and grandma-style pumps appeared from one of the doors off the side of the altar. "Good morning. Today we're gathered to celebrate the life of Darla Barrows."

Nora's throat closed up. She struggled for air. The chapel disappeared and all around her stood tall Ponderosas. The casket turned into a pine box full of her husband's ashes. Death. Everywhere.

Nora could almost feel Charlie's arm circling her for support and Abbey sitting at her feet. Scott's friends paid tribute, giving tale after tale of Scott's crazy antics. Nora's insides felt scraped raw and hollow.

She'd been sure she'd never feel happy again.

Two weeks later she'd huddled between Abigail and Cole on a pew in a Flagstaff church. The casket on the altar contained Heather's body. Nora squeezed her eyes closed and fought for control. Heather was young, so alive. Nora couldn't hold all her grief.

Of course, today she sat in a church in downtown Boulder, Colorado, but it couldn't convince that panic-prone mush serving as her mind. She thrust herself out of the pew and stumbled over Petal and Abigail to rush down the aisle to the narthex. Cold sweat filmed her body as she cast about for someplace to hide. Tears threatened her throat and eyes. She didn't want to explain her flight from the funeral to her new co-workers.

A stairway to the side of the narthex offered escape. She gripped the rail and lurched up, focused on slowing her racing heart and steadying her breathing. The stairway led to a choir loft, giving her full view of the altar and the casket. She whirled around and exited, plopping herself on the top stair.

Damn. Another panic attack. Did this herald the end to sanity? Soon she'd lock herself inside her apartment amid a maze of old newspapers and magazines, with food delivered to her door, afraid of the sunshine. She'd hold endless conversations with a long-dead Hopi *kikmongwi*.

Get a grip.

Cole shot from the chapel. He scanned the lobby and his eyes locked on the stairs. His gaze followed it up and he spotted Nora slumped at the top. He bounded the stairs two at a time.

Ugh. Why did he have to be here?

He sat next to her. "What's the matter? Are you okay?" he whispered.

She swallowed. Maybe Cole showing up was the best thing for a panic attack. It got her torqued up and helped her focus. "What are you doing here? Following me to a funeral is really low." She matched his whisper.

He opened his mouth to speak. The outside doors opened and the two police officers entered. Nora recognized them from the board meeting. She searched her brain for their names. Langston and Kirby. They wandered to the chapel and slipped inside.

The organ music swelled and weak strains of attendees' singing filtered up to them.

Cole blushed. "I thought you might have a hard time going to another funeral."

"Did Abigail call you?"

He studied his hands. "She's concerned about you."

"She's trying to set us up."

"Ya think?"

Nora felt the tingle of a smile.

"She was right, though. It's tough on you and I thought you could use a friend"

Was he her friend? Did she want him to be?

A man in jeans and work shirt trudged into the narthex from an entryway across from the choir loft stairs where they sat. It must be a basement. He taped a computer printed sign to the wall and disappeared downstairs again.

Nora needed to shift from her memories. "Okay. If you're my friend, help me figure out who killed Darla."

His jaw dropped. "You're kidding, right? That's the cops' job."

She waved that off. "I found some money missing from Sylvia's accounts. A lot of it."

His whisper grew stronger. "The cops already have enough evidence to suspect her. Let them know about this and be done. Get out of there."

The man appeared from downstairs carrying a long folding table. He glared at Nora and Cole before setting up the table and heading down the stairs.

She shook her head and lowered her voice. "It's a little too clean, don't you think? They find a gun in Sylvia's office. Someone tells the cops Sylvia has plane tickets and plans to flee the country—which she denies. Suddenly money goes missing in Sylvia's accounts?"

"Sounds like Sylvia killed Darla."

Nora thought about it. "Sounds more like she was set up. She's too smart to leave all those clues."

The man popped up from downstairs carrying a giant coffee urn he placed on the table.

Always the reasonable one, Cole said, "Tell the cops about the missing money and let them deal with it."

"I haven't gone through all the accounts yet. It could have been transferred somewhere or in an account I don't know about. I'm going to ask Mark."

Cole's eyebrows drew down and shielded his eyes in doubt. "Stay away from him."

She waved that off. "He's harmless. Just creepy and Sylvia-obsessed."

"He probably tried to kill you. I don't suppose you told the cops about that, either."

Two well-dressed woman stepped from downstairs carrying trays of cookies and coffee cups. They must be volunteers from the church to help with services. They eyed Nora and Cole with distaste before returning to the stairs.

He sounded impatient. "Would you let the cops do their job? This isn't a game, Nora. Darla was murdered."

Nora went cold. "Wouldn't it be stupid to murder two Finance Directors within a week? I think I'm safe."

The service must be over. People started to filter out of the chapel. A few coworkers formed a solemn knot in the middle of the lobby. Fay wiped at tears and Bill hugged her.

The small crowd milled around the coffee and cookies.

Nora stood. "I'm going to take Petal and Abigail home before I go back to work."

They walked down the stairs. "Let me get you some coffee." Cole headed toward the refreshments.

Nora stood at the foot of the stairs apart from the smattering of people. She watched the chapel doors for Abigail and Petal. The sooner they got out of here the better.

Sylvia swooped out from the chapel and Mark followed. He grasped her elbow and turned her toward the coffee. She pulled her arm away, surveyed the table and started toward the front door.

Fay glared at Sylvia, as did several of the other staffers. Sylvia smirked at them.

Daniel walked out of the chapel with the grace of a tiger. He burned three degrees hotter than handsome in his Armani suit. Sylvia's eyes focused on him.

Mark said something and Sylvia nodded. He scurried to the coffee with a stupid grin on his face. Abigail and Petal finally made it from the chapel. Abigail propped Petal against a wall next to the chapel doors and headed for the coffee. Her eyes scanned the lobby, probably trying to locate Nora.

Nora should try to be sociable but she didn't feel up to mingling and making small talk to people she didn't know, about a dead person she'd never met. Instead, she watched.

The group of half a dozen staffers congregated at one end of the refreshment table. Three or four other people held foam cups and spoke in hushed tones. Maybe they were family. The two church volunteers chatted with the basement guy, helping themselves to the cookies. Petal leaned against the chapel entrance like a lost puppy. Sylvia stood in the middle of the narthex. The minister and Daniel seemed deep in conversation with the Langston and Kirby by the basement stairs.

Cole filled two cups. He might be annoying but having him with her did help quell her panic. Mark handed Sylvia a cup and Nora watched him giggle, thankful she didn't have to hear it.

Cole returned with the coffee. It tasted better than Mark's Mr. Green Beans but still reminded her of acid. "Thanks."

"So what do you know about Daniel Cubrero?" Cole asked.

"Aside from being handsome and rich?"

Cole rolled his eyes.

"His big concern is fighting oil mining in the Amazon basin so I'm not sure why he's on the Trust board. He's from Ecuador and his family has money." She didn't have to tell Cole she'd had a nice dinner with Daniel recently and found him interesting.

Cole considered her. "Against mining in the Amazon basin? His family made their fortune in oil. A substantial fortune, by the way."

"And you know this how?"

He shook his head. "Do you think I research everyone you've come in contact with?"

"Sounds paranoid when you say it."

He laughed. "Did you forget I spent the bulk of my career in mining? I know who the biggest players are. And Cubreros are the biggest of the big."

The cops moved from Daniel and the minister to the knot of staffers.

Daniel spotted Nora and started across the lobby to her. When he arrived, he clasped Nora's hand and brushed it with his lips. "Did you feel ill during the service? Not quite over the food poisoning?"

Self-conscious at the hand-kissing silliness, Nora sounded more brusque than she intended. "I'm fine. Just needed some air."

Cole frowned at Daniel and didn't say anything.

Abigail butted next to Cole, dragging Petal with her. "There you are, dear," she said to Nora, all the while eying Daniel as if might be there to eat Nora.

Before Nora could introduce Daniel to her mother, Sylvia slinked next to him. "Well, hello." Her voice dropped low. "How nice of you to come to Darla's service when we know how important and busy you are."

Puke. Food poisoning might be better than listening Sylvia's gushing. "Well, I'd better get back to the office. Ready to go?" Nora said to Abigail and Petal.

Mark appeared, hovering behind Sylvia like a broken satellite.

"Oh, Petal," Sylvia said, her voice losing the pseudo-sexy lilt. "I need you to run out to the tower this afternoon. I checked the angle measurements you submitted and they're accurate. We just need to make sure the tower is functioning."

Petal lowered her eyes and nodded.

Sylvia beamed at Daniel. "You can report to the board that we're working. We'll be sending an ELF wave to gather the latest data associated with this cold front."

Petal shivered noticeably.

Abigail slid an arm around her. "Where is this tower? Is it far?"

Sylvia puffed up. "It's on Mount Evans."

Abigail saw Sylvia's ego-puff and raised her a her regal head-tilt. "You shouldn't go up there alone when they're predicting snow. Nora will go with you."

Wait. What?

Nora didn't want to go to Mount Evans this afternoon. But there didn't seem to be a gracious way out. *Thank you, Abigail.* Nora ignored Sylvia's glare. "Sure. Yeah. I've got some stuff to do first and we can go."

Cole's tone didn't invite argument. "I'm going, too."

Abigail smiled with satisfaction. "Thank you."

Nora focused over Sylvia's shoulder at Mark. "If you're going to be around I'd like to talk to you about something when I get to the Trust."

He barely made eye contact. His attention shifted between Sylvia and Daniel. "What do you want to talk about?"

Just four-hundred grand that's gone missing that I think has something to do with a murder. "I have a couple of questions, that's all."

Obviously irritated, he grabbed her arm and pulled her to a corner of the narthex. "What is it?"

She caught Cole zeroed in on her. He scowled. "I'm not sure if it's anything or not, but I found $400,000 missing from Sylvia's restricted account."

He threw back his head and let out a shrill cackle. "That's crazy. There's a mistake, obviously. We'll check into it, of course. Of course." *Snort.*

Freak. "Okay. Can we get together later today?"

His attention slid to Sylvia. "Yes. I'll be at the Trust soon."

Nora nodded and walked away, unsettled by his overwhelming strangeness.

Nora, Abigail, and Petal donned their coats and wraps and braced themselves before opening the church doors. Cold air blasted them as they stepped from the church and hurried toward the parking garage.

Abigail bent her head to Petal. "Do you think the killer was there?"

Petal kept her head down.

Abigail continued. "If he was, he wouldn't dare do anything suspicious with those cops. But he'll make a move sometime, don't you think?"

Nora caught Abigail's eye and whipped her finger across her throat to tell Abigail to drop it.

Abigail tilted her head. "I'm glad Cole is going with you this afternoon."

Maybe they could go back to talking about murder.

Petal peeked out from her dreds. "He's really hot. And his aura is orange. That means he's detailed and scientific and has a good soul."

"I don't want to talk about it." The fact is, being with Cole did feel good.

"You can't keep saying you don't want to talk about it whenever someone brings up a touchy topic. What color is my aura?" Abigail asked.

Petal smiled shyly. "Yours is pink. It means you're creative and sensitive. You're loving and tender."

Abigail beamed.

They stepped from the curb to cross to the parking lot. A gust of icy wind, bringing a smattering of dry snow, hit Nora full in the face. The three of them drew together, lowering their heads against the onslaught.

Abigail's voice floated out from her tightly-wrapped pashmina. "Cole is more than a good soul, Nora. He's got integrity and is a commanding presence."

The overcast sky blended with the gray of the street. Nora kept her head down to avoid the wind. "He's not rich, you know that, right?"

Abigail huffed. "I'm not that shallow. You're perfectly capable of earning your own living."

Damn right. Maybe Abigail was evolving.

"Besides, his family owns one of the largest ranches in Wyoming. There's money there."

And then again, maybe not. They crossed the street, huddled together as the pedestrian light blinked a warning.

The roar of an engine cut through the icy air. Startled, Nora instinctively reached for Petal.

A shiny black widow of a sports car careened toward them in the far right lane. The crazy driver must not see them. He accelerated.

Petal froze in the sights of the deadly bullet.

Good thing Abigail and Nora had her by either arm. They weren't willing to be smashed on the pavement by some careless driver. Both of them lurched for the curb, dragging Petal with them.

At the last minute the car veered from them and screeched around the corner. Nora's hair blew back from her face in the rush of wind from the retreating car.

Her heart thundered in her ears.

Abigail caught her eye over the wild tangle of Petal's dreds. "Was that...?"

"Sylvia." Nora finished the sentence for her.

Petal's red-rimmed eyes traveled from Abigail to Nora. "She doesn't like me."

27

Sylvia hummed as she lay back and savored the beauty of her bedroom. She'd had Petal set the beam to send into the ionosphere in a few hours. The fruits of years of study and sacrifice would culminate in this monumental success. It was only a sample, but Eduardo would understand her genius. Then the money would flow.

What a perfect way to wrap up a morning. The snowy Egyptian cotton sheets with a weave so tight it felt like silk, made her skin glow, and the color contrasted nicely with her dark hair. She resembled Cleopatra in all her royal splendor.

Her broad-shouldered Latin lover, lay next to her, caching his breath from his final passion. She'd provided the kind of lovemaking he could only dream about with younger, less experienced women.

The day hadn't started out well. She'd had a fight with Mark. He wanted her to wait for any money until the heat died down from the board. She'd had to attend that tacky funeral, nothing more than a waste of time. Then there was that nasty episode with Nora trying to hone in on Daniel.

Sylvia teased Daniel's nipple. "It's pathetic the way Nora Abbott throws herself at you. I suppose it's to be expected. You are a Cubrero."

Sylvia had succumbed to that silly moment of jealousy. The pressure of her genius sometimes needed to blow off steam. She wouldn't really have plowed into Petal and Nora and her pretentious mother. But it made Sylvia chuckle to think of them scrambling to the curb.

"Nora is not an ordinary woman and she isn't throwing herself at me." He sounded bored. As he should be with someone as common as Nora.

Sylvia needed to be subtle. "She doesn't like me much. I think she senses you and I are... close and she's jealous. You know, I think she's the one who set me up with the police."

He studied her. "You were set up?"

"Of course I was, darling. Someone told the police about my gun and stole my credit card number to make plane reservations. I'm positive Nora did it."

"It is your gun, then? So, if it is your gun, did you kill Darla?"

Sylvia laughed. "I couldn't kill anyone." She didn't kill Darla any more than she'd run down Nora. It was all just releasing the pressure valve.

He didn't say anything as he enjoyed the feel of her hands on his chest.

She scooted close to Daniel and traced his mouth with the tip of her tongue. He jerked his head away and she laughed. "Did I tickle you?"

He stared at the ceiling, ignoring her.

She knew what he wanted and it wasn't conversation. She'd give it to him, slow and excruciatingly delicious. She swirled her tongue along the skin of his belly, tantalizing him as she worked her way lower. A young man like him wouldn't be done with one blast. She'd make him explode with desire for her. Then he'd protect her from Eduardo, if needed. To keep her in his life, in his bed, he'd do anything.

He definitely rose to her bait. Her mouth closed around him, teasing him with her tongue.

Her phone blared. Daniel pushed her head away.

She smiled at him. "I'll call them back." She leaned over him again.

"Answer it. I've got to get back to the Trust anyway." The sheets bunched around the bottom of the bed and the duvet spilled to the side, splashing scarlet orchids on the white carpet.

The Trust and Nora.

Stupid ignorant people always calling, always needing something from her. They wouldn't leave her alone for a minute.

She reached for the phone. Every great leader dealt with idiots. "Yes," she said, sounding powerful and competent.

"Sylvia, it's Adrianne."

She couldn't place the name or voice.

"Your attorney?"

"Yes. What is it?"

"We need to go over your deposition as soon as possible. Can you meet me at my office in two hours?"

Sylvia laid a perfectly manicured hand on Daniel's chest. Taking the phone from her face she whispered, "Stay. This won't take a second."

He sat up and her hand fell away. He didn't say anything as he stood and reached for his pants.

Adrianne ruined everything. "Your office is in Denver. With the traffic, I'd have to leave now. That won't work for me."

Daniel pulled a cobalt blue shirt on and worked at the buttons. He didn't pay any attention to Sylvia. Damn Adrianne for destroying her perfect afternoon.

"You realize you're being indicted for murder? This isn't a picnic, Sylvia. It's your top priority."

Sylvia employed Adrianne, not the other way around and she needed to realize that. "I can't drop everything and run up there. Just because some idiot police want to accuse me of killing someone doesn't make my work any less important. We'll have to schedule something later and it must be in Boulder."

Daniel sat at the edge of the bed to pull on his shoes and socks. Sylvia ran her nails lightly down his back. He arched away from her, stood and tucked his shirt in.

"Maybe you don't understand the serious nature of the charges," Adrianne said.

Daniel zipped his jeans and buckled his belt. He walked out the bedroom door.

"I understand that I have important work to do. This is your job and you're being paid a fortune." Sylvia punched the call off and wound up her arm, ready to fling the phone at the wall to watch it splinter. She lowered her arm.

Dignity. Control. Poise.

Then she threw the phone anyway.

She climbed out of bed and considered herself in the full wall of mirrors attached to the closet doors. Daniel must have important business to leave this.

Sylvia pulled a silk kimono from the closet.

A shower would restore her composure, and she'd scurry back to the Trust to make sure all was ready for tonight's launch of the ELF beam.

She hummed as she turned on the shower sauna to let it warm. She'd be more energetic and productive after relaxing for a bit. Maybe a glass of wine would help her unwind as she let the heat soak into her skin.

28

Nora leaned back in her desk chair and rubbed her eyes. After she'd taken Petal and Abigail home and made plans for going to Mount Evans later, Nora changed into her hiking boots and jeans and hurried back to the Trust. Abbey settled in his now-usual place by the coat closet and Nora pulled her chair up to her desk.

For two hours she'd been waiting for her meeting with Mark and going through the financial statements and monthly project reports. She'd discovered the $400,000 had been withdrawn from a long-term investment account over a year ago, though the Trust's accounting program didn't reflect that. She guessed Darla didn't actually reconcile savings and investment statements often. If they weren't used for general transactions, they shouldn't change and maybe Darla counted on that. If someone else had passwords and could transfer and if the financial director didn't pay attention, $400,000 could go missing.

Who would have those passwords besides Darla?

Mark.

The initial transfer was deposited in a short term savings account one month. It had been moved from one account to another over the course of several months, sometimes in a lump sum but more often in two or three transactions. If you weren't zoned in on that sum, and you weren't a particularly good accountant—or lazy—you'd never notice it.

Last month, the money had been transferred to Sylvia's restricted account and soon after, an ACH payment went out to an unnamed bank account.

"Excuse me, Ms. Abbott?" The authoritative voice belonged to a thin man in his mid-fifties standing at her office door. He combed his gray-streaked hair neatly from his head and smelled of Old Spice. He wore khakis and a navy blue blazer. "I'm Detective Ross from the Sheriff's office. Can I ask you a few questions?"

She stood and shook his hand and indicated the wicker chair. "Have a seat." She wheeled her desk chair over.

Detective Ross sat and pulled a small notebook from his blazer pocket. "I was supposed to meet with Mark Monstain but he's out. Do you know when he'll be back?"

Guess she wasn't the only one Mark had stood up today. She shook her head. "Sorry."

He flipped open the notebook. "That's okay. Can you answer some questions?"

"I'll try."

He clicked his pen. "Did you know Darla Barrows?"

She shook her head. "No. I was hired to replace her." She indicated a box on the floor near the door. "That's all the personal stuff I found here. I didn't know who might want it."

He gazed at the box. "No one's come to claim it?"

Nora studied the framed picture of Abbey on her desk, her iPod dock, a silly figurine of a polar bear and her Tree Hugger mug. If Nora disappeared suddenly, Abigail would collect her things. Darla's remained unclaimed.

He studied her. "I understand you were here when they were notified about Darla."

The thought of that scream sent a chill over her skin. "Petal found out. She was a friend of Darla's. I think the police called her."

"Petal. I see. What's her last name?"

Good question. Part of Nora's duties involved payroll and some HR. Nora fished in a desk drawer and produced the file cabinet key. She unlocked the employee file drawer. She flipped through searching for Petal's file. She finally found it and pulled it out. "Petal Rainbow."

The detective didn't crack a smile. He flipped open his notebook. "Address?"

Nora scanned the papers inside the folder. "62 Canyon Boulevard."

He started to write and stopped. "That's Loving Earth's address."

That was stupid. "You're right." She paged through the rest of the forms. "They all have the same address."

"Do you have a phone number for Petal?"

Nora snatched a staff contract printout off a bulletin board next to the desk. She ran her finger down the list. "I guess not."

He closed his notebook and stuffed it into the chest pocket of his shirt. "One last question. Do you have any theories why someone would want to kill Darla Barrows?"

She really needed to talk to Mark about the missing money before going to the police. Maybe he had a perfectly good explanation. If she didn't meet with him by the end of the day, she'd go the cops with her financials tomorrow. "Sorry," she said again.

He picked up Darla's things and walked to the door. "Thanks for talking to me."

Nora wanted to dive back into the books. Why had Abigail volunteered her to go with Petal to Mount Evans? She needed to investigate the missing money.

Bright blue flashed in the corner of her eye and she jumped and gasped.

Daniel stood in the doorway wearing a deep blue shirt. "Sorry I couldn't get here any sooner."

His jeans hugged his long legs and all his shapely... shape. The top buttons of his shirt were undone, showing a bit of black hair. Man, oh man. "No problem. I need to go to the mountains with Petal in a few minutes, anyway."

"And Cole, no?" He stepped into her office and rolled up his sleeves. Like a strip tease, his fingers played with the fabric. Dark hair lay soft against his forearms. Who knew arms could be so sexy?

"Where would you like me to start today, boss?" His lips formed a smile but Nora imagined those lips kissing someone. Okay, kissing her.

She grabbed a handful of files and set them on the work surface. "These are invoices and payments. I've been going through them for this fiscal year, sort of hunting for..."

A light touch on her shoulder startled her. She paused and saw Daniel's dark eyes fixed on her face. She straightened.

His hand traced down her arm, his fingers light. "You are beautiful."

How did her legs continue to support her weight when her knees felt like peanut butter? Breathing was out of the question. "Um." That was witty conversation.

His hand traveled up to her cheek, his touch like satin. "Not only beautiful but brilliant. Do you have any idea how sexy you are?"

Tongue-tied would be super compared to how she felt. Good thing he didn't seem to expect a response.

Daniel leaned into her. His lips captured hers with the same gentle touch of his fingers on her skin. He kissed her slowly, and even if it sounded like a bodice-ripper novel, he kissed her thoroughly. Her knees weren't the only body part melting.

He drew away slightly and gazed at her with intensity from his bottomless, fire-lit eyes.

He kissed her again. Sweet, with deep undertones and a hint of restrained passion. For dog's sake, she sounded like she described a glass of wine. Really good wine. Like the five-hundred-dollar a bottle kind. The sort of wine she couldn't afford.

Right. She didn't drink wine like that because, well, because. It would end up making her throw up in the morning... or something like that. What she meant was that she didn't really want him.

Nora stepped back. "Okay. Well. So."

He laughed. "Nora. You can take a little pleasure, no?"

She reached for her coat. "I think I ought to go find Petal."

He leaned back on the counter with a cat-chomping-canary smile on those full, warm lips. "You looked radiant this morning. You should wear a dress more often. Your legs are exquisite."

If only he weren't so gorgeous. She zipped her coat. "Knock it off."

"Life is short, *mi amor*. Why not enjoy each other?"

"I'm an accountant. We don't enjoy things." She unzipped her coat.

He laughed. "You are ripe for pleasure."

Her face could not burn any hotter. She zipped up again.

A vibration in Daniel's pocket—not the kind he'd been hinting about—thankfully ended the talk of juicy fruit.

Daniel's face clouded with annoyance as he listened to the phone call. He slid the phone back in his pocket. "Sadly, we will finish this conversation at another time. I must go."

He hurried away and Nora plopped into her desk chair. It took a few moments for her vital signs to return to normal.

"'You should wear a dress more often. Your legs are exquisite.'" Cole's mocking voice made her jump. He leaned against the door frame.

"You were spying on me!" She flamed in embarrassment.

He walked into the room grinning. "Petal's waiting in the pickup. Are you ready to go?"

How long had he been there? Had he seen Daniel kiss her?

Nora followed him out the door, wondering why she cared what he thought.

29

The doorbell rang as Sylvia opened the shower sauna door. She set her wine glass on the bathroom counter and tightened the kimono. Had she ordered anything and forgot about a delivery?

Sylvia padded down the stairs and peered out the window at the side of the door. The irritating stray cat would be a more welcome sight than what stood on her porch. What was Mark doing here? She unlocked the door and opened it. A whoosh of cold air followed him in, making the kimono feel like a sheet of ice. A few flakes swirled outside. "I'm in a hurry to get back to the Trust. What do you want?"

That supercilious grin begged for a slap. "Sorry. I need to talk to you."

She left him in the foyer and started up the stairs. "Can we schedule a meeting? How about sometime tomorrow?"

He seemed to be trying for coy. "Oh, I think you'll want to talk to me."

"What is it?" The sauna would be warming up nicely by now.

He stayed just inside the door. "Nora Abbott and Daniel Cubrero are combing through everything."

She stopped and gave him a frosty stare. "So what? I have nothing to hide."

He licked his fat lips. "We know better, don't we?"

"What are you talking about?"

His eyes had a weird gleam. "It can be our secret. We take care of each other, isn't that right? We're special friends."

What would get him out of here the quickest? "Yes, Mark. We're good friends. But I don't think I need to be protected."

His voice rose in a hysterical giggle. "They could find the four hundred thousand dollars you stole last month."

More ways to waste her time. "Don't be ridiculous. I didn't take any money."

He sniggered. "You don't need to play stupid with me anymore. I know you have it. Darla made the approval and the money disappeared in an electronic transaction. No record."

All the oxygen suddenly left the room. Someone took her money. "Where did it go?"

He shrugged. "Only you and Darla know that. And Darla turned up dead. Do you suppose the cops will suspect you had a motive?"

She stared at him.

"I won't tell. That is, if you show me what good friends we are."

She didn't have time for this. She stomped up the stairs in search of her phone. Eduardo needed to know her money was stolen. It proved Nora set her up. Sylvia didn't know how Nora could have done it when she didn't work at the Trust until a few days ago, but she'd figure it out.

Her toes sank into the deep pile of her white carpet as she hurried down the hallway.

Mark's heavy breathing startled her. He'd followed her. "Oh, I know that with someone like Daniel Cubrero around no one notices me. But, Sylvia, I promise you, whatever Daniel has to offer, I can do better."

She couldn't concentrate on what his words meant.

Mark followed her into the bedroom.

Sylvia strode to her black lacquered dresser but the phone didn't sit in its usual place. She hurried to the bedside table but it wasn't there. She spun around scanning the spacious room and her gaze found it. Her phone lay in a heap at the base of the wall by the bathroom.

Mark minced his way across the room and stepped close to her, his fetid breath warm on her neck. "You're a beautiful woman."

She skirted him and walked to the end of the bed. "Where would Darla have hidden the money?"

Mark brushed his hand against his crotch. "You won't be disappointed."

She glared at him. "I'm trying to save your butt. If four-hundred-thousand dollars is missing, it'll be your fault. If you don't go to prison, at the very least, the board will fire you."

He closed the space between them. "I can make you feel like a woman."

"Are you sure the money is missing?"

His hand snaked out and brushed her waist. "We've denied our desire for three years. Here we are. Your bedroom. Now is the perfect time for us. I'm more than you would suspect."

The hiss of the shower sauna filled the silence while Sylvia stared at him in disgust. The faint odor of stale coffee and sweat seeped from him.

He reached out and stroked her breast through the silk of the kimono.

She sprang back. "What is the matter with you?"

His eyes glazed and his moist lips slackened as he stared at her breast. "You think I'm stupid, don't you?" He spoke with a whine, like a four year-old.

What a hideous man. She backed up.

He stepped toward her. "I've treated you like a goddess. I left you alone so you could work on your oh-so-important research."

"You're way over the line. Leave now."

Sweat glistened on his face. "But now you need me even more. You don't want me to tell the cops about the money, do you?"

He wouldn't have the *cojones* to go against her.

He stepped toward her again. "You're not really working on climate change and beetle kill, are you? You never were. Where are the reports, Sylvia? Where is all that money going? Who are you really working for?"

She laid a hand on his sweaty chest and shoved him back. "You're crazy. I'm calling the cops."

His shrill laughter sent a chill up her spine. "The cops? When they get here let's tell them about the night Darla died."

Sylvia didn't kill Darla. Of that, she was certain. "What do you know about that?"

He crowded her against a cabinet and slid his fingers under the kimono belt. "I know she came to see you. You argued. She left and I heard shots fired. Next thing we know, Darla is a goner."

Her mind reeled. She needed to shut him up.

The kimono slipped open and Mark slobbered on his fat lips. His gaze traveled to her face. "Do you want to know what I was doing there?"

Think Sylvia. How can you shut him up?

He touched her nipple and moaned. "I've waited for you for a long time. And I've watched. I know your favorite coffee shop. I know where you buy your lingerie." He panted. "I'm good for you, Sylvia. And I can make you feel so good. Even Daniel Cubrero can't do what I can."

"You need help," she said, letting her contempt drip from her voice in a hiss like the sauna. She jerked her kimono closed and strode to the other side of the bed. "You're a disgusting little man."

"I would kill for you. In fact, if Nora hadn't thrown up all the drugs I gave her, I would have been successful. As it is, I destroyed all the bank statements for the climate mapping account. That will slow her down."

"Get out."

He followed her. "You don't need to fight it, Sylvia. I've loved you and protected you. Now let me pleasure you as only I can."

She pointed to the door and shouted. "GET OUT!"

He ignored her demand. "I know you were here. With him."

Sylvia curled her lip. "Leave."

He stalked her around the bed. "Not until I get what I came for. Only I can protect you."

She laughed, a cruel sound meant to emasculate him. "You think I'd sleep with you? You really are crazy."

"I'm not planning to sleep."

He grabbed her wrist, leveraging her to toss her onto the bed.

Sylvia wrenched her wrist free and whirled around to the bedside table. Her fingers clasped the handle and jerked open the drawer. Keeping her eyes on Mark, she felt around for the plain Smith and Wesson Airweight she kept there. It didn't have the sex appeal of her gold-plated model, but it was as deadly.

He only had a nanosecond to register his surprise before she slipped off the safety, buried the small barrel in the soft flesh of his chin, and pulled the trigger.

30

Nora drove her Jeep and Cole sat in the passenger side. Petal huddled in back with Abbey's head on her knee. They headed south out of Boulder in the light early afternoon traffic. Clouds still hung heavy and low, blocking their view of the front range of the Rockies. The air carried the smell of snow and a few dry flakes swirled in the wind.

The Jeep rumbled along with its noisy cadence and they barely spoke. Petal's occasional sniffs and quiet tears wrenched Nora's heart. Cole seemed lost in his own thoughts, now and then glancing at Nora as if he'd like to start a conversation, then deciding against it.

They worked their way through a few stop lights in the foothills town of Golden then up I-70 into the mountains. Too early for commuters and few people out to play in the middle of the week left the six-lane Interstate feeling empty. The green slopes with scattered houses turned into sheer rock faces hidden in shadow.

After forty-five minutes of driving, Nora pulled off the Interstate onto the road leading to Mount Evans. She hated this treacherous drive and to have to face it so soon after her last climbing attempt stretched her courage. Familiarity ought to ease her tension but she dreaded the narrow road winding up above timberline.

"What's your ranch in Wyoming like?" She wanted to distract herself from the anxiety building inside her.

Cole seemed startled to have a question directed his way. "It's up by Sheridan. A hundred thousand acres."

"You grew up there?" Keep him talking.

He seemed to understand her need for distraction and launched into a monologue. "My great-grandfather homesteaded it. My father inherited it from his father and they both added land to it. My younger brother runs it now. I've been working there since I left Flagstaff last year. It's about time for me to move on, though. I'm weighing my options."

She quizzed him and he answered, telling her anecdotes about growing up on the range. Wild horses, wild cows and two wild boys.

It helped, and they eventually pulled into the parking lot at the top of the mountain. Nora held the front seat up for Petal and Abbey to exit.

The wind tugged at Nora's hair and battered her cheeks. She reached into the glove box and pulled out an elastic band to gather her hair back. Technically, Abbey wasn't allowed on the trail up to the top but since the Jeep was the only vehicle in the lot, Nora broke the leash law and let him go.

They headed toward the trail and the series of five switchbacks that led them to the top. Cold, brittle air felt so thin Nora was soon puffing to fill her lungs. The snow still struggled and miniscule drifts accumulated in rocky crags along the trail. When they reached the top, low clouds hid the view.

Petal pointed to the east. "It's around that outcropping there. It's hidden behind two sharp ledges so no one will mess with it."

"I can't believe the Trust let her install a tower someplace so dangerous to get to," Nora said, her stomach lurching at the thought of scrambling over the rocks to find it.

Petal climbed toward the outcropping. "I don't think they know. Sylvia told Mark it's up here and he never checked. She had me take a picture for the board and it doesn't show how remote it is."

"If you can climb out there," Cole said. "What keeps vandals away?"

Petal dug in a pocket of her skirt and brandished a key. "There's a fence and padlock. But Sylvia needs me to check it every once in a while to make sure it's okay."

The summit was long and flat, but boulders and rocks piled in a jumble across the surface to create precarious footing to climb from one smooth surface to the next. Petal clambered with the surety of a mountain goat and soon disappeared around a bend in the east.

Nora and Cole followed Petal up the rocky pile to the bend. Abbey explored on his own, pausing occasionally to keep Nora in sight.

Nora's heart thundered against her ribs. She glanced at Cole. Did he see her fighting with the panic?

He squinted against the wind and snow and watched Petal climb on all fours around another bend.

Nora gritted her teeth and focused on the forest green of Cole's down jacket in front of her. She'd follow him and it would be okay. No reason for panic.

Cole stopped and waited for her to catch up. He lowered his head, suddenly serious. "Can I ask you something?"

She tried to still her heavy breathing. Fourteen thousand feet in elevation left little air for her lungs. "Sure."

The flush of his skin didn't come from the wind. "Is there something going on between you and Daniel?"

"What?" She laughed.

"I'd like to know."

One thing about Cole, he didn't play games. "No. Absolutely not."

Well, one kiss—but it wasn't her idea and she had no plans of repeating it.

He eyed her, and then seemed to accept her answer. He turned and followed Petal's course.

The wind howled with a menacing sound. They scrambled up a boulder in time to see Petal disappear again. They had to be getting to the edge of the summit. How many more crags, boulders, or bends could there be before they reached the eastern side of the mountain?

She stumbled up a smooth, cold rock to see Petal just one bend away.

Panting and using her hands to maneuver up a slick rock Nora spotted the tower. Similar to any number of weather stations she'd seen, one metal rod extended about twenty feet into the air. The rod had a twelve-inch circumference with a four-foot dome at the top. Smaller legs extended from the dome to the ground in a tripod configuration, probably for stability. The stem must be anchored deep into the stone of the mountain to hold it steady in the high altitude storms. A chain-link fence about five feet high encircled it. Someone could climb the fence, but only a fool would try because the whole fixture perched on an overhang. Only a few inches of rock bordered the fence before solid ground ended. From there, a sheer drop of several hundred feet would mean certain death.

A gust buffeted Nora from behind and she stumbled. "Ah!" Despite herself, she screamed.

Cole whipped around and grabbed her arm. "Are you okay?"

She started to nod then shook her head, not trusting her voice.

"Here. Sit." He helped her off the boulder to a crag, out of the wind.

She dropped to the rock and leaned back. "Thanks."

"Abigail said you have panic attacks in the mountains."

The cold stone radiated through her jeans. She glared at him. "That's why you offered to come up here. To protect me again, right?"

He nodded. "What are you going to do about them?"

Time to change the subject. "So, I've been thinking about Benny coming to Boulder and wondering what he meant about the prophecies."

Cole gave his head a slight shake as if acknowledging her conversational duck and weave. "End of the world stuff?"

"That seems extreme. But Benny is worried." Should she tell Cole that Benny worried because Nakwaiyamtewa him some warning? "Maybe there's something in the prophecies we should think about."

Cole chuckled. "Hopi corn and now prophecies? Doesn't sound like the skeptical Nora I know."

"And the Hopi Instructions. I've been studying those, too."

His eyes registered surprise. "Since when?"

She played with a pebble while the wind whistled above them. "Since I left Flagstaff."

"Benny got to you, didn't he?" Cole grinned at her.

Nakwaiyamtewa had the real powers of persuasion. "I guess. And then..."

He tilted his head and waited.

She swallowed and viewed the gray sky. "Turns out I'm half Hopi."

He slapped his hand over his heart in exaggerated surprise.

It took Nora a beat to understand. "Abigail told you."

He nodded.

"You guys are a regular best-friends club."

Abbey bounded over the ridge above them and bumped Nora's side. He sat and panted in her face.

Cole reached over to pet Abbey. "So what about the prophecies?"

Nora ticked off the list in her head. "Okay, these all came to the Hopi over a thousand years ago. They say there will be roads in the sky. There will be moving houses of iron and horseless carriages. People will have the ability to speak through cobwebs and to speak through space. Women will take on men's clothing and wear skirts above the knee which devalues the sacred female body. Apparently that demonstrates how low society sinks."

"Not much to go on there." Cole said.

She agreed. "There are more. People of the cross will lead Hopi away from the Great Creator. Short hairs of the Hopi will join the *pahana* government and dilute Hopi beliefs." She paused and explained to Cole. "*Pahana* is the white man"

Cole narrowed his eyes. "I know that much."

She thought about the list of prophecies, trying to remember. "Do not bring anything home from the moon or it will lead to weather disturbances..."

Cole interrupted. "Now we're getting somewhere. Weather disturbances. Sylvia is working on climate-change modeling isn't she? That's disturbed weather."

"I don't know. That seems like a stretch. Prophecies can mean anything. There's one that talks about inverted gourds of ashes that will boil rivers and cause disease no medicine can cure." A lump formed in Nora's throat when she remembered Heather's excitement to tell her about the prophesies and that the one about the inverted gourd that referred to nuclear weapons.

"Maybe we should try to get Benny back to Boulder," Cole said.

They'd never be able to figure out what these obscure predictions meant. "There's one about the Earth turning four times and then mankind will crawl on all fours and only the brother and sister will survive to recycle the Earth."

"There you go. Recycling. Definitely your bailiwick."

Didn't a board member wonder if the HAARP research would flip the Earth on its axis?

Petal appeared at the top of the boulder above them. "It's fine. Sylvia can run her procedure now."

Cole helped Nora up.

Nora's shoulders tensed but she felt in control enough she didn't think the panic would return. She shouted above the wind. "Is that safe up here?"

Petal nodded. "It's sturdy. If someone punctured the tower the energy would leak out, sort of like if you drove a copper nail into a tree and the energy leaks out and the tree dies. But it would be hard to do that."

The wind changed directions. Nora said, "That's the only way someone can ruin it?"

Petal spoke matter-of-factly. "Well, you could take the tunable inductor out of the tower. It's just two PVC pipes with wire coiled around them. When you tune the capacitor just right, it oscillates with the ionosphere. So if that's removed, the energy won't transfer through the spark gap."

Riiight.

Petal stared at the tower. "This is a simple concept for creating energy and the world should know about it. They could shut down the coal and the nuclear plants. This is natural and how we are meant to power our planet. It's the resonance we can all connect to. We can align our chakras with the power. We should build more of these towers on every mountain and they should become places of worship. Because it's a place of creativity."

Nora didn't know what to say. Her eyes met Cole's and she realized he was at a loss, too. "I guess we'd better head back," Nora said.

They scrambled over the ridge toward the trail. "If Sylvia is sending out beams to bounce off the ionosphere, wouldn't that require a lot of energy? I don't see bills that would show that?"

They made it to the switchbacks. Abbey trotted ahead.

Petal stopped beside the cliff wall, out of the wind. "Tesla came up with all sorts of discoveries but they were stolen by the government and kept secret. They use them at HAARP. One study they did is an expansion of the Tesla Coil and it's what we've adapted here. That's an electrical resonant transformer used to produce high-voltage, low-current, high-frequency alternating-current electricity."

Nora gaped at Petal.

Petal wore a shy smile. "It's like this: the tower here uses electricity from the atmosphere. Like in a thunderstorm with a lot of lightening. You know that impressive energy? That energy is the most dominant outward factor in all kinds of storms. So the energy at just the right ELF frequency can create the power of storms."

They walked down the trail in single file. Petal first, then Cole and Nora last. Nora studied her feet to choose each step on the rocky path. She had to project her voice over the wind and with her shortness of breath, her sentences came out in two-to-three word bursts. "So she gets all this energy and she's going to shoot out a beam to collect climate data and she's figured out how to aim it down here, in the Rockies?"

Petal stumbled. Cole jumped forward to help her up.

"And you just checked to make sure it's all functional but she sets it where she wants it to go with her equipment at the Trust?"

Petal mumbled and kept her head down.

"I'm sorry," Nora shouted. "I didn't hear you."

Petal stopped and faced Nora. "She's going to run it tonight."

31

Sylvia paced the foyer, her heels pounding. She'd chosen three-inch pumps tonight because of the solemn occasion. It wouldn't be appropriate to dress flamboyantly with a dead body in her bedroom.

She'd left Eduardo a message on his voicemail over an hour ago. Why didn't he call her back? She told him she needed to speak to him immediately. There was nothing to do but wait.

Eduardo must have a fixer who handled situations like this. Maybe Juan.

The sheer volume of blood surprised Sylvia. It splattered the white walls and carpet and ruined the black lacquered furniture. It soaked her silk duvet clashing with the scarlet orchids. All of that would be ruined.

Maybe she'd change it up now. Go contemporary with splashes of primary colors. On second thought, she'd avoid red.

The phone distracted her from redecorating plans. She punched it on. "Eduardo. Oh, thank god."

He didn't greet her. "Juan says there's problem."

How did Juan know? "He came at me. He wanted to kill me."

Silence met her outburst. "Are you talking about the Director?"

"Mark. Yes. Mark. It was awful."

"Why did Mark Monstain want to kill you?"

His voice made her think of her father's yellowed toenails. "I don't know. He was crazy." She broke off and swallowed horrified tears.

"So you shot him?"

"He was going to rape me! He would have exposed our plans. I protected you!" Sylvia stomped up the foyer stairs and pounded down the hallway. She paced back.

Again, the dead-sounding voice. "Do you know the problem you've created?"

Why wasn't he outraged? He should have wanted to kill Mark himself for attacking Sylvia. "I didn't ask Mark to defile me."

Despite his velvety accent, Eduardo's voice drove ice into her veins. "First you kill Darla and now Mark."

"I didn't kill Darla!" What was that odor drifting down the stairs? Death smelled like a rotten forest.

"And you did not take thousands of dollars from the Trust?"

He was turning on her. She dropped down the two steps into the great room and stared at the foothills outside her windows. "I've been set up. Nora Abbott is behind all this."

"If you've not taken money from them, how do you afford the Ferrari? The crystal? The leather, furs—my god—the shoes?" He paused. "And the Chihuly? Do not worry about that. Your order was cancelled."

Her glass? "That was mine!"

"Where did the money come from for all your indulgences if it did not come from the Trust?"

How did they know all of this? Eduardo was out to get her. But he didn't know everything. He thought she got money from the Trust. He didn't know of her masterful system of borrowing from one card and another and juggling money from friends willing to donate to a brilliant scientist.

"You're a liability."

Icicles pierced her heart. Damn him for upsetting her like this. She needed to play it cool. "I've done it, Eduardo. I've given you a taste of what I can do. Watch the news tonight."

"Have you really accomplished our task?" Eduardo asked, a little perk to his voice.

"Yes. And I need you to clean this mess." She thought of the blood splattered across her bedroom.

"We'll see." Eduardo said.

"The police might come here. I'm still under suspicion for Darla's murder. If you don't take care of Mark it will all be over. You won't get what you want."

"How about this, Sylvia." His tone was slow and deliberate. "You give me what I want and we'll see about cleaning up your mess."

He hung up.

She stood at the foot of the stairs staring up, the coppery stench of blood filling her nostrils.

32

Another day done. In the glow of the eternal parking lot lights, Nora trudged up the stairs to her apartment. The air smelled of snow and wood burning in someone's fireplace. A door below her opened and loud music momentarily disturbed the night and then the door closed again.

They'd returned from the mountain at dusk. Cole left in his pickup and Petal disappeared to Sylvia's office. Nora had spent the next few hours creating a spreadsheet to trace the missing money's journey. She waited for Mark. She wanted to show it to him before taking it to the police. She eventually gave up, resolved to take the spreadsheet to the police in the morning and headed home exhausted.

Maybe Abigail had a delicious dinner cooked and waiting. More likely, she had reservations for some fancy restaurant Nora couldn't afford. What else were credit cards for if not to overspend on her mother one month and live on cheap noodles the next?

First things first. She'd take Abbey for a long walk. She'd convince Abigail to come along. They'd stop and get a few groceries for dinner and instead of going out, prepare it together. And maybe, just maybe, she and Abigail could enjoy each other's company.

She slipped the key in the lock and opened the apartment door. Abbey trotted in and Nora unzipped her jacket.

A burst of laughter drew Nora's attention to the living room. She blinked at what she saw.

Abigail sat on the floor in yoga pants and tunic, legs spread out. She bent from the waist to grasp her bare feet. She let out another bout of giggles.

Petal sat across from her in a similar pose. Her bare feet stuck out from black leggings that disappeared under three layers of skirts. "You need to breathe, Abigail. That's the essence of yoga."

Abigail swung her head around to the doorway, tears of hilarity shining in her eyes. "Oh, Nora. I didn't hear you come in."

Nora pulled off her jacket. "How did you not notice me? The door is right here."

Petal giggled. "I guess we were preoccupied."

Abigail burst out laughing. She covered her mouth with her hand. "We were concentrating."

The both cracked up. Abigail fell back, her chest and belly rising and falling with her howls. Petal fell to her side with her head resting on Abigail's stomach. She snorted and laughed all the harder.

Nora addressed Abbey. "What's up with them?" She inspected the galley kitchen, hoping for some kind of dinner. Instead, chip bags and a package of Oreos littered the counter.

Nora stepped into the living room and her nose itched with the tell-tale smell. She stared at the giggling women on the floor. "You've been smoking pot!"

Abigail sobered. She lifted Petal's head off her belly and sat up. She grew serious for five seconds and then cracked up. "I told Petal you'd know."

Fear clouded Petal's eyes. "I'm sorry."

Abigail stoned? With Petal? The whole scenario twisted so far from reality Nora could only stand mute and watch as Abigail and Petal fell back into giggles.

Nora reached for her jacket and the leash. "I'm taking Abbey for his walk. We'll discuss this when I get back."

The labyrinth of paved paths running through Boulder intersected with the parking lot in her apartment complex. Students used these trails as bicycle highways to campus. Runners trod up and down at all hours and the general, outdoor-loving Boulder population found them necessary to their lifestyle. Access to the trail system was one of the big advantages to Nora's apartment.

Nora and Abbey tromped along the Boulder Creek trail. The creek babbled and leaves rustled in the brisk wind. For the first fifteen minutes Nora railed in her head about Petal. How dare she get Abigail stoned? The next ten minutes involved blaming Abigail. After that came the question of why Abigail would experiment with pot. And just before they returned to the apartment, Nora started to chuckle at the idea of her mother, Abigail the Perfect, sprawled on the floor experimenting with yoga. Smoking a little pot might not be such a bad thing for someone as uptight at her mother.

By the time Nora and Abbey stepped from the cold into the apartment, Petal and Abigail had cleaned the kitchen. They sat in the living room with steaming mugs, watching the evening news.

It seemed strange to have the television on. Nora rarely watched it.

Abigail stood. "Can I get you a cup of tea?"

Nora motioned her to sit. "I'll get it. Are there any more of those cookies?"

Abigail smiled sheepishly. "A few. In the cupboard." She leaned against the counter bar.

Nora fixed her tea and found the cookies. "You didn't drive to get your snacks, did you?"

Abigail regarded her tea mug. "I.... I rode Petal's bike."

Nora stopped steeping her tea and gaped at Abigail.

The only sound was a commercial chirping in the living room.

They held each other's gaze for a heartbeat and Nora lost it, nearly spewing cookie crumbs at Abigail. "I wish I'd seen that."

Abigail smiled. "I'm glad you didn't."

Nora carried her tea into the living room and sank into the green chair while Abigail settled herself on the couch next to Petal.

Petal hadn't said anything, just watched Nora with big, fearful eyes.

Why was it that Petal could get stoned with Abigail, laugh and carry on, yet she seemed afraid of Nora? Furthermore, how old was Petal? It was impossible to tell under all that hair. "You know," Nora said to her, "I'm not mad."

"'Let not anger snuff out the youthful delight of new life.'" Abigail considered the line and wisely shook her head rejecting it.

Petal twisted her hands in her lap. "You're not?"

"I was at first. It's not every day I discover my mother is a pot head."

"Nora!" Abigail exploded in indignation. "One shared joint does not make me a pot head."

Nora struggled to keep a straight face. "I think you should be able to cut loose once in a while. In fact, why don't we do it together? Have you got any more, Petal? We could make brownies."

Petal looked from Nora to Abigail and back again. She didn't say anything and kept wringing her hands.

"So why are you smoking pot, Mother?"

"I wanted to see what all the hoopla is about. Is there anything wrong with that?"

Nora sipped her tea. "The 'hoopla' has been going on for decades."

Petal's voice squeaked from the end of the couch. "It's not her fault. I invited her. I was feeling so sad about Darla and I asked if she'd mind if I smoked a little, just to take my mind off Darla for a while."

"So Abigail joined in to be supportive?"

Petal stared at her hands.

"This has something to do with Charlie, doesn't it?"

Abigail pursed her lips. "Charlie is out of my life. I don't even think about him anymore."

Might as well talk about this now. "There's no way Charlie had an affair."

"Of course you'd defend him."

A low moan escaped from Petal. Abigail and Nora both turned to her.

Even paler than usual, Petal's eyes formed giant dark circles in her face. Her mouth gaped and she seemed drawn into the television.

The news announcer's voice spoke over the image of what might have once been a meadow but now appeared to be a field of mud. The wide-angle shot showed an open area ringed by trees with fall leaves. As the view closed in the trees faded and ground came more into focus.

Petal dropped to her knees in front of the screen. "No. No. No." She covered her mouth with her thin hands.

Abigail grabbed the remote and punched up the volume.

While the camera narrowed in on the ground, showing mounds of black feathers, the announcer said, "Hundreds of thousands of blackbirds fell from the sky in an unexplained rain of death." The image on the screen showed piles of dead birds. "Apparently the kill happened sometime in the late afternoon when the birds dropped onto this Georgia meadow. No explanation is forthcoming although Timothy Peterson, Professor of Ornithology at the University of Georgia had this to say."

The screen switched to a tall man standing outside a collegiate-looking brick building. "It could be the result of a washing machine-type thunderstorm extremely high in the atmosphere. This type of storm would agitate and create a vortex, suddenly appearing and sucking the red-winged blackbirds into its midst and spitting them back onto the ground."

Petal rocked back and forth. "How could she?"

The announcer, a blonde woman with skin like rosy plastic and eyes so rimmed in makeup they might have been painted on, held the microphone to her full-lipped mouth. She stood at the edge of the meadow with a view of the carnage behind her. "Of course, there are other explanations for the bizarre phenomenon."

The camera drew back to reveal a bony woman with gray hair down to the middle of her back. Her face burned with intensity. "This is obviously a government conspiracy. It's the result of a doomsday weapon experiment. Wake up, America!"

Behind her, a small group carried signs and chanted. The scene reminded Nora of the activists who hounded her about manmade snow on the peaks. Her stomach churned.

The announcer smiled knowingly. "According to conspiracy theorists, there is such a doomsday weapon in development since the 1970s. The HAARP facility in Gakona, Alaska is home to what was once touted as Star Wars Defense." The screen flipped from the announcer's face to a photograph of a group standing in front of an array of towers.

Petal gasped. She pointed. "Sylvia," she whispered.

Nora leaned forward. It was difficult to tell with the grainy shot, but a petite woman with curly black hair stood in the front row. It could be Sylvia.

The announcer continued. "The government and private contractors insist they are performing ionospheric research for better communications. But some, including former Minnesota Governor, Jesse Ventura, say HAARP is creating weapons of mass destruction." The screen flashed a video of Jesse Ventura at the gates of a government facility, presumably HAARP, being pushed back and refused entry.

Back to the announcer. "Midnight thunderstorms, government weapons testing, or signs that the world is coming to an end? Whatever the reason, residents of Harris County will be cleaning up for some time." The plastic-faced reporter signed off on her segment of the day's bizarre stories from around the country.

The program cut to a commercial and Petal collapsed into sobs. "I did this. It's my fault!"

33

Petal fell to the floor in a heap and Abigail patted her back. "You had nothing to do with this, dear."

Nora's first instinct was to console and protect Petal's total vulnerability. That's the thing, though. You can't protect people from the world.

Abigail jabbed the Off button and huddled over Petal. "I know it's hard to see all that death." With her facial gyrations, Abigail signaled Nora for help.

Petal pulled away and rolled into a ball, sobbing. "She promised. Never again. She promised. She promised."

Abigail sent Nora a puzzled expression. Maybe Mark and Sylvia were right about Petal: Don't feed the drama.

Abbey whined. He sniffed at Petal and came to Nora, thrusting his nose into her hand.

"Who promised? What did they promise?" Abigail asked.

Petal inhabited her own world. "No more death. She said it. No more."

Abigail and Nora half-lifted Petal and plopped her on the couch. Abigail snugged in beside her and Nora knelt in front. "Calm down, Petal. Tell us what you mean."

Petal swiped her sleeve across her eyes and nose. "First it was the fish kill in Missouri. And now this." Sob, sob, sob. "They were innocent birds. They didn't need to die." Even more sobbing. "She lied. She *lied*."

Maybe Nora should call an ambulance to take Petal to the nearest psych ward. "You're going to have to start at the beginning if you want us to understand."

Petal hiccupped and turned her red-rimmed eyes to Nora. "Sylvia."

No surprise there. "Sylvia what?"

Petal sniffed. "She killed those birds."

While Abigail rubbed Petal's back, she opened her eyes wide, tilted her head, and dropped her jaw. She either had a sudden stroke or she tried to communicate silently with Nora. If Nora had to guess, Abigail was saying Petal was one enchilada short of a combination plate.

Her silent message delivered, Abigail concentrated on Petal. "How could Sylvia have anything to do with those birds? She was here in Boulder at the funeral this morning."

Petal shook her head, eyes watering again. "She can do it all from here. She did it."

Nora had nothing to say.

In between intense eye roll signals to Nora, Abigail said to Petal, "When you calm down you'll see you're not making sense."

Nora tried to fit the bits of Petal's scattered thoughts into some shape. "Does this have to do with the tower? Is it linked to the HAARP research?"

Petal grew still, like a frightened kitten hiding in a corner. "Yes," she squeaked.

"What is *harp*?" Abigail asked, impatience fraying her words.

Nora answered for Petal. "Sylvia worked there before she came to the Trust."

"What does that have to do with birds dying?" Abigail asked.

Nora answered Abigail. "I don't know. She said she researched sending a beam up to bounce in the ionosphere. She's using that technology to gather data on climate and beetle kill. What do you know, Petal?"

Irritation colored Abigail's voice. "You're speaking Greek."

Petal sniffed. "It's more than that. The HAARP facility is in Alaska because it's close to the atmospheric conditions like the aurora borealis. It's all really secure with government soldiers and things."

"I still don't see where this has anything to do with birds," Abigail said.

Nora understood that Petal needed to wind down the path of her brain to get to any meaningful destination. Abigail might as well slow her pace.

"Tell us everything," Nora said.

Petal inhaled a shaky breath. "When we worked for the private contractor who worked for the government, we studied communication systems based on bouncing lasers off the ionosphere. But we also worked secretly on weapons research."

Abigail opened her mouth, probably to hurry Petal along.

Nora jumped in. "You worked with Sylvia before?"

Tears seeped from Petal's eyes. "I've been with her for seven years."

That was one clue to Petal's age. "Go on."

Petal searched Nora's face as if to test her worthiness. "While we were with HAARP, we found Nikola Tesla's secret studies and they showed the exact frequencies needed for incredible power. The technology we discovered can be used to alter the weather."

Right. And Santa Claus kept a list with Nora perpetually in the wrong column.

"So Sylvia learned to alter the weather. Why did she quit HAARP?" Nora said.

"She didn't quit. She was fired." Petal swiped her nose with her sleeve.

"Why?" Abigail asked.

"She wasn't doing any of the work but taking credit for it and they finally figured it out."

"Why didn't she publish her findings?" Nora asked gently.

"They made her sign a document about government secrets and that she wouldn't continue her research."

"But she has?" Abigail crossed the room and grabbed another tissue from a box on the counter bar. She handed it to Petal.

Petal wiped her eyes and nodded. "Besides, if Sylvia tried to publish her work there's a good chance someone would kill her."

Abigail's eyes narrowed in offense. "From our government? That's preposterous."

It sounded more like a spy novel than real life. Maybe that's where Petal came up the plot.

"Now all those innocent birds are dead." Her voice faded into sobs.

Abigail did some weird eye roll thing that Nora thought meant Petal was not just crazy but a full-out Looney Tunes.

Nora tried to ground Petal. "But changing weather doesn't have anything to do with thousands of dead birds."

Changing weather. One of the prophecies had to do with weather.

Petal gulped. "It's the freak thunderstorm like the ornithologist said."

"But he said there was no record of the phenomenon," Abigail said.

"That's because it happened so far up in the atmosphere the only indication was the impact it had on the birds."

The pieces didn't fit together any better than Petal's outfit. "Even if this is what happened and Sylvia is behind it, why would she do it?"

Petal looked from Abigail to Nora. She lowered her voice. "Because she's really not working for the Trust. That's just her cover."

"Cover for what?"

"She's continuing to work on controlling the weather."

Abigail stood. "I think we need coffee. Nora, can you help me find the beans you like?"

Even a flake like Petal could see through that obvious ploy. Nora rose and followed Abigail into the kitchen. Abigail opened and shut cupboards, all the time keeping an eye on Petal over the breakfast bar. "If it were me, I'd keep them here." She nearly yelled and banged a cupboard door closed.

She leaned close to Nora and whispered. "Do you think we should call a doctor?"

They should call somebody skilled with delusional hippies but Nora had no idea who that would be. "Let's just—."

"Nope, not here, either," Abigail yelled and opened and slammed a door.

"—see if we can talk some sense into her."

Abigail opened and closed a door and whisper. "Do you think that will work? She's really nuts."

"Make her some hot milk and maybe we can get her to sleep." They kept their eyes on Petal.

Petal hugged herself and rocked on the couch.

"She can smoke some more pot," Abigail said.

"Petal has a flimsy enough grasp of reality. She doesn't need that kind of encouragement from us." Nora slid a canister of coffee from its spot on the counter and stopped it in front of Abigail. She walked back to the living room.

The doorbell rang and Petal sprang from the couch and sprinted down the hall toward the bedrooms. Abigail patted Nora's arm. "You get the door. I'll go see about Petal."

"No illegal drugs, Mother."

34

Nora pulled open the front door to see Cole standing there with a pizza box balanced on his outstretched hand

It smelled like cheesy, spicy wonderfulness. Now it made sense that Abigail hadn't cautioned Nora to take a weapon with her when she answered the doorbell. "Let me guess," she said, grinning and stepping back to let him in. "Abigail and Petal called and asked you to bring this."

He stepped inside. "How did you know?"

She closed the door against the increased wind. "Lucky guess."

He set the box on the kitchen counter. "I thought it might be another of her tricks to get us together."

She laughed. "You're becoming as skeptical as me."

"But she swore it wasn't." He unzipped his green down jacket. "And she sounded so desperate I couldn't say no."

The cold clung to his coat as Nora hung it up. She was strangely glad to see him. Cole carried assurance as comforting as a warm sleeping bag.

That sounded like Abigail's poetry.

She reminded herself how unpredictable Cole could be. If he thought she was in danger, he might chain her up in a basement.

He folded his arms and leaned back on a kitchen counter. "In the interest of full disclosure, I should tell you I didn't believe her."

She walked to the hallway and shouted to the closed bedroom door. "It's safe. It's only Cole and pizza."

He shook his head. "*Only* me."

"Hey, you got top billing over the pizza." She grinned.

Abigail appeared with her arm around Petal. "Let's get something in your stomach. You'll feel better." They stood beside the table.

"You mean something besides Oreos and Doritos?" Nora headed into the kitchen.

Cole set the pizza on the dining table and opened the box. The spicy aroma of sausage and cheese made Nora's mouth water.

Petal paled as if no blood circulated in her veins. She wouldn't make eye contact with Cole. "Where did you get it?"

Abigail only cringed slightly at Petal's rudeness.

Cole carried the plates and spatula Nora handed him to the table. He slid a piece of pizza on a plate and held it out to Petal. "That place down the street."

Petal waved it away. "No. I can't eat that. They use pork sausage and cow's milk cheese."

Right. "Vegan," Nora explained to Cole.

He offered the plate to Abigail.

She waved it away, too. "It seemed like a good idea at the time but I'm not hungry anymore."

Nora accepted a plate. "Munchies all satisfied?" Petal had eaten the chips and Oreos. Did dietary restrictions take second place to THC cravings?

Cole piled a couple of slices on his plate. He raised a questioning eyebrow at Nora. "I guess pizza *was* another of Abigail's matchmaking tricks."

Abigail sniffed. "It was no trick. We were very hungry. Now we're not."

Abigail led Petal into the living room and settled her on the couch.

Nora opened the refrigerator and found two beers hanging out with the leftovers from last night's arranged dinner. She handed one to Cole.

Nora hiked herself to sit on the kitchen counter and Cole leaned back across from her.

Nora gulped the cold beer. "Petal and Abigail spent the afternoon taking the edge off their problems in a haze of smoke."

Cole's eyes widened. Around a mouthful of pizza he said, "I thought I smelled something and chocked it up to residue on Petal's clothes." He swallowed. "Abigail stoned. What led to that apocalyptic event?"

Nora hated the reference to End of the World, even in jest. All that Hopi Fourth World-ending stuff didn't seem like a joke to her.

"She claims Charlie had an affair and she's leaving him." The pizza tasted as good as it smelled.

Cole nearly spit out his mouthful of beer. "You better invest in long underwear because hell is freezing over."

She finished her pizza and hopped down. She reached for his plate and piled pizza onto both and returned. "Speaking of the end of the world, a bunch of birds fell from the sky in Georgia and sent Petal into a meltdown. We've been teetering on the edge of reason ever since."

Nora gave Cole the skinny on the escalating events leading up to the pizza delivery. The warm, gooey pie might be the single best thing that happened to Nora all day. Having a rational person to provide and share it with didn't feel too awful, either.

They left their plates in the sink and Nora set the beer bottles on the counter for recycling. Cole leaned on the counter and watched her. "What are you going to do?"

"Bring this all back to reality." She walked into the living room where Abigail and Petal sat on the couch talking quietly. They seemed calm, Petal's hysterics a thing of the past. Perching on the edge of a chair, she addressed Petal. "If what you say is true, we need to go to the police."

Petal jumped from the couch and screamed as if Nora poked her with a torch. Abbey leaped up and let out a few barks.

Crazy was back in fashion.

"No, no, no. I can't." Petal folded herself into the corner between two pots of corn.

Now would be a good time to call the folks with the white jackets.

Cole stood by the kitchen table watching it all with a blank face.

Abigail squatted in the corner with Petal. "It's okay, honey. Why don't you want us to call the police?"

"She'll kill me, too." Petal whimpered and drew even tighter into the corner.

Abbey sat by Nora, welcoming her fingers in his fur. Why couldn't everyone in her life be like him? He didn't need expensive trappings, stayed calm most of the time, gave her affection and comfort, and having an affair amounted to sniffing another dog's rear end. All this in exchange for a daily walk and a full food dish.

She regarded Cole. Actually, he didn't require much, either. And he showed up with his own food.

"Sylvia's not a killer." Abigail sounded reasonable

Petal shook her head. "No. You don't understand."

"What don't we understand, honey?" Abigail drew Petal from the corner.

"She killed Darla and if she finds out I know, she'll kill me, too."

Abigail and Nora exchanged helpless expressions. What would they do with Petal?

Petal gazed from one to the other. "Sylvia stole a bunch of money from the Trust. Made it look like Darla took it and then she killed her."

Using only her eyes, Nora asked Abigail what to do.

Petal saw their silent exchange. "You don't believe me. But it's true. I saw her kill Darla. I was there."

"Oh, my," Abigail said.

Petal continued in a halting voice. "I was with Darla that night when she went to ask Sylvia about the missing money. I waited in Darla's office and I heard her run outside. I watched out the window to the backyard and I heard a gunshot. Darla fell. I didn't know what to do so I hid. And then Darla died."

"But she was found closer to the road," Nora said.

Petal sobbed and they waited until she could talk. "I carried her out there."

Aside from Petal being too weak to carry a dead cat, it seemed strange. "Why?"

"To protect Sylvia." The weirdness compounded the longer she spoke.

Nora said, "You have to go to the cops."

"I can't. If the cops arrest Sylvia she won't be able to do her work and if she can't, they'll find someone else."

"'They' who, dear?" Abigail asked.

Petal sniffed. "And if they don't arrest her, Sylvia or the people she works for will kill me." Petal gulped air. "If she kills me, who will stop her?"

"Stop her from what?" Nora asked.

Petal's eyes acquired a desperate gleam. "I don't know. But something awful."

Abigail sat back in disbelief.

Nothing about Petal's story sounded the least bit sane. Still, it made Nora's heart pound with dread for Petal. "It's too dangerous for you to do this alone. You have to go to the police."

Petal squeezed Nora's hands with more strength than Nora thought possible. "Please, please. Not tonight. I'll go tomorrow. Please, let me just stay here and rest tonight."

True or not, Petal was terrified. Nora didn't have the heart to rip her from the slight comfort of Abigail's mothering.

35

Sylvia's Ferrari squealed off the road and across the bridge and into the Trust's lot. The parking lot light was out again. She was sick of this rinky-dink facility and their slip-shod maintenance. It was wrong. Everything was wrong tonight. She slammed on the brakes and skidded on the gravel. The few flakes falling hadn't started to accumulate.

Birds! Goddamn birds. How did this happen? Petal had calculated the angle, and Sylvia trusted her. Petal should have known. How could Petal make this mistake?

Eduardo would have been watching the news anticipating his victory. What would happen when he saw a sea of dead birds instead?

Brittle flakes of snow whirled through the frigid air. Clouds threatened to drop more before the storm moved on. Sylvia climbed from her car and hugged her fox-lined jacket close, thankful for the fur-topped, snow boots with the rubber tipped-heels. She may have to live in an inhospitable climate but at least she could maintain some style. Not like Alaska where she'd had to wear clothes straight out of survival catalogues.

Sylvia hurried across the front porch and unlocked the front door. She didn't bother turning on lights and ran through the kitchen to her office suite.

Where was Petal? Sylvia needed her to recalculate the refractory angles of the tower and reset the beam.

But no, she couldn't trust Petal. Sylvia should have known that girl didn't have the brain power to accomplish something so delicate. Why hadn't she checked Petal's calculations?

Because Mark had shown up and ruined it all.

Think, Sylvia! But her mind chased itself. Dead cats, Daniel's body in her bed, blood on her carpet, the black Town Car, her fur-topped boots, Daniel's naked body, Mark's bloody body, Mark, Daniel. Stupid, stupid Petal.

She leaned against the door jamb and held her hands to her head trying to push the random thoughts into order.

Sylvia snapped on the light and ran across her office. She flung her bag onto her desk and booted up her computer. She'd checked the coordinates Petal calculated. They should have been correct.

Sylvia entered her passwords and navigated beyond the firewalls. In a matter of minutes she understood Petal's mistake. The moron had transposed two numbers. Perspiration lined her body as she reset the program. Her fingers shook and her nails kept hitting the wrong keys.

Finally she sat back, her insides a molten stew of acid, her skin chilled from sweat. She'd done it. As only she could do.

Sylvia rummaged inside her bag for her phone before she remembered where it lay—hurled against the wall after Eduardo's last call—broken on the floor of her bedroom, spattered with Mark's brains.

She grabbed the headset of the ancient landline phone on her desk. Her fingernail tapped the buttons and she dialed the country code, area code, and private number. She waited while it ran.

Finally he answered. "Ah, Sylvia, *carina.*"

"Eduardo. Listen, I can explain."

His robust laugh sounded cheerful. "No need. Truly."

She didn't trust his good cheer. "It was an error. I'm fixing it right now. I can send another ELF wave at dawn. You'll see. I'll do it for you, Eduardo."

"Yes. Yes. That will be excellent. Good bye, Sylvia."

"Wait! Don't—"

He hung up on her. Again.

Thud.

What was that? Sylvia ran across the room and slapped off her office light. She couldn't stop her rapid breathing as she snuck into the dark kitchen. She stood on tiptoe to see out of the window above the sink. In the unlit parking lot she made out the Lincoln Town Car sitting next to her Ferrari.

The knob on the front door rattled and she felt the pressure in her ears as it opened.

Sylvia tiptoed to the back door and stealthily turned the lock. She grabbed the knob, twisted, yanked. She didn't bother to shut the door, knowing that Juan—or whoever it was Eduardo sent to kill her—would already be chasing her.

She sprinted across the icy lawn, slipping. *Is this what Darla felt like just before the bullet ripped into her back?*

36

Abigail had coaxed Petal into Nora's bedroom, convincing her to lie down. Petal would only relax if Abigail stayed with her. Both were sleeping when Nora checked on them a half hour ago. Cole hadn't made any move to leave and Nora hadn't asked him to. They'd been sitting on the couch ever since, staring at the television.

After the Petal drama and the exhausting day, Nora didn't know what to do. Tomorrow morning she'd take Petal and the spreadsheets to the police. Tonight, she felt helpless. She plopped down on the sofa and turned on a daily news satire show. Uninvited, Cole sat next to her. She didn't complain. The host reported on the day's events with pithy political commentary. Cole stared at the screen without any reaction and Nora assumed he heard as little of the show as she did.

Too bad Nora didn't have any more beer. She could use another cold one.

Too many questions banged around her brain to concentrate on television. What if what Petal said was true? Did Sylvia really possess the means to alter the weather and kill birds? If so, did that mean Petal's life was in danger?

Abbey lay in his bed under the corn plants, snoring softly.

Cole stirred. "What was Petal saying about Tesla?"

Nora sat up. "I don't have any idea. I thought Tesla was a car. I didn't know it was a person."

Cole scanned the apartment. "Do you have a computer?"

Nora hurried to a small desk in the corner of the room. She shoved the leaves of a corn plant out of the way and grabbed her laptop. She booted up. "Okay. We've got weather and Tesla and HAARP." She typed them all into the search engine and hit enter.

Cole leaned into her and read the screen. "Might want to narrow that down."

She grinned at him as results appeared and she clicked on one. She scanned it then read to Cole. *Tesla was also reportedly working on resonance machines, or devices whereby he could shake one or many large city buildings from some distance away.*

This capability has now blossomed into the ability to create earthquakes in any desired location on earth, of the desired magnitude, and desired depth. HAARP can create such earthquakes.

Cole lifted the computer, settled it on his lap and kept reading. *Tesla's experiments in Colorado produced powerful artificial lightning, in the millions of volts. Producing this lightening was one of the earliest examples of Tesla being able to create weather phenomenon. A mushroom-shaped radio tower was instrumental in Tesla fine-tuning his ability to create all manner of weather. As he beamed radio waves at the exact ELF frequency by which earth's weather is naturally created, Tesla discovered he could alter the weather.*

A chill spiked up her neck. "Syliva is going to create an earthquake."

Cole's eyebrows shot up. "Not jumping to conclusions, are you?"

"Well, maybe. It could be."

Cole laughed. "You're sounding like Petal. Just because the first site you randomly hit spouts crazy conspiracy theories, it doesn't mean it's true."

Maybe she was getting carried away. She shot him a sheepish grin.

Instead of teasing, as she'd expected, he grew serious and his eyes darkened.

She caught her breath. She tried to tell herself she didn't know him well, but she understood his expression. He leaned into her, sliding his warm fingers along the back of her neck. With the gentlest touch, he drew her toward him.

"Is it okay if I kiss you?" he whispered.

She nodded, not trusting her voice.

They'd only kissed once before and yet his touch felt natural and familiar. She closed her eyes and blood rushed through her ears. His lips moved with soft pressure against hers and suddenly her arms and legs felt like pudding. She smoldered against him.

Cole stopped long enough for Nora to set the computer on the floor.

His arms encircled her, pulling her against him as his heat matched hers. They paused for breath and Nora sank into his eyes, dark with passion. Without thinking, she allowed herself to fall into another kiss. And another.

How many years since she'd made out on a couch with her mother asleep in another room? It was as exciting and erotic now as it had been at seventeen. The bad tension eased from her shoulders, replaced with the good kind—the tingly kind that accelerated her pulse and made her warm all over, some places downright steamy. She could go on like this forever. No guilt, no expectations, no past or future.

She was so far gone she didn't hear anything until Abbey woofed and focused on the door. That's when she realized the pounding came from fists on the door and not the blood in her ears.

"Oh." She stood up and yanked at her shirt that had twisted around her belly. She walked to the door on shaky legs, rubbing her mouth and struggling to regain some dignity.

In the year Nora lived in the apartment, she could count visitors at her door in the single digits. They'd all been trying to sell her wrapping paper or hoping she'd help fund a grade school field trip or wanting her to buy magazine subscriptions to help an inner-city delinquent on the road to better himself. Maybe this time the cops waited on the other side. They might have found out Petal witnessed Darla's murder and needed to question her. Or it could be the bad guys that Sylvia supposedly worked for, come to pop a cap in Petal's brain. In which case, they'd kill everyone in the apartment.

Not overreacting or anything.

Nora slipped the chain on the door and opened it to peek outside. What waited outside trumped whatever fantasy she concocted. She slammed the door, unhooked the chain and swung it open again. She threw herself into waiting arms. "Charlie!"

He hugged her hard, his grizzled face roughing her cheek. "You are sunshine and light and give me reason to live."

The snow fell in giant white flakes, swirling in the gusts. She drew Charlie inside, out of the storm. She'd missed his forest smell, the gravelly voice, and his strange way of speaking as though he were in a soap opera.

Abbey wagged his whole body in delight to see his old hiking buddy and Cole grinned.

Charlie scratched Abbey's ears. "You're a fine fellow. Fine fellow." He straightened and surveyed the apartment. "Nice crop of corn."

She hugged him again.

He grinned at her. "In a world of sorrow and pain you are a bright angel of joy."

Cole grasped Charlie's hand. "Good to see you, man."

Charlie's bright eyes traveled from Cole to Nora. "Awfully good to see you here."

Nora grasped his cold hand in both of hers. "Why didn't you call and let me know you were coming?"

His face grew serious. "A wise soldier relies on the element of surprise." Charlie didn't often speak in war metaphors. His eyes drooped with weariness.

"Take your coat off and tell me what's the matter."

"Element of surprise, is it?" They all whirled around to see Abigail standing in the dining area. Her hair smashed against one side of her head and a dark rim of mascara smudged under one eye. Only a life-threatening emergency would bring Abigail out in in such disarray. "Don't you mean ambush?"

"Now, Abbie…"

Nora tugged at the neck of Charlie's army jacket as he shrugged to shed it.

"Don't you 'now Abbie' me." She pointed at Nora. "Don't take his jacket. He's leaving." Abigail made a chameleon seem consistent. She could go from pothead to Florence Nightingale to a panther all in the course of a few hours.

Charlie gazed at Abigail with sad eyes. "I've come to take you home."

"I'm not going anywhere with you. My home is here now, with my daughter."

Whoa! Cole and Nora watched like spectators in the Thunderdome.

Charlie stepped toward Abigail. "You are my very breath. My home and my bed are cold and empty without you."

Nora cringed.

Abigail held her hand up to stop him. "You've destroyed whatever home we had together. And as for your bed…"

"Okay, okay." Nora stepped between the two. She had to stop this talk before she was scarred for life. "I'll make some tea and we can sit down and discuss this like adults."

Abigail's voice rose an octave or three. "He won't drink anything but beer so unless you have a twelve pack on hand, don't bother."

"Hey," Nora said. "You knew he drank beer when you married him." Everyone knew Charlie drank beer. He kept the pockets of his army jacket well supplied. Come to think of it, she hadn't felt any cans when she'd hugged him. Maybe he wisely didn't drink and drive.

"'The heady party of our love has faded to the painful pounding of a hangover.'" Abigail cast about, probably for paper to record her poetry. The universe would be forever grateful to lose that particular verse. Abigail turned her attention on Nora. Her eyes glistened with tears. "I won't sit down with you and Charlie together. You always take his side."

Nora stammered. "What side?"

Abigail ignored her and shot back at Charlie. "Are you so immune to your effect on women?"

Charlie? He didn't stand more than five feet, eight. He smelled of pine forest and beer and wore baggy-butted jeans and a faded plaid shirt. He had a kind and gentle nature like a benevolent dwarf in a Disney movie. He was Nora's dear friend but she'd never thought of him as romantic. Using the word sexy in the same sentence as Charlie would be a stretch.

"Can't we talk about it?" Charlie asked.

"No. No. And no. You ruined our wonderful love with your thoughtless, selfish ways."

Nora knew Charlie to be one of the most caring and considerate people in the world. "Come on, let Charlie explain."

With all four of them standing in the apartment it felt as crowded as a Japanese commuter train at rush hour. And at least as uncomfortable.

Abigail tossed her head back. "You!" She shot a finger at Nora. "I would think after what you went through with that philandering husband of yours, you'd understand."

Nora tried again. "Charlie wouldn't cheat on you."

"See? I told you. You're taking his side and you haven't even heard the facts. Fine."

Charlie started, "I'm not—"

Abigail whirled around. "As far as I'm concerned, you deserve each other. I'm through with both of you." Abigail stomped down the hallway and into her room. It surprised Nora that Abigail didn't slam the door. She probably did that out of consideration for Petal.

Nora exhaled and said to Charlie. "I have to ask. Did you have an affair?"

Sorrow wafted around him like flies on a corpse. "No."

Nora pulled out a chair at the table and sank into it. Cole and Charlie followed her. "Then what is she talking about?"

Abbey sat next to Charlie and rested his muzzle on Charlie's lap.

Charlie stared down the hall and petted Abbey. His face grew rigid. "I would walk across hot coals for your mother. I would chase the great white whale to please her. I would rope the wind, cage the man in the moon. I would..."

Nora rested a hand on his. "Okay. But what did you do?"

He focused on Nora. "I gave up beer."

Those were the last words she expected from Charlie.

Cole's chair creaked as he sat back acting as astonished as Nora felt. "That's a pretty big deal."

Charlie nodded. "I thought she wanted me to."

"What does giving up beer have to do with you having an affair?" The connection didn't seem obvious to Nora.

Charlie went back to staring down the hallway. "I had a little trouble giving it up cold turkey so I went to someone the VA paid for."

"A therapist?" Cole asked.

"Yep. A pretty young thing about your age." Charlie propped his elbow on the table and leaned his face against his hand.

Nora stood and slipped around to the kitchen. She spoke over the counter bar. "Good for you. Did she help you?" Nora filled her tea kettle and set it on a burner.

Charlie lifted his head to answer her. "Oh, sure. She helped me a whole lot. But she had me start going to meetings."

Cole nodded. "AA meetings." A gust rattled the patio slider.

Abbey placed a paw on Charlie's knee as if commiserating. "And they helped. So I went to them every day. And I quit."

"That's great. Was Abigail happy?"

He turned his sad eyes to Nora. "If she noticed she never said a word."

Nora leaned over the counter. "Ouch. Did you ask her about it?"

Charlie stroked Abbey's paw. "She had other things on her mind. She wanted to know where I went every day. I lied and told her I went to the forest, like I always do."

"Why didn't you tell her the truth?" She pulled out three heavy mugs.

"I was ashamed I couldn't quit on my own."

Nora grabbed a few boxes of tea bags from her cupboard. She caught Cole's eye and started tossing them to him. "So you kept going to meetings and lying, and she knew you were lying."

He shrugged. "I guess so. She followed me."

She brought the mugs around and placed them on the table. "And she saw you went to a meeting right? So why does she think you were having an affair?"

Abbey dropped his paw and closed his eyes, still leaning into Charlie. "Because the day she followed me was a big test day. I met my therapist at a bar downtown and she ordered a beer. I had a club soda, which is a poor substitute, by the way. We stayed there for a few rounds so I could get a feel for what it was like to say no."

"And Abigail saw you," Cole said.

"That would be my guess."

Nora brought the kettle from the kitchen. "You didn't talk to her?"

Charlie's chin fell to his chest. "I didn't know she was there. When I got home, her bags were packed and she was gone."

"So tell her now." Nora picked an Earl Gray tea bag for Charlie, dropped it in his cup and poured the water.

He wrapped a hand around the mug. "Nope."

Oh no. Charlie needed to make up to Abigail, and the sooner the better. If not, Nora would be stuck living with her in perpetuity. "You have to talk to her, tell her the truth."

Cole chose orange flavored black tea and steeped it in his mug.

Charlie stared at his tea. "Don't you see, sweet child? If she doesn't have faith in me, there's really nothing for us."

Cole stared down the hall. "Does it feel cold to you?"

Nora noticed the chill. She stood and started down the hallway to investigate a draft. Cole followed.

She opened her bedroom door expecting to find Petal curled up on her bed. Instead, the bed held nothing but a pile of rumpled blankets. The curtains billowed with the storm blowing in the open window.

37

Nora raced to the window and scanned the balcony that ran along the second floor of the building. Most of the well-lit parking lot was visible from that vantage point. Snow accumulated where it caught in ridges and tiny drifts. The wind grabbed the bent screen and banged against the building. Nora slammed the window closed.

"Is she out there?" Cole asked.

Charlie appeared uncharacteristically rattled. "She ran from me? Why would she have to steal into the frigid night to escape from me. My Abigail angel."

Abigail answered from behind him. "I haven't gone anywhere, you old fool. It's Petal who's jumped ship."

"Thank the morning star you're safe," Charlie said. "Who is Petal?"

Abigail now wore one of her velour jogging suits with matching jacket. She'd repaired her hair and makeup. "How long has she been gone? What did you do to her?"

Nora snapped on a bedside lamp but it did little to illuminate the room. She made her way around the rustic log footboard of the bed and squeezed past Abigail to check the closet. "I didn't do anything. Last I knew, you were napping together."

"Humph." Abigail watched Nora as she closed the closet door and scanned the small space between the matching log night stand and the wall, then turned and focused on the corner by the dresser. "You need a bigger bedroom. Or smaller furniture. Or both, would be my opinion. That rustic decor is…"

Nora glared at her.

Abigail sounded disdainful. "I suppose you think Petal running off is my fault, as you think everything is my fault."

Nora held back a retort. She wished she had more light in the dim room.

Cole squinted out the window. "Why would she take off?" He pulled down the mini blinds.

Now that she looked at her room through others' eyes, it did feel over furnished and generic. She'd only hung a couple of prints she'd found at Target and the comforter and curtains were a solid shade of light blue. All of it serviceable because, she admitted, not much exciting happened in her bedroom these days. Her eyes strayed to Cole and she blushed.

Abigail knew where to place the blame. "She's scared to death Sylvia or someone else is going to kill her. And along comes Charlie. He storms into our home. I'm sure she heard his angry voice and fled for her life."

They all stared at Abigail for a moment then Cole said quietly, "Charlie didn't sound threatening to me."

Nora ran a hand through her hair. "Doesn't matter what set her off. She's gone."

"Who is Petal?" Charlie asked again.

Cole started for the door. "Come on. I'll explain while we'll search outside."

Charlie reluctantly followed Cole out the door, his eyes still pleading with Abigail.

Abigail slammed her hands on her hips. "We should go after Petal. She's had very rough life."

Nora didn't want to get involved with Petal. It was okay to let her stay the night, to feed her and listen to stories and to tuck her into bed. But Nora wasn't responsible for every stray that wandered into her path. "What did Petal tell you?"

"She grew up poor and her mother is ill. She has an aunt who, apparently, is well off. But she won't help with Petal's mother. I think she has some resentment issues with the aunt and she ought to see a therapist. If you don't take care of these negative feelings they can fester—"

"Mother!"

Abigail smoothed her jacket. "For heaven's sake, Nora, she worships you because she thinks you've been so kind to her and frankly, you barely notice her."

"Notice her? She's living in my home!"

"At *my* invitation."

"Thank you for finally giving me the sister I always wanted. Maybe we can play Monopoly and read *Teen* magazine together."

Abigail lasered a withering shot at Nora, creating instant guilt. "What's happened to you? You used to be generous and kind and giving. Now you're locked up like a clam, holding back all your love lest it wither in the salty waves of life." She pulled her notebook from her pocket, uncapped her special pen, and scribbled.

Out of nervous energy, Nora pulled the comforter up and straightened the bed. "You're nuts."

"Is that so? I remember a little girl who always included the most forlorn and ostracized child on the playground."

"That was only because no one else would play with me." Nora plumped a pillow and tossed it onto the bed.

Abigail tsked. "That's not true. You were always the leader and the most popular."

"Whatever." Nora didn't like this conversation.

"This's why you're so unhappy these days." Abigail was rolling on the Nora-improvement wagon and there was no stopping her.

Nora walked out of the bedroom. "I'm not unhappy."

Abigail followed. "Of course you are. You can't hide it from me."

"How could I hide anything from you? You're living in my back pocket." Nora stopped in the middle of the living room, not knowing what to do. She stomped to the kitchen and leaned on the counter.

"I know you're refusing to let yourself care about Petal because of what happened to Heather." Abigail paused in the kitchen doorway.

Nora froze. They said time would heal but after a year, it still felt like an open wound.

Abigail took out her chisel and hammered away on Nora's heart. "You push Cole away with both hands. Just because Scott betrayed you."

"Enough!" Nora brushed past Abigail.

Abigail watched Nora pace into the living room again. "You need Petal as much as she needs you."

Nora walked to a corn plant and held a broad leaf. She wanted to be left alone to take care of Abbey and herself.

Snow swirled outside the window. Petal didn't have a coat. Nora spun around and searched the side of the couch where Petal had curled up. Petal's Chacos peeked from beneath the blanket. No shoes, either. Damn it.

Abigail nudged her. "It's a nasty night out there."

"I don't know where she would have gone."

Abigail considered. "She talked about wanting to stop Sylvia."

"Do you think she'd go to the Trust?"

Abigail shook her head. "I think she'd go to Sylvia's house."

"I wonder where that is."

Abigail grinned. "I know."

"How do you know?"

Abigail rolled her eyes. "There's this thing called the Google. You might have heard of it."

"Why...?"

"I was curious." Abigail defended herself. "It's a swanky neighborhood. When Berle and I lived here it wasn't much but since then, they've scraped off most of the older homes and built new. It's where the people with money live. We'll GPS it."

Abigail grabbed her phone from the corner of the counter bar. "Got it. Let's go." She opened the coat closet by the front door. "I didn't bring a causal cold-weather coat." Abigail slipped into Nora's newest, warmest down coat. Of course Abigail would commandeer that coat and leave Nora digging in the closet for a lighter-weight, beat-up version.

They headed out the door to Nora's Jeep. Abbey bounded toward them across the parking lot enjoying the snowy evening. Abigail opened her door and before she could climb in Abbey scrambled into the passenger seat. Abigail waved him into the back.

"Nora, wait." Cole jogged from the end of the parking lot.

Nora walked to her side of the Jeep and watched him approach.

"Where're you going?" His breath puffed in a white stream.

"To find Petal." Her fingers tingled in the cold.

He stood motionless between her and the car door.

"So, we'll see you later." She reached behind him for the door handle.

He placed a hand over hers. He gazed down at her, the struggle for words visible in his eyes. Finally he said, "I know you've had a rough year and I've stayed away because I wanted to give you space, or whatever."

Nora studied Abbey in the Jeep. He sat in back, staring out the windshield, unaware of her thudding heart and rushing blood.

Cole let out a breath. "Here's the deal. I understand you're afraid of commitment because Scott had an affair and you don't know if you can trust anyone. And you think I kidnapped you and—"

"You did kidnap me."

He flared. "That was becau—never mind. What I want to say is this. I like you, Nora. I mean, probably more than like you."

She wanted him to stop talking but he kept going.

"The timing might not be ideal for you but I can't put my life on hold waiting for you any longer."

She turned to get in the Jeep.

Again, he tugged her hand so she'd face him. "I'm not asking you to move away with me. I just want to know if there's a chance for us."

Why did he force this on her? "I don't know."

"What about tonight? I thought maybe you felt..."

She jerked her hand away. Jobs, mothers, runaways, discovered fathers, weather manipulation. She couldn't bring anything else into her life. "I'm going to find Petal. If you want me to confess undying love and fidelity to you, forget it. I'm not ready for this. With you or anyone."

Nora slid onto the icy car seat and started the engine. She refused to make eye contact with Cole, didn't want to know if he still stood there or if he'd walked away.

Abigail rubbed her arms. "Get that heater going."

Nora eyed Abigail's coat with envy. She shivered inside her second-best coat. And Petal was loose out there somewhere with no coat at all.

Abigail punched her phone. "Go east from the parking lot."

Nora started the wipers. Snow stuck in small patches to the pavement.

"What did Cole have to say?" Abigail pointed to the left and Nora turned.

"Private conversation."

"He told you he loves you, didn't he?" She clapped her gloved hands together. "That's romantic. He could have chosen a more intimate moment but men don't always think things through."

Either Abigail was blind to body language or she hadn't been watching the exchange. Nora maneuvered down Arapahoe Street, thankful for light traffic.

Abigail's giddy planning bubbled along. "You're going to start slowly, right? Dinner, outings, that sort of thing. Will he move to Boulder? He's not suited to that ranch anyway. Turn right at the next light."

The Jeep slid at the turn and Nora slowed. The wipers flapped at accumulating flakes. "Cole and I aren't an item. Let's drop it. Where next?"

"You should have a smart phone like mine instead of that ancient model you have. It's as bad as Charlie's. Turn here."

Nora did. "Charlie has a cell phone?"

Abigail stared out the window. "Of course."

They hit a puddle and the water splashed on the windshield. By morning it would be ice. "That doesn't seem like something Charlie would care about."

Abigail spun toward her. "I suppose you two are simpatico on this subject too."

Let's jump off one tangent and onto another. "Don't know what you're talking about."

"The two of you. Always judging me about how I live. Abusing Mother Earth. He wouldn't get a cell phone because he said it made him too dependent on others. He wanted to commune with nature and rely on his wits. Of course, he didn't care that I worried day and night he'd get hurt in the wilderness, lying on the ground, dying alone. I finally bought him a phone and insisted he carry it." Abigail pointed.

Nora turned right onto Table Mesa Road. They were heading in a giant circle. Way to go, smart phone. "Good. Did he?"

Abigail's voice faltered. "He said he only did it to humor me. But he never called me and the minutes usage went up."

Nora squinted against the barrage of flakes in the headlights. "Who was he calling?"

Abigail's voice hardened. "I did a little research and found out he was calling that woman."

"What woman?"

"That woman from the bar. Beth Ann Troutman."

Nora flopped her hand against her thigh in frustration. "Are we anywhere close to Sylvia's house?"

Abigail exhaled in frustration. "We're discussing my marriage, my life. Why must it always be about you?"

"You drag me out to save Petal and you're upset because I won't tell you that Charlie isn't having an affair."

Abigail folded her arms in a huff. "Oh, what do you know?" She pulled one arm loose and pointed a right turn into a neighborhood with two elephant-sized sandstone slabs as neighborhood signs.

Nora slowed and drove through the dark neighborhood, the splash of her wheels on the wet pavement accompanying the wipers. Nora had hit her limit for games.

"He wanted to quit drinking because he thinks it will make you happy and all you can do is ride him and accuse him of things that if you really knew him, you'd know he wouldn't do."

Abigail's jaw went slack. "He's quitting?"

"Yes, Mother. And you haven't noticed. That woman, Beth Ann, is his therapist."

Abigail sat motionless for a moment and Nora peeked at her phone. It indicated another left so she headed that way.

Abigail's eyes went soft as she thought. "You're right. I haven't seen him with an open beer for a long time." She came back to the present. "He said he's doing this for me?"

Nora nodded. "Can we get back to the drama at hand?"

Abigail kept her satisfied smile. She checked the phone. "The next house."

Abigail had the expression of a twitterpated teenager. "Why didn't he tell me? I would have supported him."

Nora slowed.

Abigail pointed to a house. "This is the place." She gave it the once over. "A bit gouch."

Nora eased the Jeep to the curve in front of a huge house. The lawn, now smooth and white under the accumulated snow, yawned in a ridiculous expanse that would need watered and mowed—the opposite of sustainable. The foothills rose from behind the multi-gabled McMansion with its covered portico and two-story front windows that must accent a great room with the mother of all vaulted ceilings. No direct lights shone through the great room windows, only a glow cast by another room. A window inside the massive stone entryway framed a crystal chandelier.

Abigail started punching numbers into the phone. "I have to call him. Tell him I was wrong."

A minuscule sliver of light escaped from the front door and sliced the front porch.

The door was open.

Abigail held the phone to her ear.

Nora slid from the Jeep and started up the walk.

38

The snow eased off but the wind continued to howl through the trees behind the Trust farmhouse. Bright moonlight reflected off the white ground, leaving Sylvia's footprints visible.

Sylvia huddled at the edge of the backyard under an evergreen shrub. Her feet felt damp in her fur-topped boots. She'd broken a heel in her flight down the back porch stairs.

She strained to see though the darkened windows inside the house. Where was Juan? He must be hunting for her. He'd be skulking around the dark building, stopping to listen.

The rumble of boards on the creek bridge sounded like machine gun fire. She barely heard the purr of a car engine but seconds later a car door slammed. More of Eduardo's thugs?

Sylvia slithered from under the branches, feeling them claw at her smooth cheeks. She limped across the yard, staying close to the outer edge along the trees. With a burst, she scurried toward the farmhouse and hugged the wall, where no one inside could see her from a window.

She peeked around the edge of the house to the parking lot. The Town Car still sat in the lot with a smattering of snow on the roof. Daniel's Prius was parked next to it. Sylvia's Ferrari was hidden on the far side of the Town Car. She couldn't get to it without running in full sight.

Pounding and what sounded like a scuffle erupted on the front porch out of Sylvia's view. Male voices rose in anger. Juan slid out from the front of the house on the slick grass as if he'd been pushed. He fell to his knees.

Daniel strode after him. He fired off a rapid string of Spanish and advanced on Juan.

Juan scrambled to his feet and hurried to his Town Car. He turned and shouted at Daniel, throwing up his hands. He yanked open the door of his car and jumped inside. In a matter of seconds he gunned the engine and spun out of the parking lot. He fishtailed and banged a back fender on the bridge before he accelerated down the highway.

Sylvia ran from hiding. "Daniel!"

He watched her.

When she grew close enough, she launched herself into his arms. "You've saved me. I knew you'd come."

He grabbed her hand and pulled her up the stairs and across the front porch. He shoved her inside and slammed the door. "Tell me now, Sylvia. What are you doing? Why did my father send Juan?"

Why was he being so rough? She settled herself and brushed her fingers through her hair. She sidled to him and ran her hand on his chest under the leather of his jacket. "Don't be grouchy. You're going to love me when I tell you."

He pushed her hand away. "Tell me."

She rose on her toes and slipped her tongue around his cold lips. "I did it for you."

"For god's sake, Sylvia. Get away from me."

Why was he acting like this? "I set it in motion, Daniel. Like you wanted me to. Like Eduardo demanded."

His face froze. "What did you do?"

She smiled and reached for his hand. "Come here, I'll show you."

39

This is not a good idea.

In fact, it could be one of her worst. That didn't stop Nora from climbing the stone steps on the front porch and approaching the open door. Wind whipped her hair and stung her ears and her hiking boots left waffles in the snow on the walk.

Abbey stayed close on her heels. She should probably have left him in the car with Abigail but she didn't mind the four-legged dose of courage at her side.

Nora rang the doorbell. She didn't expect anyone to answer and they didn't.

She pushed the door open and stood outside. "Hello!"

Silence.

She should call the cops. Tell them Petal had gone missing. And that Sylvia was involved in a mysterious and deadly venture involving Tesla towers and dead birds, and the powerful people Sylvia worked for would kill Petal if the police didn't intervene.

They'd have no trouble believing that.

Abbey trotted in front of her, leaving muddy paw prints on the marble foyer.

A wide staircase to the right of the entryway swept to the second floor.

The curved wood railing shone with polish in the light from the foyer. Splashes of bright oranges, blues, and reds blazed from abstract oil paintings on the wall.

Abbey's claws clicked on the marble and his breath sounded like an elephant snuffle as he sniffed the floor.

"Hello?" she said again. Silence in a house this size was a big silence.

Directly in front of them, the marble of the foyer gave way to a white-carpeted sitting room. A baby grand piano left room for two white upholstered chairs. The night darkened on the other side of a floor-to-ceiling window.

Nora chose to head left down a short hallway. It opened onto the great room facing away from the street.

She stepped around a stone pillar and Nora nearly gasped at the expanse and opulence. Down three steps that ran the length of the room and across the wide space covered with the impossibly thick white carpet, floor--o cathedral ceiling windows faced the Flatirons. In the daytime, the view would be breathtaking. Tonight, with snow swirling outside, was merely spectacular. A huge stone fireplace occupied one whole wall and several white couches and chairs made up a couple of conversation areas. It resembled the lobby of a posh hotel more than a real person's living room.

How often did Sylvia entertain? Nora couldn't imagine one person wanting to spend time with Sylvia, let alone a team large enough to make this room practical.

"She's not much for color."

Nora gasped and whirled around at the sound.

Snap. The room burst into light and Abigail adjusted the dimmer from spotlight to natural. She stepped from behind a pillar and surveyed the room from the top stair, hands on her hips.

"My god, Mother, you scared me. I thought you were in the Jeep talking to Charlie."

Abigail waved her hand. "A phone only works when you turn it on. I can't make him understand that. I left some voicemails but I don't think he knows how to retrieve them."

Nora gazed out the tall windows at the swirling snow. Petal might be out there.

"Did you see that chandelier in the entryway?" Abigail asked, disgust ringing her words.

The fireplace gaped at Nora as if waiting for a sacrifice. "I didn't pay any attention."

Abigail loved to tour houses. She wasn't shy about giving her decorating opinions. "It's ostentatious. The entryway calls for something smaller and more tasteful. This place reeks of new money."

As if Abigail came from a long line of aristocrats. She'd grown up in Nebraska and only later, married money. Lots of it. Mostly gone now.

Nora started for the stairs. "We shouldn't be here. I think it's breaking and entering."

Abigail scrutinized the room. "Nonsense. The door was wide open. As friends we're obligated to check things out and make sure Sylvia is all right."

"Friends?"

"Small detail," Abigail said and descended the stairs. "The carpet is a nice weave but the white is much too risky if you want to actually live in your home."

"This is a bad idea," Nora said to Abbey.

"It's too stark with all this white. Although I do appreciate the natural elements of the stone. And, oh Nora, look at those beams. Those are very nice. I can't identify the wood. Not pine."

Who cared? Nora gave up the sane notion of high-tailing it out of there and advanced on a bookshelf inset into the wall opposite the fireplace. Framed photos sat amid glass sculptures. Compared to the sharp angles and abstract contemporary art on the walls, the frames twisted in ornate gold gilt.

Abigail stood in front of one of the furniture groupings assessing the accent pillows. Abbey plopped down and rested his head on his paws.

The photos mostly showed professional studio shots of Sylvia. From the headshots at various angles and the posed casuals, it seemed Sylvia loved playing fashion model. There were a few photos not done with the intent of making Sylvia gorgeous.

Abigail abruptly walked from the furniture to the fireplace. "This room is a mosh-posh of mixed styles. Most unsettling."

"Shhhh." Nora cocked her head. "Do you hear anything?"

Abigail paused a moment. "No. You're letting your imagine loose again."

Nora turned back to the photos and Abigail walked over to peer over her shoulder.

Abigail pointed to a picture. "What about this?" Sylvia stood next to a dark-haired, older and more-worn version of herself. An awkward girl of about thirteen stood in front of the two women, shooting a cheesy grin at the camera. From the style of clothes, the picture must have been taken twenty years ago.

Nora studied the picture. "Must be family. At least it proves she didn't rise from a lagoon on a dark, stormy night."

Abigail picked it up and stared at it. "That little girl is Petal."

Nora focused on another interesting shot. "Right. Now who's imagination is running wild?"

Abigail thrust the frame under Nora's nose. "Look at it."

Nora hadn't seen Petal's impish side as much as Abigail had, but the little face did bear a resemblance to Petal in her rare happy moments. "I can see how you'd think that. But it's a coincidence."

Abigail pursed her lips and set the photo on the shelf.

Nora picked up the frame she'd been studying. "Whoa." She handed Abigail the snapshot of Sylvia arm in arm, gazing adoringly at someone.

Abigail gasped. "It's Daniel!"

Nora pointed at the picture. "See in the background? They're standing in front of World Petro."

Abigail shrugged and handed it back. "She's having an affair with that Latin lover. I knew there was something fishy about him."

"World Petro is his father's company." Nora stared at the picture. "Supposedly, Daniel is trying to stop them and others from drilling for oil in the Amazon basin."

Abigail trod across the room and up the steps. "It's shocking that a woman Sylvia's age would cavort with someone like Daniel but it happens."

"Cavort?" Nora set the picture down and followed Abigail.

They continued down the hall toward what appeared to be the kitchen. "You know what I mean," Abigail said.

Nora noticed the muddy paw prints Abbey left on the white carpet.

Sylvia wasn't going to be pleased. "If Daniel and Sylvia are having an affair, why are they keeping it a secret?"

Abigail felt around on the wall of the dark kitchen. "It isn't good policy for a board member to be sleeping with the hired help."

If the dark, silent house weren't so creepy, and if they weren't breaking the law, and if she didn't think that Petal might be in some kind of danger, she might find the idea of Sylvia being called hired help amusing.

Abigail slapped on the light to reveal a kitchen fit for the Iron Chef himself. Copper cookware hung from a rack above a center island covered with gleaming granite big enough to dance a tango on. The cook top had more burners than the Octomom had babies. Two ovens, two refrigerators, miles of counter space and gadgets Nora could only guess at. If anything had been used, Nora couldn't tell.

Abigail didn't sound impressed. "It's all for show. She clearly doesn't cook."

"Daniel's been helping me to sort out the financials. If he and Sylvia are together, why would he do that?"

Abigail slapped off the light and brushed past Nora. "Maybe he's trying to keep you from finding something that incriminates her."

Could he be protecting Sylvia? But if he loved her, why didn't he just give her $400,000? For someone with his resources, that wouldn't be much.

Next up was the dining room. Abigail found a dimmer switch and turned it up. "Oh my. My, oh my."

The dining room table was a mass of wrought iron and glass. The chairs twisted in bizarre shapes like torture devices. Dinner in this room would be about as much fun as an evening in the dungeons of the Spanish Inquisition.

Abigail tsked. "I suppose Sylvia thinks this passes for art. She's obviously trying too hard."

"Petal said Sylvia worked for someone powerful. With World Petro behind him, Daniel is certainly powerful."

Abigail stared at the dining table as if considering how to destroy it. "The only thing worth keeping in this room is the chandelier. That's quite lovely, actually."

She brushed her hands as if to get rid of the room and strode down the hall. "Let's check upstairs."

"No," Nora said. "This has gone too far already."

Abigail waved her off. "We need to make sure Petal isn't hiding up there. Besides, I want to see the bedrooms."

"Big mistake," Nora grumbled to Abbey. He sat in the foyer watching her.

Abigail trotted up the stairs, scowling at the abstract oil paintings and shaking her head. She reached the landing halfway up and her phone jangled.

Abigail held it up and frowned. "Why is Cole calling me?" She answered and her face lit up like Rockefeller Center on Christmas Eve. She pulled the phone away and said to Nora, "My knight in shining armor. His battery died but he was dying to talk to me." She turned her back on Nora and spoke into the phone. "I'm so sorry!"

Nora stopped several steps down. Abbey hadn't moved.

"Just a minute, dear." Abigail pulled the phone from her ear. "I need to take this in privacy. You check upstairs and I'll wait for you in the Jeep."

"I'll come with you."

Abigail lowered her eyebrows. "Private conversation, Nora." She skipped down the stairs, knocking Nora to the wall.

Nora watched Abigail hurry outside. Abbey sat at the base of the stairs. Once more Nora eyed the front door and escape. "Did I mention what a mistake this is?" She said to Abbey. The golden retriever wisely kept his own counsel. She climbed the stairs, feeling the weight of the silence grow more dense with each step. "Abbey, come."

Abbey gave her the I-don't-wanna attitude.

"Stop being lazy," Nora said. "Come."

Reluctantly, he got to his feet and climbed after her.

A strange odor crept into her nostrils like a hairy caterpillar. Was Sylvia's toilet clogged? But no, it didn't smell like bad sewer. Whatever it was, it stunk.

The hallway ran the length of the foyer, looking down on the chandelier—now that Nora noticed, it really was gaudy. To the right a few doors opened onto dark rooms.

The slightly worn path in the thick pile led to the left. Must be the master bedroom.

Nora leaned down and scratched Abbey's head. *Stupid, stupid, stupid.* And yet, her feet carried her down the hall, however slowly.

The stench was like thick Yuck Chowder.

Nora glanced behind her to make sure Abbey followed close behind.

She snaked her hand around the wall to the dark room and felt for the light.

40

At first the muted light of the bedroom didn't reveal much. Sylvia must keep the lights dim in here to set the mood. The bedroom was only slightly smaller than the great room. The section closest to the door contained a sitting area with a fireplace. A television the size of a child's wading pool hung on the wall.

The massive four-poster bed jutted from the far corner of the room and black dressers accented the room. Even with all the furniture, someone could still perform a gymnastics floor routine. Who needed this much space?

The covers bunched at the foot of bed and spilled onto the floor. The carpet seemed to have a splotchy pattern in a dark color by the bathroom door. Odd.

A nightlight cast a glow from the bathroom across the room. Sylvia was not the neatest person because she'd left shoes and clothes strewn on the floor.

Abbey whined. He'd retreated to the stairs.

Nora found the light switch and toggled it up. The wall sconces brightened, as did the chandelier. How many crystal chandeliers does it take to please Sylvia?

Nora stepped tentatively into the room.

Dear god.

Nora gasped and stepped back, running into the doorjamb.

She wanted to run but couldn't make her feet move.

What she'd thought was a pattern on the rug so obviously wasn't.

Blood. So much blood. Crimson splashes on the wall by the bathroom. Deep ruby on the white carpet. The smell. It made horrible sense.

Scuffed black men's shoes with thick leather soles, black socks and the bottom of black trousers made up what she'd thought was a pile of Sylvia's clothes.

Nora gagged. The walls and white sheet of the bed resembled a macabre Jackson Pollock interpretation of red, with enough lighter colored chunks to add texture and depth.

Nora spun and raced down the hallway. Abbey barked. Nora lunged into the closest bathroom and made it in time to vomit into the toilet. Shaking and slimed with cold sweat, she braced herself on the counter and turned on the tap. She rinsed her mouth, her legs trembling and threatening to give out.

She had to go back. The shoes and pants gave Nora an awful sense of recognition.

Nora knelt and buried her face in Abbey's fur. She hesitated a moment to calm down enough to force herself return to the room. She pulled herself up and step by awful step, made her way back to the bedroom. She stopped in the doorway, staring at the black shoes.

Nora needed to see around the foot of the bed. She swallowed but her mouth felt like a desert.

Step. Step. Bit by bit the body came into view. Dress pants covered the legs. A white shirt pulled out of the waistband over a soft, pudgy belly.

One more step revealed the entire body.

Nora held her hand over her mouth. "Oh, no." The head had been blown away. Bits of it stuck to the wall and the side of the bed. White pieces of skull with wisps of black hair clumped amid globs of bloody brain.

Nora backed away. Tears ran down her face and she gagged again. There was no face, but she'd seen enough to know it was Mark Monstain.

A voice squeaked from the dark corner of the room next to a tall armoire. "Nora?"

She whirled around, heart in her throat.

The wad of fabric and hair wedged between a dresser and the corner of the room mewled. "Oh Nora."

Nora rushed to Petal. "What happened? Are you all right?"

Scarlet slashes marked Petal's cheeks, matching the rings around her eyes. Tears streamed down her face. "Sylvia and Daniel. They were here."

Nora kept her face turned away from the gruesomeness at the other end of the bedroom. Waves of toxic fear sloshed inside her. She reached for Petal and tugged at her to stand. Together they lumbered to the hallway. "Did Daniel do this? Is he still here?"

Petal shook her head. "I don't know. Mark was dead when I got here."

Nora kept her arm around Petal as they moved toward the stairs. "Where did they go?"

Petal trembled against Nora as they descended one stair at a time. "They went to the Trust. Sylvia wanted to set the coordinates. They're going to send a beam at dawn."

Abbey squeezed around them and plodded down the stairs to the foyer.

"Sylvia's not gathering data on climate change, is she"

Petal shook her head.

They made it to the foyer and both sat on the bottom step, huddled together. "Tell me what's going on."

Petal swiped her sleeve across her nose. "The beam is set at a refractory angle to strike in Ecuador."

Now it made sense. "Daniel isn't really trying to protect the rainforest. Why are they targeting Ecuador?"

Petal shivered despite all her layers. "The beam will start an earthquake. That will trigger the volcanoes and they'll erupt. They'll wipe out whole cities. After that happens, the government will sell the oil rights so the companies will pump money into the country and they can rebuild."

Heat surged over Nora's body and her ears rang. "They're staging a massive natural disaster so World Petro can get richer? They can't do that."

Petal stared at her with round, watery eyes. "They can."

Nora jerked her to her feet and noticed she wore damp wool socks and no shoes. "We have to stop them!"

She pulled Petal to the door and reached for the knob. A movement through the side windows stopped her.

She caught her breath and watched through the window as a Lincoln Town Car stopped at the curb and shut off its lights. The driver's side door opened and a tall man dressed in black started up the front walk.

41

Nora dropped to the marble floor, pulling Petal down. "Someone's coming," she whispered.

"No." Petal's cry sounded plaintive.

Nora crawled toward the hallway. "This way. I think there's a door in the kitchen."

Abbey plodded after Nora, unconcerned with her strange behavior.

As soon as Nora was far enough into the hall she couldn't be seen through the foyer windows, she jumped to her feet and sprinted toward the kitchen.

Petal ran after her, small moans escaping with each step.

Nora pushed the kitchen door open and halted in the darkness, remembering the layout. Island, stove, sub-zero freezer, more counters. Her mind found escape just as her eyes adjusted to the dark.

They heard the front door open. Why hadn't they locked it? It snicked closed.

She grabbed Petal's hand and patted her thigh to bring Abbey closer.

"Here." They skirted the kitchen island, heading for the garage door. All three of them hurried through the door.

If they had the time, they could have had a barn dance in the garage. With no windows, it was even darker than the kitchen. Nora's feet clattered on the textured concrete floor as she dragged Petal toward the back where she hoped she'd find escape.

She fumbled beside the large overhead garage door, desperate to find a regular door knob. If they used the automatic door it would sound like buffalo stampede and they'd lose any chance of sneaking away.

She couldn't find a door. Frantic, Nora stopped and searched the dark garage. A small light by the kitchen showed the overhead door control. They might be able to escape if the man in black had started upstairs in his search.

At any rate, they had no choice.

Nora ran back to the kitchen door and punched the control.

The motor roared with the sound of a freight train. The overhead light burst on.

Nora sprinted for the opening, grabbing Petal's hand on the way. "Come, Abbey!"

The garage door rose with the speed of a frozen river.

The kitchen door swung outward. "Hey!" The man shouted at them.

Nora dove and rolled under the door.

Petal copied her.

Abbey ran after them.

"Stop!" The man yelled.

"Run!" Nora leapt to her feet, heading toward the Jeep.

A gunshot exploded from the garage, shattering the wood of the door.

Petal screamed.

42

Nora skidded on the snow in the driveway. "Petal!" Had she been shot?

She'd barely turned when Petal plowed into her, knocking her on her tailbone.

Another shot pegged the driveway next to them.

Nora must have jumped to her feet and dashed across the driveway and street to open the Jeep door, but she didn't remember it. Now she held the door open for Abbey and Petal to dive into the back seat.

Abigail gasped. "Whatever is—?"

Nora vaulted into the driver's seat. "Hang on." She cranked the key and jammed it into gear.

"Hurry!" Petal screamed form the backseat.

Nora peeled away from the curb, the back end slipping in the slush.

She caught a glimpse of Sylvia's house in the rearview mirror. The man stood in the light from the garage watching them.

"What's happening?" Abigail asked.

Nora pointed at the phone. "Is that Charlie?"

"Well, yes it's Cole's phone because he didn't char—"

Nora careened around a corner and gunned it. "Tell him to meet us at Baseline and Foothills. In the Safeway parking lot."

Abigail swiveled in her sit and gasped. "Who is that man?"

"Mother! Tell Charlie."

Abigail repeated the instructions into the phone.

Nora slid around the next corner and ran a red light.

Abigail pulled the phone away from her ear. "He doesn't know where that is."

Another light at the intersection on Broadway turned from yellow to red. Nora glanced left and right, saw headlights, and slammed on the brakes. Abbey crashed into the back of her seat. "Cole can get him there."

Nora waited for the sparse traffic to pass in front of her, and then crossed the intersection despite the red.

Abigail spoke into the phone and ended the call. She twisted to see into the back seat. "Petal, are you all right?"

Nora didn't hear any response. She concentrated on the street. The pavement ran with melted snow and slush. If you headed to the grocery store for milk, it would be a matter of slowing down to be safe. If you were running for your lives, it meant some sliding turns.

Abigail braced her arms against the dash. "You're going to kill us."

Nora whipped into the Safeway parking lot and slid to a stop behind a bank building.

"Now, will you tell me what's going on?" Abigail folded her arms, the slick fabric of Nora's best ski jacket whizzing in the silence.

"Sylvia and Daniel killed Mark."

"Oh my god!"

"They plan to send out a beam to cause an earthquake in Ecuador."

Abigail's lips turned down in skepticism. "Well, that's just silly."

Nora didn't have time to convince Abigail. "I've got to stop them. So you and Petal have to stay with Charlie."

Abigail held up her phone. "We need to go to the police. I don't know who that man at Sylvia's house was, but he shot at you and that's against the law."

"No!" Petal came to life in the back seat.

Nora and Abigail wrenched around.

Petal placed her hands on the back of their seats. "I need to go up to the tower. It's the only way to stop this. I can disable it."

"Can't we stop the beam from the office?" Nora asked.

"Yes" Petal squeaked. "But it's very secure and Sylvia is the only one who knows the codes to get in and cancel the launch. If she's got it set there's nothing we can do."

Nora straightened and stared ahead. The Town Car sat at a red light on Baseline.

Duck! Hide! Run! But all she could do was pray he didn't see them.

If the shooter twisted in his seat and surveyed the parking lot, he could spot them parked behind the bank.

Abigail's no-nonsense tone set the course. "The police can take you there."

Petal trembled. "They won't believe me. They'll waste time and the beam will go off before we can get there."

The light turned green and the Town Car eased across Foothills Highway, heading east.

People live in Ecuador. Cities lie at the base of several volcanoes. An eruption or a high magnitude earthquake would kill… Nora had no idea how many people. Not to mention the devastation to the rainforest and what long term, world-wide environmental problems that would create.

She addressed Petal. "Cole will take you to Mount Evans. I'll go to the office and see if I can cancel the launch."

"What am I going to do?" Abigail asked.

Nora rubbed her forehead. "You stay with Charlie and Abbey. I don't want to worry about you."

Abigail reached for her handbag on the floor of the Jeep. She unzipped a pouch on the bottom of the bag Nora had never noticed and pulled out a small pistol. She held it out to Nora. "You'd better take this."

What the—? "Mother, why are you carrying a gun? Is it loaded?"

Abigail wore a satisfied smile. "The gun isn't real, dear. I saw it in SkyMall. It's an authentic replica designed to scare muggers. You pull that out and they run away."

"And this will do me what kind of good?"

"You didn't know it was fake. How do you expect Sylvia to know the difference? Wave it around, demand she cancel the death beam, call the cops, save Petal, easy as pie."

Nora doubted it would be that easy.

Headlights appeared around the west corner of the bank. Cole eased his pickup beside them. Charlie's door opened and he raced around the front of the Jeep toward Abigail's door.

Cole climbed from the driver's side.

Nora scanned the intersection of Baseline and Foothills for the Town Car's return. All clear. She jumped out of the Jeep and stepped in a puddle. She met Cole by the bed of his pickup. "You need to take Petal to Mount Evans."

He scowled. "You want me to do you a favor?"

"It's not for me. It's—" She couldn't explain it all again. There was no time. "Please. Just trust me."

He folded his arms. "I'll do this for you. But this is it. No more."

"What do you mean?"

He ran a hand through his hair, now damp with falling snow. "I need to get on with my life. Right now, that means going back to the ranch in Wyoming."

She didn't want him to leave. But did that mean she wanted him to stay? She couldn't deal with this now. "Do what you need to do." It sounded more harsh than she intended.

Nora sped back to the Jeep and helped Petal from the back seat. She'd removed the wet socks and was now barefoot. Nora settled her into the passenger side of Cole's pickup. The heater made it cozy away from the wintery wind. "Be careful. Cole will help you."

Petal reached out and hugged Nora. Her voice choked. "Thank you. You're a good friend."

Charlie and Abigail huddled together under the portico of the bank. Their heads bent together in quiet conversation. Abbey sat at their feet.

When Nora ran to them, Abigail pulled out her phone. "I already called a taxi. Get going."

Nora gave her a quick hug. "Take care of her," she said to Charlie.

"She is my galaxy," he said. Crazy old Charlie.

Nora followed Cole's pickup out of the parking lot and west on Baseline. At Broadway he turned south toward the mountains and she turned north.

Toward...

She didn't know.

43

Despite the broken boot heel and the snow-dampened hair, Sylvia knew she carried herself with class as she led Daniel through the darkened kitchen to her office suite.

There, she laid out the maps of Ecuador showing the Cotopaxi volcano and the oil fields in the rainforest. He was suitably impressed by her brilliance.

At first he acted angry. She assumed that was because he felt inferior to her genius as he struggled to understand the difficult principles behind the plan.

He studied the maps on the banquet table in front of him. "If you actually make the volcano erupt..."

She kissed the back of his neck. "Oh, it will."

He ducked away from her kiss. "You will kill thousands of people."

They weren't the kind of people who mattered. It was far better to accentuate the positive. "But the Cubrero family will be rich. We can have whatever we want, whenever we want it."

He walked to her desk where her monitor showed a diagram of the tower on Mount Evans and the angle of refraction of the beam that would send it directly into the volcano. "When will this event occur?"

She ran her hands through her hair pulling her arm back to give him a view of her breast outlined through her cashmere sweater. She sauntered to where he leaned over the monitor and hiked a hip on the desk. "It's scheduled to activate at dawn. About three hours from now."

He stepped back from the screen and paced across the office. "And you are the only one who knows of this?"

He was starting to understand how special she was. "I designed it. I set it in motion. Yes, my love, it is all mine."

"My father paid for all of this and yet does not know about the dawn launch?"

She sprang to her feet. "Eduardo! He's so unreasonable. I tried to tell him but he hung up on me. Hung up!"

"And sent Juan."

She purred. "But you saved me."

Daniel frowned. "If you're doing my fahter's bidding, why does he want you dead?"

She couldn't stay still and strode across the office. Her skin suddenly felt too small. "He's irrational. He thinks I killed Darla and Mark and that I stole Trust money. And when last night's launch misdirected and killed birds, he wouldn't listen to me."

His face froze and he stared at her. "You killed Mark? And you are behind the birds dying?"

She hurried to him and slid an arm around his neck. She snuggled her cheek into the warm spot where she felt his heart beating. "But you can talk to him. You can tell him about our love and how I am doing what he wants."

"Can you stop this beam or whatever it is?" He lifted her hand from his neck and stepped back.

"Of course I can, but why would I?" She couldn't stop it, though.

He ran a hand back from his forehead across his short, black curls. "What if someone tampers with the tower?"

She waved her hand toward the window. "It's snowing. Petal was up there earlier today and it's working correctly. Believe me, it's safe."

"Does Petal know of your plan?"

She tickled his chest just above the button of his shirt. "She might suspect something but she's not bright enough to figure it out."

"But she could be out there now."

A warning flashed in Sylvia's brain. "Petal. You're right. She hates me. She and Nora are out to get me."

Daniel grabbed her arms. "Why does Petal hate you?"

"Because I won't give her mother unlimited money. Because she thinks I stole her ideas. She thinks *she* deserves the credit at HAARP for taking Tesla's technology forward. But she worked for me. She couldn't have done it if I hadn't nurtured her. If I hadn't given her the opportunity."

He glared at her. "Petal developed this?"

No. He would *not* dismiss her the same way they did at HARRP. "No. *I* did it. *I'm* the one."

He spun toward the door and strode into the kitchen. "I've got to stop her."

Sylvia ran after him, tripping on her broken heel. "Yes. Go. Don't let her destroy my tower."

She hurried after him from the kitchen to the dark lobby. She bumped into his back. "What?"

Daniel stood motionless.

Sylvia shoved him to send him to the mountain. But he wouldn't move.

Sylvia stepped around him to pull him forward and she suddenly understood what stopped him.

Nora Abbott stood just inside the front door, pointing a gun at them.

44

Great. Now that Nora pointed Abigail's gun at Daniel she didn't know what to do. Fake gun, fake bullets, fake courage. "You aren't going anywhere." She sounded a lot tougher than she felt.

Sylvia whirled around and raced through the kitchen.

Daniel backed up, keeping his eyes on Nora. "Why are you here?"

Good question. "To stop you."

Daniel held his palms out. "You don't understand, Nora. I'm not the bad guy."

Was Sylvia getting a gun? A butcher knife? Nora was outnumbered, out-experienced, and—wielding a SkyMall Special—out-gunned. With Sylvia probably on her way back with a Katyusha rocket—or just a real gun—Nora had to come up with something.

Nora spotted the old-school landline on a side table. She walked to it, keeping the gun pointed at Daniel. She picked it up and pushed 9, heading for the 1. She took her eyes off Daniel for the splittest of seconds.

He charged. With all of his sexy muscle he rammed into her, sending her flying several feet.

She cracked a hip and her elbow when she landed against the fireplace and slid to the floor. Blood filled her mouth where she bit her tongue on impact. Amazingly, she still gripped the gun.

He came at her again and she raised it as if taking aim. "I'll shoot!"

It didn't faze him. Maybe he suspected she'd never fire on him. Or maybe he wasn't afraid of a toy gun.

He dove on top of her and clawed for the gun. She raised it above her head and he boosted himself across her with his knees to reach for it.

"Uff." It felt as though his knees pushed all her organs out of the way and ground her spine into the floor. His hand closed on the wrist that held the gun.

Nora twisted beneath him. She pushed off with one foot and kicked the knee of her other leg. She knocked him in the back, causing him to lose balance and tip to the side, slipping off her.

She rose to her hands and knees and scrambled to get away.

He grabbed her ankle and fell on her again.

This time he grabbed her gun hand with both of his. He slammed her hand onto the ground and wrested the gun from her grip. Pain shot through her forefinger as though he'd snapped it from her hand.

He sprang to his feet, waving the gun at her. Abigail's fake-out fooled him.

What did it matter if the gun could kill her or not? Even without a weapon Daniel was bigger, stronger, and more lethal than Nora.

He stood above her, hesitating. Nora readied herself to jump up, grab his ankles, tackle him to the floor. And then?

She might bring him down but Sylvia would show up to kill her any minute. Nora anticipated the bullet ripping into her, shredding her kidneys, mangling her guts. Blood would splatter across the fireplace and soak into the carpet.

The sound of a gunshot tore open the night.

Bullets didn't shred Nora.

Abigail said it was a fake gun but that was a real gunshot. Nora rolled to the right before Daniel could fire again.

But the shot hadn't come from Daniel's gun. She realized the sound hadn't come from this room.

Daniel's head jerked toward the kitchen. He hesitated only a second then he sprinted to the front door, yanked it open, and dashed into the night.

The old farmhouse fell silent. Nora lay still, straining to hear Sylvia rushing from the kitchen ready to fire off more shots. This time, the bullets would find Nora.

Nothing.

45

Nora got to her knees and pushed herself up. Someone had stolen her femurs and her legs wobbled. She considered following Daniel out the door and heading directly to the police station.

Instead, she tiptoed to the kitchen. The back door stood open allowing flakes to blow into the narrow passage. The brisk air washed away the smell of burnt toast.

With careful steps she snuck past the door heading toward the light spilling from Sylvia's office. Her footsteps caused the old floors to creak. She inched closer to the lighted office. She didn't want to see inside.

But she had to.

A smell like spent firecrackers and hot oil hung in the air and Nora froze. She listened to the nothingness around her.

Bang, whoosh, groan. She jerked and catch her breath. The heater kicked to life in answer to the open kitchen door.

Nora focused on the office door hoping to hear something, anything, moving inside. She slid her foot forward and leaned toward the door. She eased around the door jamb and surveyed the room.

The office appeared empty. The overhead light glared, reflecting on the maps spread on the table. The computer monitor on Sylvia's desk cast a faint glow as if she'd been working. Petal's chair snugged up to her desk and the lamp with the pink silk scarf was off. The papers stacked neatly on Petal's desk. Nora stepped into the room and moved tentatively toward the desk. Something creeping along the floor caught her eye. She narrowed her gaze to the floor in front of Sylvia's desk.

Not creeping. Leaking. Deep crimson, it spread like gruesome syrup, dripping from the edge of the plastic chair runner and soaking into the thin carpet.

A low moan escaped from Nora's throat. She held her breath to silence herself. Fighting every step, she advanced until she saw the whole scene.

Nora fell back against the wall. Part of her fought to deny the image while the other part struggled to understand it. She gagged on the smell of death.

Sylvia sat wedged in the far corner under the desk. Mascara smeared under her eyes and her black curls flopped in wild disarray. Her eyes stared sightlessly at Nora.

A river of blood flowed from the mangled flesh that had been Sylvia's chest.

46

Nora staggered out of the office. The kitchen door still stood ajar and freezing night air blew in. She slid down from the sink and sat in front of the blast.

Earthquakes of revulsion and fear cracked her surface. She couldn't do this. She shivered and stared into the backyard.

Get control. Think.

Sylvia was dead. But Daniel, the man who stood to profit from the rainforest's destruction, was on his way to the mountain to stop Petal from dismantling the tower.

Cole.

He was on the other end of Daniel's deadly quest. Nora had sent him there. And Charlie had Cole's phone so she couldn't warn him.

She shot to her feet and clattered through the kitchen and foyer, out the front door, and across the porch. She lurched down the stairs two at a time, slipping on the last one and crashing a knee on the ground. The snow had tapered off and the temperatures weren't at their winter worst. The wet snow stuck to the grass in clumps and would be gone before lunch. She bounded to her feet and sprinted toward the Jeep.

The Town Car sat next to hers.

She dove to the ground and rolled under a shrub. Not the smartest move she'd made. If he'd been in the car he'd have already killed her. Now she was wet and muddy.

The Town Car Guy had killed Sylvia and he wouldn't think twice about doing Nora the same. She pulled her feet under her and crouched next to the shrub. Obviously he'd used the kitchen door to the back yard. Where was he now? At the edge of the house waiting to gun her down?

She had no choice.

Nora dashed to the Jeep. The roar of a pistol did not shatter the silence. The bullets didn't burn into her exposed body. In fact, she made it to the Jeep without incident even if she couldn't breathe from terror. She jerked open the door, dove inside and turned the ignition key, seemingly at the same time.

Hunched over the wheel to make as small a target as possible, Nora punched the gas and sped away. She studied her rearview mirror. Nothing moved at the Trust farmhouse. The black rectangle where the front door stood open gaped back at her.

Since it was a weeknight—technically a week morning now—it was too late for people to be out and too early for them to be up. She raced through Boulder heedless of the stoplights. The snow had melted on the pavement leaving the streets wet but not icy.

Nora punched on the heat and let it blast from the vents. Her damp jeans and coat made a comforting wet-Abbey smell in the Jeep.

She climbed out of town south on Highway 93 toward Golden. As soon as she dipped over a hill the lights of town disappeared. Starless night closed around her. The Jeep's heater tried, but in the drafty vehicle it couldn't keep up with the winter chill. Shivers ran through Nora at irregular intervals, nerves and cold vying for credit.

Two glowing pinpricks at the side of the road alerted her to deer. She tapped her brakes in response. The steering wheel jerked from her hand and the back end of the Jeep swerved to the right. Black ice.

Heart pumping, she counter-steered. The back end slid the other way, gaining momentum like a deadly pendulum. She yanked the wheel back. This time, the Jeep responded with a *swoosh* to the right that kept going. And going. The Jeep spun across the road like a drunk ice skater. It finally stopped with two wheels off the pavement, facing back toward Boulder.

The engine idled. The headlights shone crazily across the center line. She wanted to break into tears and sit still to gather herself. She needed to take the time to stop her shaking. She felt like tearing the seat belt off and jumping out to walk off the adrenaline pumping through her.

There was only one thing she could do. Nora locked her jaws tight, rammed the Jeep into gear and pulled onto the highway. At least the wild ride warmed her but the sweat would chill her.

She made it through Golden and onto to I-70 heading into the mountains. It seemed to take ten years to find the exit from I-70. The whole time she expected death to arrive in any number of ways. She could slide across the median and into oncoming traffic; Town Car guy could catch up to her; she could keel over from fear alone. Or she might arrive too late to save Cole and Petal.

Nora exited the Interstate and began her long climb up Mount Evans.

Another mountain. Another fight for life. Why did it always happen on mountains? Why did it have to happen at all?

White, fluffy flakes started falling again. "Of course," she said aloud.

Shutters covered the windows of the Park Service toll house and a bar blocked access to the road. Nora eased the Jeep off the road and around the barrier. Shoulders hunched up high enough to be ear muffs, she gripped the wheel.

In daylight, the harrowing road pushed Nora to the limit. At night, the switchbacks, narrow ledges, darkness, and ice became a nightmare.

She inched her way along the cliff-side road. Snow accumulated over packed ruts. Cole's pickup probably made those, followed by Daniel's Prius. She shifted up and down around each precarious switchback. Her headlights revealed a frustratingly small section of the mountain. She knew the edge dropped forever down the mountain but she couldn't see it. She stayed in the middle of the road, praying her tires would grip the snow.

What was happening on the dark summit? Her progress seemed like swimming through quicksand. Every time she tried to gain speed she fishtailed. But every second she lost gave Daniel more time to kill.

She pictured Cole smiling at her on the Pearl Street Mall. The fall leaves a swirl of golds and reds. He had been shy and uncertain about her but he'd been happy to see her.

"You were happy to see him, too." She scowled at the shadowy road. "Quit talking to yourself."

Was she happy to see him? What about earlier tonight, in her apartment? Didn't that feel right?

She'd spent the last year wrapped in a cocoon, gluing herself back together.

How long are you going to stay shrouded in self-pity? See, you don't even need Abigail around to harass you with her sloppy poetry.

She slipped the lever into first gear and pulled around a steep U-turn.

What if she died tonight? Or worse, what if Cole died? What would all the protecting and taking time to repair her heart get her? She didn't want to waste any more time shielding herself from life for fear that something might hurt again.

She wanted Cole.

Nora turned the last switchback into the parking lot. She ought to slap her headlights off for stealth but she wouldn't be able to see. Besides, anyone up here would have heard the Jeep's engine.

Four inches of snow sat atop Cole's pickup. Daniel's Prius still dripped melted snow from the warm engine.

Nora pulled next to Cole's pickup, cut the motor, and climbed out. The dry, cold air caused her nostrils to stick. The air burned into her lungs and out again in puffs.

The trailhead to the summit should be at the corner of the lot but in the darkness and covered with snow, Nora couldn't make it out. In a matter of seconds her fingers grew numb and her ears ached. She ducked back into the Jeep. A knitted purple ski cap with bright braids peeked from under the back seat. She yanked it on her head and found a cheap pair of thin knit gloves she kept in the Jeep to protect her from a chilly steering wheel. They wouldn't keep her hands warm, but they'd help a little. Her headlamp rested in the glove box and she pulled it over the ski cap and snapped it on.

The weak beam from the headlamp held the darkness at bay a few feet in front of her. She shuffled toward the trailhead, swinging her neck back and forth to sweep the area for footprints. The fluffy flakes had erased even Daniel's tracks.

Though not easy to make out, she found the start of the trail by locating a flat area about three feet wide between two boulders covered with snow. Feeling for each foot step along the bumpy, rock strewn path, Nora started toward the summit.

The headlamp provided a faded glow and snow plunked in her eyes. Her feet slid along under several inches of fluff, stubbing into rocks. She leaned as close to the cliff face as possible, using it to catch her when she slipped.

After two switchbacks she found the terrain becoming increasingly rugged as she headed around the side of the mountain. She must have missed the spot where the trail turned back up. The somewhat level path she'd been following became a jumble of snow covered rocks edging away from the cliff face. She soaked her gloves scrambling over a mound of stones. Her jeans wicked melted snow from the hem and her knees where she'd had to climb on all fours.

Shivering and panting in the thin air, she swung her head to the side. Her headlamp disappeared into nothing. She hung on the very edge of the mountain. Nora swung the beam back to where she suspected she lost the trail. She tilted her neck up, gauging whether it would be better to bushwhack up the side or try to find the trail.

Uneven and full of rocks, the trail wasn't an easy way to go. Backtracking to find it would eat up valuable time. She held her breathe, listening for voices or sounds of a struggle.

Nothing.

She reached her hand upward to feel under the snow for a solid hold. Her frozen fingers felt like clubs. She searched for a platform for her numb feet and pushed upward.

One movement and pause for a breath. Still, she panted. Despite frozen fingers and toes, sweat slicked her body, creating an even deeper chill. She could only see as far as her next hand hold.

She pushed off again. Her sole slid off the rock and she careened to the side.

No!

She flailed at the snow-covered rocks trying to find something to grab. Her fingers wouldn't grip. Her arms splayed out and her chin whacked the boulder under a pile of cold snow, sending a shower of lights behind her eyes. She cried out.

Desperate to keep upright, she scrabbled, but her fingers only raked the icy surface of the rock.

Nora couldn't get her balance. Her other foot twisted and she toppled to her right. She crashed to her knee and momentarily paralyzed her leg.

Her body sailed onto her side, kicking and fighting, she managed only to skid around so her head pointed downhill. Nora started to slide.

She threw her arms out trying to wedge them against any rocks. She gathered speed like a luge. If she didn't arrest herself she'd go over the side. She'd land in a pile of broken bones. Dead. Like Scott. Like Heather.

Like Cole.

Her forehead crashed into a boulder. Her body accordioned into her neck like a train hitting a brick wall. She stopped in a burst of white hot pain.

She lay with her head slammed against the boulder, her body in a heap uphill. Snow accumulated all around her, freezing her neck and cheek. At least she wouldn't fall all the way to her death at the bottom of a fourteener.

But she might never walk again.

Nora couldn't feel anything below her neck.

They'd pull her out of here, prop her in a wheelchair in front of a TV for the rest of her life. Over and over again she'd have to relive her failures and mourn the loss of Heather. Of Petal. Of Cole.

No more negative talk. She couldn't quit. Nora rolled onto her stomach and pushed herself up. Her hands ached with the cold and wet. "Ow!"

Her neck was nothing but frozen pain. But her arm—gave new meaning to *agony*. Excruciating molten bone somewhere just below her elbow. She wanted to scream. Or curl into the snow and wait for help.

She had to keep going. What choice did she have?

Slowly she maneuvered her legs and feet to push herself to stand. Okay, she wasn't a quadriplegic...yet.

She surveyed the side of the mountain where she'd slid. The rock strewn slope would be a challenge to scale in the best of circumstances. With a broken arm, it might be impossible.

She tucked her damaged arm close. With shaking legs, shivering and gasping for air, she climbed.

Find solid footing, brace your numb hand against a rock, push off. Repeat.

She gritted her teeth against shrieks of pain but nothing could stop her grunting and yes, even a moan or two.

She searched for handholds with her good hand and fell to her knees, pushing off with her feet. She slid, banging her chin again and sort of hopped by shoving with her feet. She gained a few inches.

Her foot slipped and she landed on her arm. "Ah!" She humped herself another few inches.

Cole. Petal. Rainforest.

Slipping and sliding and earning a foot to losing six inches, she finally made it to a spot where the trail reversed direction for the last climb to the summit.

She pulled herself over the side and lay on her back, resting for just a moment to ease her broken arm. At least the climb would be easier now. She dug in her feet and pushed to roll over.

A brilliant beam of light lit up the snow two feet to her right. It swerved to illuminate her. Snow puffed and metal skidded on rock.

The sound of the gunshot ricocheted in the darkness.

47

Nora rolled to the side of the trail and tucked into the cliff face. She turned off her headlamp. Daniel wouldn't be able to hit her now without climbing down the trail. The cliff provided shelter for the time being.

But she couldn't stay there.

A slight gray appeared on the eastern horizon. While it afforded Nora enough light to make out large objects, it reminded her that time was running out. Dawn was near and the beam would go off soon.

A boulder sat ten feet up the trail. She lurched for it and slid behind it, out of line of fire from the summit. Snow blew into her eyes. No gunshots.

She made another dash up the trail to the cliff face. She gulped in air. Again, no shots.

He must be busy with Cole and Petal.

Nora cantered up the trail watching her feet carefully. Each step jogged her bad arm, firing pain through her, but the thought of Cole in danger kept her moving forward. She pushed herself until black dots formed around the edges of her vision and she had to stop to fill herself with oxygen and windmill her arm to force blood into her fingers.

She hadn't gone too far before tracks appeared in the snow. They led up a rocky side and disappeared around an outcropping of stone. The summit lay ten feet straight up or another hundred feet if she stayed on the safer and more level trail. Even knowing the last time she'd bushwhacked she'd ended up with a broken arm, Nora couldn't opt for easy. She leaned into the cliff and planted her frozen hand in the snow, searching for leverage. She lurched up.

A noise made her freeze and she fought against her loud panting, trying to hear around the pounding of blood in her temples. The voices came as a relief. At least Petal was still alive.

On her hand and knees, she crawled the last few feet to peer over a rock to the summit.

Petal held a flashlight toward the ground and the light cast large shadows.

Daniel stood with his back to Nora, facing Petal. He wore a black down jacket with a cap pulled over his head. Somewhere he'd acquired a much larger gun. A real one. He held it in his hand, ready to pull it up and shoot Petal.

Petal stood swallowed in a barn coat, obviously one of Cole's. Her various skirts flowed in the gusts. She wore cowboy boots too large for her and they made her appear even more loopy than usual. They must also have been borrowed from Cole too.

Nora pushed with her feet and pulled with her hand to slide over the top of the cliff. She lay on her belly, the snow soaking through her jeans, seeping under her coat to her stomach. She shivered uncontrollably.

"Why are you doing this?" Daniel asked. His voice didn't sound nearly as sexy to Nora as it used to. It carried the sour note of threat.

Petal wasn't crying. Her mouth turned down in a fierce scowl. "You know why. Sylvia cheated me out of what was mine and I want what I deserve."

Where was Cole? Was he okay? He must be injured. If not, he'd be standing in front of Petal, protecting her. But he could be out at the tower now. He'd climb the fence and somehow destroy the tower.

Despite dawn threatening, darkness made it difficult to see much outside the circle of Petal's flashlight.

Even though he didn't have his normal bedroom voice, Daniel seemed to gentle his tone. "You know you needed her."

Petal shrieked, frightening in its sudden intensity. "That's not true. It was Sylvia who needed me."

"Now she's gone and she won't hurt you anymore."

Petal started to cry. "I'm glad she's dead. She deserved to die. She stole my science like she stole my mother's life."

Daniel didn't argue. He slid in another step closer.

He was getting ready to attack and all Petal did was rattle on in her disjointed sobs.

Daniel sounded soothing. "I know you were instrumental in her research. You should be rewarded. We could get you a position back with HAARP if you want."

Petal backed up and when she shifted her weight a pile of gear appeared behind her in the gloom.

Another step and Daniel was within striking distance of Petal. "This is not the way."

Petal pleaded with him. "It's the only way."

Nora squinted in the ashy light. The lump of gear moved.

No. Oh no.

It wasn't gear. That was Cole's green coat. She couldn't detect any blood but her vantage point wasn't good. Daniel must have shot him!

Nora cast around for a weapon. She crawled a few feet to a pile of rocks under the snow. Moving with as much stealth as possible, Nora pushed herself up. With her broken arm hugged to her side, she bent down and picked the biggest rock she could hold. It would have to do.

Ten minutes ago she'd have been hidden in darkness. Now she crept forward in half light. She faced Petal and Daniel in slow motion, praying that she wouldn't give her away when she noticed.

Petal's eyes flicked to Nora and widened slightly. She refocused on Daniel, who thankfully, seemed clueless.

Nora slid another foot forward, arm raised, ready to lunge in and smash the rock on Daniel's head. It wouldn't be enough to knock him out but it should throw him off balance and Nora could tackle him to the ground.

She couldn't fight him at the Trust with two good arms so she'd need a miracle to stop him now. It all rested on Petal. With any luck, Petal would come to her senses and help. Once they had Daniel contained, Nora could hold the gun on him and see to Cole, while Petal disabled Sylvia's doomsday machine.

It was a plan. Not a good one, but a plan.

One more step. She tensed, ready to spring.

Whether he noticed the slight change in Petal or heard Nora's movement, Daniel's instincts kicked in. He glanced over his shoulder.

Nora didn't hesitate. She yelled and jumped forward, bringing the rock down with all her strength.

The blow landed squarely on Daniel's head, bounced off his ski cap, hit his shoulder of well-padded down, rebounded up and skidded off his arm. It caused no more damage than if she'd spit at him.

"What?" he demanded before Nora plowed into him. She screamed at the jolt of fire in her arm.

He outweighed her and was a whole lot stronger, but she couldn't back down. Everything depended on her. She crashed into him. They tumbled backward and landed in the snow. The gun sailed behind them.

Despite ending up beneath her, Daniel gained the advantage. He grabbed her arms and she howled in pain. He held her arms and looked up at her. Desperation lined his face. "Stop. You don't understand."

"You want to destroy the rainforest and kill thousands of people." She struggled for release, wishing her arm would fall off and stop the torture.

He held her arms in an iron grip. He bucked her off never losing his hold. He flipped her and planted her on the ground. "You have it wrong."

They struggled in the snow, the rocks bruising and scraping her.

"Petal!" Nora yelled. The girl needed to help her.

As long as Daniel had hold of her arms, he couldn't reach for the gun. This might be their only chance. "Petal. Get the gun!"

Daniel shook his head, panic in his eyes. Obviously he didn't like it when the tables were turned and he might be hurt. "No. You're wrong."

From the corner of Nora's eye she saw Petal dive for the gun. The cowboy boots slid on the snow and rocks as Petal scrambled to help.

"You have to stop her," Daniel said.

In the high altitude and with Daniel on top, Nora could barely breathe, let alone give a good fight. *Hurry, Petal.*

It seemed Petal didn't feel the urgency but finally she stood over

Daniel's shoulder. Thank god it wasn't too late. Nora waited for Petal's warning for Daniel to stop.

Daniel knew Petal stood behind him and he tried to swivel around while keeping Nora under control. Nora might be able to take advantage of his distraction and wrench free.

She threw herself backward and bucked against Daniel.

"No. Don't." He sounded frantic.

Please, just let Petal do something effective. We might get out of here alive.

Nora expected Petal to knock Daniel in the head with the gun but she leaned down slowly. She reached toward his back.

Daniel pulled away. "NO! Nora, stop her!" He started to get to his feet, knocking into Petal and sending her off balance. She stumbled backward.

He whirled around, ready to lunge for the gun. It wouldn't be hard for Daniel to overpower Petal. Then he'd shoot them both.

Petal brought the gun up with both hands. Daniel surged forward.

The bang of the gunshot exploded in Nora's ears as Daniel's his arms flew out. Down puffed from the blackened hole in his chest, just above his heart. He was airborne momentarily then his full weight crashed onto Nora, knocking the wind out of her.

The echo of the shot faded and Nora realized the sound ringing in her ears was her own screaming.

Daniel sprawled on top of her. His head slipped off her shoulder into the snow. Blood gushed from the gaping hole in his left shoulder blade. Petal had aimed for his heart and missed. He groaned.

Maybe he wanted to kill them both the way he'd murdered Mark, but this was horrible. Beyond horrible.

"Stop screaming," Petal said, deadly calm.

It might have been Petal's uncharacteristic chill that shocked Nora to silence.

Nora squeezed out from underneath Daniel, her arm numb from the pain and cold. His blood gushed over her coat and jeans, leaving a sticky, warm mess.

Nora's hands shook as she leaned over Daniel. "We need an ambulance." She searched for something to use to apply pressure. There was so much blood.

She wanted to help him but she needed to be with Cole.

The fresh scent of the mountain and the snow couldn't wash away the stench of Daniel's blood. She wanted to vomit to rid herself of the sight, the smell, the memory. Mark, Sylvia, Daniel.

Heather.

Petal remained motionless, the gun weighing down her arm. She watched Nora with no expression.

Nora ran to Cole. He lay on his side, trembling in the snow. She managed to roll him onto his back.

He opened his eyes, cloudy with shock. "Nora."

The jeans covering his right calf were dark and soaked with blood. It stained the snow, so much like the carpet in Sylvia's bedroom covered in Mark's blood. "He shot you?"

Cole shook his head. "Petal…"

Petal. The tower. Nora twisted to locate Petal watching the point on the horizon where the sun would appear. She shouted at Petal. "Did you dismantle the tower, yet?"

Petal shook her head.

"We don't have much time." Nora yelled.

Still Petal didn't move.

Nora bent toward Cole. "Hang on. I have to go."

Cole's hand shot out and grabbed her wrist. "No."

She pulled from his weak grasp. "I'll be right back."

Nora stumbled and slid over the rocks. She fell to her knees and fought to keep moving. Over the first ridge.

Petal finally came to life and followed her.

Nora slipped going down the second ridge and landed on her tailbone. She had to wait until her legs would move again. Petal caught up to her.

It surprised Nora that Petal still held the gun. She must be more shocked than Nora thought.

"Go to the tower," Nora said. "I've got to help Cole. Daniel shot him."

"Daniel didn't shoot Cole." Petal's voice held a flat calm that sounded eerie.

Nora started back to Cole, only paying slight attention to Petal.

"I did."

48

Relief flooded Nora. "You did? You dismantled the tower? Before Daniel got here? Good. Let's go." She grabbed Petal's arm.

Petal shook her off. "No," Petal said, again with the strange flat voice. Her face didn't have the typical Petal vulnerability. Instead, her eyes glittered with lethal intent. "I shot Cole."

Nora couldn't comprehend Petal's words. "What?"

"I shot Cole and if Daniel hadn't attacked me I would have shot him, too. Then I would have killed you." Petal raised the gun and pointed it at Nora.

"Petal, no!" Nora didn't understand.

Petal's face contorted in rage. "What a condescending, arrogant bitch you are. You have to take care of helpless Petal. Be big and strong for her, make sure no one hurts her feelings. Do you know how I laughed while I manipulated you to do exactly what I planned?"

The sky lightened. How long until dawn? Minutes? Seconds? "I thought we were friends."

"I needed you to turn Sylvia in for embezzlement and the project would have been mine. As it should have been. Once the missing money was discovered it wouldn't be hard to pin Darla's murder on Sylvia."

"You stole the money? Sylvia didn't kill Darla?" She focused on Petal's gun.

"Don't you dare think I enjoyed shooting Darla. It was terrible. But I had to do it. For my mother."

Keep her talking. "Does your mother know what you've done?"

Petal's face reflected a frightening combination of tears and pride. "I'm protecting her. Like she protected Sylvia."

How would Nora get to the tower before Petal shot her? "It sounds complicated."

"What's complicated is creating a technology and setting it up to cause a volcanic eruption." Her voice rose to a shriek and she wiped her sleeve across her runny nose.

"So you killed Mark?"

Petal's eyebrows angled into angry slashes. Her lips drew back in a sneer. "Sylvia did that. I told you, I don't like killing."

"But you're about to kill thousands and thousands."

"I have no choice." Where the old Petal would have been sobbing, this new monster twisted her mouth into a grimace of hate.

Nora calculated the distance to Petal. "There's always a choice." One more step.

Petal shoved the gun at Nora. "You can't stop me."

Oh yeah? Nora jumped to the right and zigzagged to fling herself at Petal.

Petal fired. The bullet struck the rock where Nora had been standing. Petal couldn't aim again before Nora smashed into her.

"Uft." Petal fell back on her butt.

Nora splayed on top of Petal, driving her into the snow. Petal's arm flung out but she still gripped the gun. Nora reached for it. How was it that petite Petal had the arms of an ape and Nora couldn't reach her hand?

Petal screeched and bucked against Nora, bringing a knee up to smash into Nora's groin. It might have been an effective move if Nora had alternative anatomy. It hurt, sure, but it didn't stop Nora from scooting on top of Petal and grabbing the gun.

She should have been able to pull it easily from Petal's grasp, but Nora's fingers cramped with cold. Petal held on.

Nora took hold of Petal's wrist, yanked her arm in the air and smashed it down on the hard ground. Petal's grip loosened and she dropped the gun.

Nora struggled to her feet and scooped up the gun and ran to the outcropping of rocks, desperate to reach the tower. The gun made it hard for her to scramble across the boulders on her hand and feet. She ratcheted her arm back and snapped it forward, sending the gun end over end into the abyss. Slipping and sliding, she finally made it to the top of the rock and located the tower. She would have to climb on the narrow ledge to the fenced enclosure and scale the chain link.

Her control slipped. A black veil threatened at the edge of her mind. She couldn't do it. Impossible to force herself to dangle on the lip of the mountain like that.

Nora dropped to her knees. Her heart threatened to rip through her chest. Her vision blurred. She gulped and choked.

And there he was. A flash of bright blue in the gray light.

The kachina.

He balanced on the ledge next to the fence. Enemy or friend?

Nora glanced over her shoulder. Petal raced toward her. But she wore Cole's too-big boots so Nora could outrun her.

The rocky surface covered with eight inches of new snow threw hidden obstacles in Nora's path. She stubbed her toes, fell to her knees, and her arm went from excruciating to debilitating. She kept her focus on the kachina.

He raised his hatchet with one hand. The other held a fistful of feathers. The blue accent of his sash flashed with brilliance. His fierce mask with the slit eyes and plug nose, the face in her nightmares, seemed to encourage her.

With the oversized coat and boots, Petal should be falling behind but she gained on Nora.

Just a few more feet.

Nora launched herself on the five-foot fence. She hoped to start high enough that she'd be able to throw her good arm around the top on the second lunge.

The toes of her boost were too wide for the narrow chain link openings. She fell back. Without hesitating she jumped to her feet to try again. This time, she worked with her momentum and kicked against the fence as soon as she touched it.

It worked. With the second lurch up, she threw her arm over the top of the fence, knocking the snow from the rail. Her feet kicked and she pulled and finally fell down the other side.

"AH!" She screamed at the jarring of her arm.

The fence clanked as Petal jumped onto it.

The enclosure left only the barest room to maneuver between the tower and the fence. Nora stared at the tower. How could she destroy it?

Petal crashed over the fence. She scrambled to her feet. "Stop. Don't touch it!"

The thingy. The conductor/transducer/transmitter/inductor. What had Petal had called it? The tunable whatever made of two PVC pipes with wire. She needed to find it and pull it out.

Petal launched herself at Nora. They careened into the fence. It stretched and swayed over the edge of the mountain. The posts at either corner loosened in their anchors.

Nora shoved back and they rolled to the ground. Petal ended up on top. The heel of Petal's hand caught Nora on the chin and pressed upward, driving Nora's head back. With her one arm, Nora knocked Petal's hand away.

Petal was little more than fragile bones wrapped in twenty layers of fabric topped with Cole's coat. Nora shoved Petal off and stood. She lunged toward the tower and bent under the structural supports. She felt along the stem. There it was! Her numb fingers fumbled with a device about the size of brick, made of two plastic pipes.

Petal collided with her. She pushed Nora toward the loose fence. Nora's boots slid on the slick rock and she lurched backward.

Petal shoved her.

Nora hit the fence. It creaked.

One corner post popped from its anchor and tipped outward. Nora screamed. The bend of the wire created a lip in the chain link that would pour her over the side. Her fingers clawed into the openings and she held on. She pushed and pulled herself back to safety.

Petal stood above her waiting for Nora to climb to the rock so she could push her over the side.

Petal's mouth turned down as if she bit into something sour. Her eyes widened. Her arms flew out just before Nora heard a shot fired.

Petal screamed. A gaping hole blew through Petal's chest. Warm blood and tissue smacked Nora's face and spattered against her coat. Petal crumpled to the ground.

Nora scurried off the fence a few feet through the snow. She stayed on her belly and turned toward the gunshot.

The man from the Town Car stared through a scope in a rifle pointed at her. He stood on the tip of a rock pile jutting over the ledge.

Twenty yards behind the man, Cole advanced, dragging his wounded leg. The fool was trying to save her.

The Town Car guy would shoot Nora, turn and plant a bullet in Cole.

Nora backed up and squatted on the far edge of the enclosure. She had to get to the tower, giving Town Car Guy an easy target.

To the east, the outline of Gray's Peak blackened against the imminent sunrise.

Nora had one chance. She'd have to spring up and grab the tunable whatever from the tower before Town Car Guy could squeeze off a round and kill her.

Impossible.

Nora closed her eyes. She exhaled, opened her eyes, and sprang up.

A shot pinged the fence, hit a rock and ricocheted a hair's width from Nora.

She dove for the tower, hitting hard rock under the snow. She lay at the base of the tower. Above her, the device sat in the stem. She'd need to grasp it immediately and when Town Car's bullet ripped into her and she flew backward, her dead fingers would clutch the bundle and dislodge it.

One more breath in this life. She jumped up. Her fingers closed on the device.

The metal of the tower rang next to her ear and she heard Town Car's gun. He missed.

She jerked on the device and looked over her shoulder.

Cole had closed the gap but he wouldn't make it to stop the next shot.

The gunman held his rifle up, sighting into the scope.

Nora caught her breath. She tugged on the device and it inched from its slot. One more pull and it fell to the snow. She knew Town Car Guy's next shot would kill her.

But it never came. She jerked her head to see him shoot.

The kachina appeared behind Town Car Guy. He held his hatchet high.

The kachina brought it down on the gunman's back. The shot fired into the air and the man lost his footing. He fought to regain his balance but he slipped to one side. His foot flew in front of him and he fell forward. He hit one boulder and slid off.

His scream echoed in the morning air.

EPILOGUE

The smell of burnt toast wafted up from the kitchen. The *tick-tick-tick* of wheels sounded as Thomas brought his bike into his office. Fay's creaky voice greeting him and Bill joined in the morning murmur of voices down the hall from Nora's office.

Creak, thump. Creak, thump. Creak, thump.

Nora smiled at the sound and continued typing the staff memo. Abbey stood and stretched. He wagged his tail while he walked to the door of Nora's office.

Creak, thump. Creak, thump. First the rubber tips of the crutches and then Cole appeared in her doorway. He grinned. "Too bad your office isn't on the first floor."

She pecked her name on the keys of her computer with her one good hand. "And too bad I don't have voice recognition software."

He bent over his crutches and scratched Abbey's ears. "We're in pretty sorry shape."

Nora pressed Send. "But happy to be alive."

Cole shook his head and eyed Nora. "I can't get over how a gust of wind could have knocked him over the side like that."

It wasn't the first time Cole seemed skeptical. He never saw the kachina, of course, but didn't quite buy a freak gust. Oh well, he could blame his fuzziness on the concussion he got when Petal shot him and he banged his head on a rock when he fell. She switched topics. "I stopped in to see Daniel this morning."

He leaned on his crutches. "Just came from there, myself."

"Any change?" She hoped Cole had good news but she didn't expect it.

"Still in a coma."

Neither one spoke of a moment. Nora sent a silent prayer into the universe and wondered if Cole did too.

Cole lumbered to one of the wicker chairs and sank down. "I thought about bringing you coffee but didn't have enough hands for all of that."

She shook her head. "I'm off the coffee for a while. I'm afraid there might be more than cream added to it."

Fay poked her head into Nora's office and croaked. "What do I need to know before you leave?"

Nora pointed to her corn plant. "He needs to be watered every few days. He likes it if you'll sing to him."

Fay questioned with her eyes.

"Okay, just talk to him when you give him water." Nora had turned into one of those eccentric plant ladies. Next thing you know she'd be wearing purple hats and talking to herself. She caught sight of the purple ski cap she'd worn that morning. At least she had dogs and plants to talk to.

And Cole. She had him to talk to.

"Anything else?" Fay asked.

"The bills are paid, payroll is set to hit at the end of next week. I'll be back in time for the staff meeting on the tenth."

Fay nodded.

"I'll check in every couple of days by cell."

"Gotcha. Have a good time." Fay waved and left.

A good time wasn't necessarily what Nora sought.

Cole studied her. "You sound like a real live Executive Director."

"I am a real live Executive Director."

"Does it feel good to be in charge again?"

She laughed. "Again? When have I ever been in charge of anything?"

Cole grew serious. "So you're leaving for the rez today?"

She turned her computer off. "Abigail is supposed to pick me up any minute. Charlie's been bugging her for the last three weeks to get home."

"How long will you be gone?"

The anxiety surged and she stood to shake it off. "Two weeks. I'll stay with Benny's cousin. Well my cousin, I guess."

"Total Hopi immersion. I won't know you."

Ask. Do it. She braced herself. "Will you be here when I get back?"

His ears turned red. "Do you want me to be?"

She trembled and a tornado roared in her brain. Commitment. Saying yes sunk her deeper. It was a bigger deal than even caring for Abbey.

What a drama queen!

If she could face down her fear of the mountain and embrace the strangeness of Hopi, maybe she could take this one more step. "I'd like that."

His grin widened. "Do you promise I won't get shot again?"

She shook her head. "With as much certainty as you can guarantee you won't break my heart."

He pulled himself up. *Creak, thump. Creak, thump.*

Nora waited. Her skin tingled with anticipation; her heart stuttered a giddy cadence. Wait a minute. That didn't feel like fear. It didn't smell of panic. She remembered happy and this felt strangely like that.

Creak, thump.

He finally stood close enough she felt the heat of him through his flannel shirt. His smile faded and his eyes turned that deep blue she recognized. He leaned forward and brushed his lips softly against hers. "Nora Abbott," he whispered. "you are dangerous."

She closed her eyes and inhaled the warmth of him. She stepped even closer and wound her good arm around his neck. Even in the city he smelled of outdoors, fresh air, pines, a breeze.

His crutches banged on the floor as he gently slid his arms around her, careful of her broken arm.

He bent his head to hers and kissed her in a way that promised more. "I guess you're worth a bullet or two."

CANYON OF LIES: Nora Abbott #3

Nora Abbott's best friend is dead.

As Nora investigates the suspicious death in the desert of southern Utah, she uncovers the dark past of a polygamist sect.

When Nora's best friend, a film director, dies in a hiking accident, Nora suspects foul play. Could a controversial film project have played a part? Intent on finding out, Nora struggles to piece together the truth.

What she finds is shocking.

What is the connection between a secretive polygamist sect, Native American lore, one of the world's richest men, and her own mother's surprising past?

Her race to weave together these seemingly unrelated threads leads Nora into harm's way. She soon finds herself at the dangerous crossroads where ancient prophecy, modern political ambition, and desperate fanaticism meet.

In the stark Utah wilderness, long-held secrets come to light. But can Nora unmask the killer in time to prevent disaster?

Murder, polygamy, Native American culture, and mystery combine for an exciting novel.

AUTHOR'S NOTE

Welcome to Nora's world, which is slightly different than the real one. I know readers are super-smart and savvy and will notice a few factual discrepancies and I want to head you off at the pass and apologize for them.

First off, kachinas belong on the Hopi mesas and the sacred San Francisco Peaks in Northern Arizona. Having one travel is a huge breach of respect for the Hopi culture. I promise not to let it happen again.

Mt. Evans, in Colorado's Rocky Mountains, is a beautiful and easily accessible mountain top. I recommend anyone who has the lung capacity to breathe at 14,000 feet to drive or hike to the top. However, don't go in October, when Nora heads up. The road will be closed and you won't be able to skirt the entrance kiosk, as Nora does. Plus, it would be stupid to try.

Although there are some wonderful stone houses in Boulder canyon and bridges cross the creek to access them, Loving Earth Trust's building is from my imagination. It certainly could be there, but it's not.

HAARP is real. The technology exists to do everything that's outlined in this book. At least, I think it can happen. The conspiracy theorists and others I researched believe it's possible. Since I don't have a physics degree and getting one would be nearly impossible for me, I decided to believe them.

Finally, I love cats. I really do.

ACKNOWLEDGMENTS

What happens when three brilliant writers go on a retreat with one very stressed and confused scribbler who can't plot herself out of a one-tree forest? A book series upon which my name gets listed as the author. Without the creative force of The Sisters of the Quill, Nora Abbott would be hiding in a computer file, growing pale and gaunt. Thank you to Janet Fogg, Julie Kaewart, and Karen Lin for giving Nora a chance to live and breathe.

Thank you to Severn River Publishing who resuscitated this book, especially Andrew Watts and Amber Hudock, who seem to work without stopping. Take a breath, guys!

To my fabulous agent, Jill Marsal, thanks for sticking with me!

Thank you to Jessica Morrell, an editor extraordinaire. If you read this before she got her hands on it, you'd thank her, too.

I bow to Boulder County Deputy Russ Nanney, who not only helped me with the nuts and bolts law stuff, he found Sylvia's sweet gun. Even though I'm kind of afraid of firearms, that's one I wouldn't mind packing!

To my Alpha litter-mates, Alan Larson and Janet Lane: your keen eyes and discerning taste have made this a much better book. Rocky Mountain Fiction Writers, hands-down the best writers group ever, encouraged and informed me from the very beginning of my writing journey and still does today.

Thank you to the Grand Canyon Trust. You took this cattle-ranching, Nebraska brain and showed it a different way to think. May you continue to do good things for the Colorado Plateau.

ABOUT THE AUTHOR

Shannon Baker is the award-winning author of *The Desert Behind Me* and the Kate Fox series, along with the Nora Abbott mysteries and the Michaela Sanchez Southwest Crime Thrillers. She is the proud recipient of the Rocky Mountain Fiction Writers 2014 and 2017-18 Writer of the Year Award.

Baker spent 20 years in the Nebraska Sandhills, where cattle outnumber people by more than 50:1. She now lives on the edge of the desert in Tucson with her crazy Weimaraner and her favorite human. A lover of the great outdoors, she can be found backpacking, traipsing to the bottom of the Grand Canyon, skiing mountains and plains, kayaking lakes, river running, hiking, cycling, and scuba diving whenever she gets a chance. Arizona sunsets notwithstanding, Baker is, and always will be a Nebraska Husker. Go Big Red.

Sign up for Shannon Baker's reader list at
severnriverbooks.com/authors/shannon-baker

Printed in the United States
by Baker & Taylor Publisher Services